The tech named Goba and a shifting handful of others took over my life after that. They told me when to eat, sleep, and wash; they gave me the food I ate and the clothes I wore and even the bed I slept in. My life was jammed into a coffin, a soft suffocating prison where every waking hour they were beating on the doors of my mind, trying to get me to answer, to come out or let them in. Nothing like it had ever happened to me before: no one had ever had that kind of control over me. No one had ever told me when to breathe, or had even cared if I kept breathing at all. The techs didn't really care, either. I was a psion, and they weren't; they didn't even like psions—nobody normal liked a freak. They didn't like this job or anyone who made them work at it. But it was their job, and they weren't going to fail because of me. Goba told me they were going to make me into a telepath if they had to crack open my skull to get what they wanted; after a couple of days I started to believe him.

JOAN D. VINGE is a two-time Hugo Award-winner for *The Snow Queen* and "Eyes of Amber." She has also written the popular *Return of the Jedi Storybook; Tarzan, Lord of the Apes; The Dune Storybook; Ladyhawke;* and *World's End,* a sequel to *The Snow Queen.* Ms. Vinge lives in Chappaqua, New York, with her husband and daughter.

JOAN D. VINGE

PSION

LAUREL-LEAF BOOKS

LAUREL-LEAF BOOKS bring together under a single imprint outstanding works of fiction and nonfiction particularly suitable for young adult readers, both in and out of the classroom. Charles F. Reasoner, Professor Emeritus of Children's Literature and Reading, New York University, is consultant to this series.

Published by
Dell Publishing Co., Inc.
1 Dag Hammarskjold Plaza
New York, New York 10017

Laurel-Leaf Library® TM 766734, Dell Publishing Co., Inc.

ISBN: 0-440-97192-6

RL: 6.8

Reprinted by arrangement with Delacorte Press
Printed in the United States of America
January 1985

10 9 8 7 6 5 4 3

To Carol Pugner,
who always believed in Cat.

And to Andre Norton,
who is Cat's spiritual godmother.

"Life and its misfortunes, isolation, abandonment, poverty, are battlefields which have their heroes; obscure heroes, sometimes greater than the illustrious heroes." — Victor Hugo,
Les Miserables

PART I

CAT

The gem-colored dream shattered, and left the kid gaping on the street. Jarred by passers-by and stunned by ugliness, he gulped humid night air. The dreamtime he had paid his last marker for was over, and somewhere in the street voices sang, "Reality is no one's dream. . . ."

A richly robed customer of the Last Chance suicide gaming house knocked him against a pitted wall, not even seeing him. He cursed wearily and fumbled his way to the end of the building. Pressure-sensitive lighting flickered beneath the heavy translucent pavement squares, trailing him as he stepped into the funnel of an alleyway. Aching with more than one kind of hunger, he crept into the darkness to sleep it off.

And one of the three Contract Labor recruiters who had been watching nodded, and said, "Now."

The kid settled into a crevice between piles of cast-off boxes, where the unsleeping gleam of the pavement was buried under layers of back-alley filth. He didn't mind dirt; he didn't even notice it. Dirt grayed his worn clothes, the pale curls of his hair, the warm brown of his skin. Dirt was a part of his life: like the smell, like the constant drip of sewage somewhere in the darkness, leaking down through the roof of his world from Quarro, the new city that had buried Oldcity alive.

Water striking a metal walkway rang like endless

bells through the fibers of his abused nerves. He raised unsteady hands to cover his ears, trying to stop the sound of the water torture and the sounds of the furious argument in a room up over his head. He felt the throbbing of distant music . . . the beat of heavy footsteps coming down the alley toward him.

He froze, sitting as still as death, caught in a sudden premonition. His eyes came open slowly, intensely green eyes with long slitted pupils like a cat's. The pupils widened, his eyes became pools of blackness absorbing every particle of available light—showing him with unhuman clarity three heavy bodies wearing shadow-black uniforms: the carrion crows of Contract Labor, a press gang searching the night for "volunteers." Searching for him.

"Jeezu!" His drug-heavy body jerked with panic. He dropped forward onto his knees, hands groping in the trash around him. His fingers closed over the plass-smooth coolness of a bottle neck. He pulled it to him as the alley filled with dazzling, confused motion and he was surrounded by men in black. Their hands caught his clothing, dragging him up, off-balance; he was slapped, shoved. Trying to find words, breath, time to protest . . . he found his arm instead, his hand, the bottle clutched in it. He brought it up in one hard sudden rush.

The heavy shatterproof plass struck the side of a man's head with a dull *sponk*; the impact jarred the kid against the greasy building wall, and the recruiter fell. Two were still coming, their faces dark with vengeance, ready to make him pay. He dodged left, right, making them counter; suddenly he kicked out and up with ruthless urgency. A second man went to his knees with a bellow of agony.

The third one was on him as he tried to break away, dragging him back and down. The kid clawed at the pile of crates beside him, twisting like a snake in the recruiter's grip. The load shifted and swayed; he felt it begin to fall—

He sprawled free as the crates came down. He was on his feet and running before the crashes and cursing ended, before any of them were even up off their knees to follow him.

"Kid!"

He had almost reached the alley mouth when the shout caught up with him. He kept running, knowing the recruiters were not armed. Something struck him in the back of the head; he cried out as painstars burst inside his eyes. Warm wetness showered over his hair, sluiced down his neck, drenched his jerkin. He lifted a hand, brought it down from his forehead wet with luminous orange dye, not blood. "Shit." He swore again, half in relief, half in fresh panic: they had marked him for a police pickup. He stripped off his jerkin as he ran, running harder out into the midnight crowds of Godshouse Circle. But the dye had already soaked through to his skin, and even the crowds could not hide him. Night was when the upsiders came slumming, came to wallow in Oldcity sin; and the Corporate Security Police came with them, to protect the rich from the poor. He elbowed aside thieves and beggars, musicians, pimps, and jugglers, along with the silken customers who fed and bled them all.

He had been a thief for most of his life; on another

night he would have welcomed this crowd. But tonight
startled heads were turning, angry voices were rising,
arms waving, pointing, clutching. Somewhere an arm
in gray would lift a stungun—

He broke through into the Street of Dreams; its
throat of golden light swallowed him up in incense and
honey and loud, rhythmic music. He had never run
down this street before. He had stood gawking in it a
thousand times, seduced by the promise that all his
wildest dreams would be fulfilled if only he would step
through this door . . . *this* door . . . *my* door . . . *no,
mine.* But none of those doors had ever let him past,
given him refuge, welcomed or even pitied him. Tonight would be no different. He pushed on through the
yielding chaos of real and holo-flesh, feeling the crowd
drain the bright energy of his panic. *A mistake, this
was a mistake*— Orange sweat ran into his eyes; the
street's glaring assault on his tortured senses was making
him sick.

Someone shouted, and this time he saw uniform
gray. He began to run again, trying to keep the crowd
between them; running through nightmare. But he
still knew the streets better than he knew his own
face. Instinct saved him, and he dodged into a narrow crack below a shadowed archway. He ran down
steps, up steps, clattering through sudden light and
blackness along a metal catwalk—out into another
alley, between rows of silent pillars; navigating by con-
stellations of distant streetlights.

Footsteps and shouting still trailed him, but they
were falling behind now, out of sight. He let himself
slow, almost missing the break between abandoned

buildings—the crumbling wall that left him room enough to squeeze through, just below the hanging entrails of Quarro. He clambered up a fallen girder, his breath coming in sobs. He crouched and leaped, straining to bridge the gap. But his legs gave way; his body had no strength left to give him. His fingers caught, clung, slipped from the lip of broken stone. He dropped back into the rubble four meters below. An ankle cracked as he came down; as his body, abused for too long, betrayed him at last.

He huddled over, cursing the white-hot pain softly, until they came for him. Again he crouched in a yellow wash of light until rough hands dragged him up and held him against the wall. This time there were guns, and this time he didn't try to struggle. He whimpered as they prodded his leg; they made him stand on the other one, hands locked behind him, until the pickup unit arrived. They knew who had marked him. They worked for the Federation Transport Authority, and the FTA took care of its own, they said. They knew his kind, they said; they knew his record, too. He couldn't do what he'd just done and think he wouldn't pay. "Get used to it, kid. This is the end of everything for you."

But they were wrong. It was only the beginning.

1

It started where it ended, in Quarro. Quarro is the main city on Ardattee, the garden spot of the galaxy, the Hub, the Heart, the Crown of the Federation. Somehow it always looked more like the garbage dump to me; but that was because I lived in Quarro's Oldcity.

My name is Cat. Cat's not my real name, but it fits, and I like it. I don't know my real name. They always called me Cat on the streets because of my eyes: green eyes that see in the dark, that don't look human. I have a face that makes people uneasy. If you want the story of my life, it goes like this: I was standing in an Oldcity alley when I was maybe three or four. I was crying, because the hunger in my belly hadn't gone away, because it was so cold that my fingers were blue—because I wanted somebody to do something about it. Somebody came out of a doorway and told me to shut up, and beat me until I did. I never cried again. But I was hungry most of the time, and cold. And doing dreamtime, when I had any money for drugs—dreaming the kind of dreams they sold on the street. No excuses. To have dreams of your own is the only way to survive, but Oldcity had killed all mine. Reality was nobody's dream.

I didn't have any reason to think it would ever be any different, either. Not at the start—or at least that piece of time where the past and the future come together and catch you in the middle, to make it seem like the start of something.

At the start I was being hauled out of an Oldcity Corporate Security detention center. I didn't really know where I was going, just what I wanted to get away from. I'd been at the station a couple of days, under arrest for beating up three Contract Labor recruiters who'd been trying to do the same to me. The Corpses had done everything they could to make me miserable; then out of nowhere they'd offered me a chance to volunteer for a "psi research project." With no sleep and nothing to do but think up worse things they could do to me, I guess by then I would have said yes to anything. So I did.

And so the Corporate Security officer took me outside into the hot, stinking afternoon and pushed me into the back of a mod with winged FTA insignias on its sides. I'd never been in a mod before; the only ones I'd even seen were the aircabs the upsiders used to get into Oldcity and get out again. Without a data bracelet all you could do was look. Without a deebee proving you were alive you weren't just poor—you didn't even exist. And without a deebee you stayed in Oldcity until you rotted. I didn't have one. The Corpse sat up front and said a few words; the mod floated up from the ground and out of the courtyard. I held my breath as it carried us over the crowds, through the streets half as old as time. I'd spent my whole life on those streets, but everyone I saw, looking down, was a stranger. They tried not to look up; I tried not to think about why they didn't.

The mod reached Godshouse Circle and began to

rise even higher: Godshouse Circle was the only place left in Oldcity where you could move between worlds, between the old and the new. We were going upside, into Quarro. I hunched down in my seat as we spiraled higher into the light, feeling a little sick, trying to remember why I'd always wanted to see Quarro. . . .

Quarro was the largest city on Ardattee, but it hadn't always been. A handful of interstellar combines had split up the planet when it was first discovered. Then after the Crab Nebula sector opened up to colonization, Ardattee became the jump-off point for the colonies.

Every corporate holding on the planet had grown fat off the trade. Finally the Federation Transport Authority moved in to get its cut. It had moved its information storage here, and claimed Quarro to set it down in. Quarro had become a Federal District, a neutral zone where no combine government had official power, but all of them had hundreds of spies and spooks trying to get one up on everybody else's. Not all the dirty deals that were made in Oldcity were made by criminals. Quarro had become the largest cityport on the planet by a hundred times. Earth lost its place as the crossroads of the Human Federation, and Ardattee became the Federation's trade center, economic center, and cultural center. And somewhere along the way somebody had decided that Quarro's old, tired Colonial town was historic and ought to be preserved.

But Quarro had been built on a thumb of peninsula between a deep harbor and the sea. There was only so much land, and the new city went on growing, feeding on open space, always needing more—until it began to eat up the space above the old city, burying it alive in a tomb of progress. The grumbling, dripping guts of someone else's palaces in the air shut Oldcity off from the sky, and no one who had any choice lived there anymore. All of that I knew from things I'd seen on the threedy, even though I didn't understand most of it; even though it didn't make me feel any better.

We were rising through color now, soft, formless, mostly greens. Plants—more plants than I'd ever seen, or even imagined. The Hanging Gardens, somebody had told me once. The Hanging Gardens were Up There. . . .

And then we were up above the gardens, tier after tier of them; moving through the honest-to-God light of day. Towers, shining and flowing, speared the bright blue air on every side, reflecting the sky until it seemed to flow into them and through them. . . . I shut my eyes, giddy and tingling. I looked out again after a minute, at the endless height of the sky and Quarro shining down below me *like . . . like . . .* Knowing there had to be words somewhere for what I saw, but not how to find them.

The Corpse sat silently with his back against the barrier between us. The city lay like a long slender hand between the bay and the sea, jeweled fingers shining into the haze. *Mother Earth—I really live here?* I felt the binders cutting into my wrists.

But then we were dropping down through the air. We settled on a ledge where a couple of aircabs already sat, halfway down the side of a silvered building wall. There was an entrance waiting for us, one that didn't look like it got much use.

It was some kind of a hospital, I knew it as soon as we stepped inside. A hospital was a hospital, no matter how much they spent to make it look like something else. I stopped dead. "What is this? What do they want with me?"

"It's Sakaffe Research Institute," the Corpse said. "I don't know, and I don't give a damn. C'mon, you asked for it." He was between me and the door, there was no way I could leave, so I went on in.

He asked a passing tech for directions. She was carrying a plastic bag with what looked like someone's liver inside it, floating in purple sauce. It didn't make me feel better. She nodded over her shoulder, and we walked on down the silent hallway to a waiting room. The far wall was a sheet of tinted glass; light poured through it in a blinding flood that made me squint.

"Over there." The Corpse pointed, and then I saw the others, sitting along a cushioned seat below the wall of glass. He reached out and demagnetized the binders on my wrists; they dropped into his hands. He gave me a shove toward the window and told me, "Siddown, shuddup, and don't pull any stunts." Then he went back out into the hall. I knew he'd be waiting for me there in case I did.

There were half a dozen people sitting under the window already. I felt them giving me the eye as I limped toward them across the thick, sunlit carpet. I knew I was something to stare at—smeared with blood and dirt and dye; wearing a paper coat the Corpses had given me to cover most of the bruises, and over my ankle brace, pants so old they were ready for a museum. I wondered why we were all here, and what I'd really got myself into. I wished I had a camph to chew on to steady my nerves.

I stopped in front of the bench and looked for a place to sit down. The group of them had spread out on it like they were staking territory, until there was no room left. There were two women and four men. All the men looked poor, a couple of them looked tough. One of the tough ones had a stretched earlobe with no combine's tag in it—a busted spacer. One of the women looked rich, the other one just looked afraid. Nobody moved. They just stared, at me and through me, or at their feet. Finally the spacer said, "Up there."

So I looked where he was looking. Past the end of the bench, in the wall on my right, there was a closed door with a blue-hazed window. "The front of the line?"

"Pretty smart, Cityboy." He thought he was smarter. "One look at you, they won't be so choosy about the rest of us." He laughed and then they all did; strained, nervous laughter.

I wasn't laughing. "You want to eat that?" I moved toward him.

"Listen, you, don't make trouble," one of the women —the rich one—said. She was dressed like all the ones who came to Oldcity for laughs. Her round face was patterned with tiny red and gold jewels, matching the color of her hair.

"Butt out. This ain't your affair." I glared at her.

But her eyes said that it was. And then I saw that so

did everyone else's; they were all looking at me now. Nobody moved.

"Any time, gutter rat." The spacer grinned. "That Corpse out in the hall would just love to see you try it."

I let my hands drop and went to the head of the line. The frightened woman moved in from the end of the bench, either to let me sit down or because she was afraid I'd touch her. I stuck my leg out into the warm sunlight and smoothed the ankle brace, pulled my paper coat tighter to my chest. Then I twisted to look out the window, letting my eyes follow the flow of clouds and towers, pretending I was alone. I looked down, and down, and thought about falling.

The door to the next room opened and someone came out. His face was grim and disappointed; he looked like a gambler who'd lost his Last Chance. And everyone was looking at me; and so was the man standing in the doorway. "All right, who's next?"

Me. I was next. I looked down at the rip in the knee of my pants, and couldn't make myself move.

But then the woman sitting next to me stood up. "I'll go," she said. She looked at me for a minute as if she knew, before she looked at the man in the doorway. "I'm next." I stared at her. She was holding something and she dropped it into my hands. It was a piece of soft cloth, a scarf.

I wanted to say, "What's it to you?" but she was already gone. I looked back at the rest of them, half heard the rich bitch say something snide. I frowned at her, and she said, "What are you staring at?"

I looked back out the window, with the face of the

frightened woman still caught inside my eyes. I tried to stop seeing it, wanting to forget about her; but I couldn't. She was older than I'd figured, somewhere in her twenties in standard years. Her hair fell almost to her hips, as black as midnight in an Oldcity alley. Her clothes were dark and peculiar, layers of shirt and shawl wrapping her in mourning shrouds. She was tall, and too thin, and tired. But her eyes: cloud-gray, up-slanting . . . and when she'd looked at me, empty. She'd gone ahead of me to help me, but it hadn't been personal. It was only a kind of reflex action, like pulling away from a flame; something you did to stop your own pain. I felt strange when I realized that; invisible. I didn't know what to think.

So I didn't think about it for long. I didn't need favors from some burned-out fem anyhow. I looked down at the scarf, as green and gentle as moss bunched between my hands. I let it slide between my fingers, feeling the clean softness of it, breathing in a spicy fragrance like incense. Then I spat on it, and began to wipe off my face.

She was in the other room for a long time. I wondered whether she read minds, if that was why we were here. If that was how she'd known. And I wondered whether knowing what everyone thought was what had made her eyes so empty. The thought of having to live like her, like a freak that everybody hated, made my skin crawl. Then I wondered why the Corpses even thought that I could do it. Because I couldn't; I wasn't some kind of freak. Someone had come and tested me at the detention center, and afterward the Corpses told me I was a psion, I could read minds. I told them they were full of it. They just looked at each other, disgusted, and said, "You're a lucky freak, Cityboy." After that they put me on a truthtester and asked me a lot of questions I couldn't answer. And the next thing I knew they were asking me if I wanted to get out of there.

But they were still crazy—I'd never read a mind in my life. That meant I didn't have a chance, if mind reading was what they wanted from me here. . . . I was almost glad, thinking about that woman with her dead eyes, every day of her life spent knowing how much everyone hated her because she *knew*. . . . But then I remembered I sure as hell wasn't glad about how I was going to end up if they didn't choose me.

"Next."

The door was open but the mind reader didn't come back, and the red-haired woman nodded as if she'd known. I got up, stuffing the scarf into my pocket. My legs still felt like they were paralyzed, but somehow I made it to the doorway.

The man who'd been standing there before was already sitting down, behind a desk terminal. Daylight poured over it from the window wall. The desk, the chairs, the tables in the room, were made of real wood. I wanted to touch something, but I didn't. I wished again that I had a pack of camphs on me. There was a genuine sculpture painting on the wall behind him, not a cheap holostill; I'd been around enough stolen goods to know quality when I saw it. I stared at the thick raised wood grain on the curve of his desk and took a deep breath, before I looked up at him.

He was about thirty-five, maybe a little older. His face had a pinched look, like the face of someone who'd been sick a long time; but something about his expression told me he was no easy mark. His hair was cut short and it was already graying. He hadn't tried to hide that. The yellow collarless summer shirt he was wearing was good stuff, imported from offworld—that must have docked him plenty. But he didn't have on a drape or even jewelry, except two plain rings on his left hand, third and fourth fingers: a widower? He wasn't smiling. I tried my best handout smile on him. His eyes were hazel—green and brown. They were staring at my face and down at my clothes, back at my face again. I figured this must be the one the Corpses in Oldcity had told me was "Dr. Siebeling," the one they were sending me to see. My leg hurt. I wanted to sit down too, but the way he looked at my clothes kept me on my feet.

"Rather young, aren't you?" That wasn't all he thought was wrong with me. His hands cupped a glass ball with a hazy image inside it. He stroked it with a kind of absentminded need, like it was helping him stay calm.

I shook my head. My own hands tightened. Everyone thought I was younger than I was—softer, stupider, easier to use or push around. It was like I'd been born a victim, somehow; like they could smell it. I had a lot of scars on me from proving they were wrong.

He said, "Prisoner nine-double-oh-five-seven." I nodded, even though it didn't mean anything. He had what must have been the report from Corporate Security on the terminal, and he stared at it for a while before he looked up again. "This says you've got a record of petty thievery, and that now you're charged with assault and battery against three recruiters for Contract Labor. That you attacked one man with a knife—"

"Is that what he said? That croach. I didn't need a knife." He looked up at me with eyes like stones. "It was a bottle."

"Attacked one man with a knife, struck another, and kicked a pile of boxes down on a third. You ran away, and were arrested by Corporate Security after you broke your ankle in a fall. You were out on drugs at the time?" He sounded like he didn't believe it.

I didn't say anything.

"Why did you do it?"

"Because I didn't want to be shipped off to some sewer world where they can't get nobody sane to go, and rot there for half my lousy life. Why the hell do you think? The stinking Crows . . ."

He looked bored. "There was kadge in your blood-stream when you were picked up. That was two days ago, and you're not climbing the walls—you're not addicted?"

I shook my head. "I can't afford it."

"None of them can afford it, but most of them aren't that lucky. In fact, I've never heard of anyone who could take it or leave it."

Neither had I, when I thought about it, but I only said, "You have now."

He glanced down at the report again. "This says you're also no mind reader. You tested wide-spectrum on telepathy but entirely dysfunctional. I've never heard of that before, either. You must have given the techs a real challenge: you show a ten-plus resistance to probe.

I show an eight; that's high. You have control like that and you've never used it?"

I was remembering the test: the veil of tingling mesh they'd fastened over my face back at the Corporate Security station, how I'd felt when my mind began to unravel. . . .

"Well? I asked you a question, Cityboy. I expect you to answer it."

"I got a name, sucker! It's Cat." I was starting to believe in hate at first sight.

His hands tightened on the desk edge; I knew I'd put my foot in my mouth. "Don't you get smart with me. I'm sick and tired of you and all the rest. Why the hell can't they send me something besides criminals and addicts?"

"Okay, okay. I didn't mean nothin' by it." I raised my hands. I hoped I looked as sorry as I felt—sorry for me. The last thing I wanted was to give him a reason to send me back out that door, back to the Corpse with the binders waiting in the hall. I tried to make my answer come out smooth and soft. "No. I didn't know I was a mind reader till the Corpses told me so. I never felt—never even f-f—" Black lightning flickering at the core of my mind, someone screaming. . .

Siebeling stared at me with a peculiar expression on his face. All his anger was gone. "What is it?"

I shook my head, rubbed my eyes, feeling cold and confused. "Nothing. . . . No. I don't want to be a mind reader; who would?" The words spilled out before I could stop them. "All the psions I ever seen were crazy. They don't call 'em freaks for nothin'." I grimaced.

"How much do you know about psionics?" His face

was empty again. He pushed the glass ball away from him on the desk top.

"Nothing. What do I care about a bunch of freaks?"

"Psionics research"—he let it sink in—"is what you volunteered to participate in."

"Oh." My ears burned.

"That's all. Thank you." He stood up. The door was open. I knew then that the interview was over. And that I'd failed it.

I went out the same way I'd gone in, wishing more than anything that I could make myself invisible. But I couldn't. I walked past the rest of the freaks like I'd lost my Last Chance, and I saw their faces. I felt mine get hot again.

"Wait a minute."

I stopped, and heard Siebeling asking if anyone there was a telepath.

One by one, they shook their heads and said, "No."

I looked at him again, even though I was afraid of what showed on my face. He frowned, and then he gestured me back. Suddenly I wanted to walk out on him. I nearly stepped on him instead, getting through that door before he changed his mind.

The first thing he said was: "Don't think this makes anything different. You're here because of your resistance level, but that's the only reason. I'll still drop you the minute you fall short anywhere. Contract Labor has requested you be turned back to them, if that means anything to you."

I laughed, but it wasn't funny.

He stood there like he was waiting for something. "Don't you even want to know what you'll be doing?"

I shook my head, as much because he wanted me to nod as because I really didn't care. "Why? Nobody's gonna miss me." Everything was lousy; at least this was a choice.

But he said, "The experiments we'll be doing involve psionics—'mind over matter.' Mainly it will be a group of people with undeveloped mental abilities working together to learn how to control those abilities. We'll teach you how to be a mind reader without going crazy. That's all you need to know for now." I shrugged. He pushed something on the desk and a door stood open in a wall again. A different door; I uncrossed my fingers. "How long have you known the woman who came in here ahead of you?"

"Why?" I frowned.

"Curiosity. She suggested that I give you a chance. I wondered why."

"I never seen her before today." I couldn't think of anything else to say, so I just stood and waited until he pointed toward the door.

"Through there. They'll tell you what to do."

2

I followed another hallway, one that didn't try so hard to look like it wasn't in a hospital. The tightness in my chest eased as I walked, and I took deep breaths. At the end of the hall a couple of people in pastel coats were sitting on the edge of an examining table, tossing out game pieces. I stopped. They looked at each other, then put the pieces back into a bowl. "Siebeling sent you?" the old man with side-whiskers asked, like he thought maybe I'd taken a wrong turn somewhere.

I nodded.

"What are you?"

I glanced down my body and up again. I put my hands on my hips. "Tired and hungry and sick of taking a lot of crap."

His face changed, first confused and then annoyed. "What's your *talent*—are you a teek, or a 'path, or what?"

"What?" I said, feeling like an echo.

"Well, he's not a mind reader, Goba." The woman pushed at her hair.

"Wrong," I said.

They traded looks again. The man leaned over and put a readout onto the screen in the tabletop beside him. He stared at it, a frown growing between his thick brows. "Take a look at that."

The woman peered past him. "Total dysfunction? We're supposed to unravel that in reasonable time? God's teeth, where do you start? What strands do you pull? How do you get through that wall?" She touched something on the screen with her finger.

"Like the Gordian knot," the man said, "I think it requires the direct approach." He chopped the air with his hand.

The woman laughed. "Well, this one's all yours, lucky son. If you can find a real telepath in that you can retire." She looked up at me. "If you can even find a human being inside this pile of rags you're doing better than I could."

He pulled at his mouth, starting to look too interested. I began to get uneasy again.

I have good instincts.

The first thing he did when she was gone was call in reinforcements. Together they stripped me and threw my clothes down the trash chute. Then they scrubbed me and disinfected me and gave me a medical that didn't leave anything to their imaginations—all the time telling me they'd tape my mouth shut if I didn't quit howling about it. After it was all over, they finally let me eat, in the hospital cafeteria. I ate until I got a bellyache, and fell asleep while they were telling me they'd told me so.

The tech named Goba and a shifting handful of others took over my life after that. They told me when to eat, sleep, and wash; they gave me the food I ate and the clothes I wore and even the bed I slept in. My life was jammed into a coffin, a soft suffocating prison where every waking hour they were beating on the doors

of my mind, trying to get me to answer, to come out or
let them in. Nothing like it had ever happened to me
before: no one had ever had that kind of control over
me. No one had ever told me when to breathe, or had
even cared if I kept breathing at all. The techs didn't
really care, either. I was a psion, and they weren't; they
didn't even like psions—nobody normal liked a freak.
They didn't like this job or anyone who made them
work at it. But it was their job, and they weren't going
to fail because of me. Goba told me they were going to
make me into a telepath if they had to crack open my
skull to get what they wanted; after a couple of days I
started to believe him.

A telepath was what I was supposed to be: a mind
reader. Goba told me that the first day. He'd explained
it all to me very slowly, like he was talking to a burnout, while I stuffed myself full of cafeteria food. There
were other psionic "talents," too: teleportation meant
that you could move your own body from one place to
another instantly, just by thinking about it; telekinesis
meant that you could move objects the same way; precognition, the wild-card power, showed you flashes of
the future—or several futures—and left you to sort out
the clues that led to the true one. Some psions could do
more than one of those things. I only had one talent,
telepathy. One too many.

They spent days hypnotizing me, putting my mental
guards to sleep while they probed around in my brain
with machines I never wanted to know about: finding
areas of resistance in my mind and walling them up,
drowning the fears, finding my telepathic sense and
dragging it out into the open. I woke up after every

session thinking everything was fine, because that was how they'd programmed me to wake up . . . but always I woke up soaked with sweat, raw-throated or red-eyed or with a headache the size of a sun. And then they'd throw me into a hundred different exercises that were supposed to loosen the tension that still held my mind shut, to force me to follow and control the strands of my thoughts, to feel the power move and reach out with it. I had to tell them things like what picture they were looking at when I couldn't see it, or what they'd eaten for breakfast, or whether they were telling me a lie.

They always told me whether I was right or wrong, but I didn't need it. I knew when something happened in my head that had never happened before; I felt the alien energy making static behind my eyes, a formless force stirring in buried rooms of my mind. But I couldn't control it. I couldn't shape it into anything like a thought message to project into someone else's mind. I couldn't even focus it clearly on somebody's sendings, no matter how much feedback they gave me.

Because from the first time I felt the psi power wake and stretch inside me, I hated the feel of it; and no matter how often they put me to sleep and made me swear I didn't, that never changed. It was like being forced to do something I was ashamed of in public, over and over, with all of them watching; being smeared with their disgust every time I brushed against their minds: *psions were scum, psions were a threat to every decent human being, because they had the power to invade another person's life. Psions were freaks and they all knew I was one. . . .*

Whenever I got anything right, I figured they ought to be grateful, under the circumstances. But usually they only got sarcastic, telling me I could do that well by guessing, and that I wasn't really trying. I told them I *was* trying, they didn't give me any choice. "What the hell's going wrong that I can't just *be* a stinking telepath? Maybe you're wrong about *me*." Wanting them to be wrong, wanting to hear Goba tell me it was all a mistake, that I was as normal as he was; even while I was afraid he might really say it, and send me back to Contract Labor.

But Goba caught my jaw with his hand, turning my face until I was looking at my reflection in the side of a metal storage cabinet. He said, "You look at that face, psion, and ask me again if I could be wrong about your mind."

I only shook my head, not understanding.

He looked disgusted, which wasn't unusual. "You are a psion; don't try to kid yourself. You've got a lot of scar tissue in there," pointing at my head, "figuratively speaking. That's what's gone wrong. Something fed you a tremendous telepathic shock once, so intense it burned out the circuits. Your mind could have repaired them itself, but whatever happened was so painful that it never did. So we're trying to do it for you. But you're still resisting. . . ." He sounded like he took it personally.

"What kind of a shock?" I wondered how something that bad could have happened and left me without even a memory of it.

He shrugged. "That doesn't matter. It's not our business to find out. We just repair the circuitry."

"I ain't a machine; you can't reprogram me. It ain't that easy." *Bastard*, wishing he could hear me think it.

"Get back to your exercises." He started to turn away.

I stayed where I was and folded my arms. "I got a headache. I don't think I want to work anymore."

He looked back at me. "Our job is to work around your problems, not to solve them. If you want to know *why*, see a psiopsychologist. Now get back to work."

And so I moved through the days like a robot, answering when Goba told me to, talking to myself if I wanted a real human conversation. The rest of the techs might as well have been robots too, for all they ever said to me. I never even knew the names of most of them. I was just one more experimental animal to them, and every night they locked me in my room. And night after night I had dreams so ugly that I started sleeping with the light on; nightmares I could never remember, that faded into the morning and left my head filled with the echoes of screaming. I never told Goba about it, or any of the others. They could all go to hell, I'd be glad to give them references, but I was damned if I'd ask them for help.

Then one day I got my visit with a psiopsychologist, without even having to ask. Nobody bothered to tell me that was what I was getting. All I knew was that I was going to see Siebeling.

He was more surprised than I was when the tech showed me into his office. He raised his eyebrows when she said, "Here's Cat," and actually looked past her out the doorway before he looked back at me. I felt the sharp stab of his surprise puncture my mind as he finally recognized me. I stopped dead, shaking the surprise loose from my thoughts, fighting my own disgust. I wasn't used to picking up strays; for some reason his mind focused much more clearly than any of the techs' did. There was an afterimage of confusion that cut off suddenly, leaving me alone again and off-balance inside my thoughts.

"Sit down," he said.

I dropped down into the sling of the nearest chair; the metal frame creaked like old bones. Siebeling grimaced. I leaned back, swaying a little, glancing past him. This wasn't the same room I'd seen him in before; this one was higher up and there was a slanting skylight instead of a glass wall. I tried to imagine what shape this building really was. The room was about like the other one except for the skylight, and Siebeling sat behind the desk like he was just visiting in this one, too. I wondered if people treated him the way they treated me around here. I stared at his clothes: probably not. He had the glass ball in front of him again; the picture inside it looked different from what I remembered.

"I almost didn't know you."

I think that was supposed to be a compliment, but somehow it didn't feel like one. I shrugged.

"How's your ankle?"

"They fixed it up all right. . . . What's the matter, did they tell you I'm no good?" My hands tightened over the metal chair frame.

"Who?" He looked blank.

"Them—the techs. They keep telling me you're

gonna throw me out of here if I don't work harder. I'm doin' the best I can!" I leaned forward, the seat shifting under me.

"I'm sure you are." He sounded like he meant it; I sat back, easing a little. "They've told me that you aren't making progress as fast as they'd hoped. They say you seem to have blocks they can't effectively break down. That's what I want to talk to you about."

"Why?" I felt my neck getting stiff.

"It's part of the research. All the volunteers here are trying to come to grips with the problems their psionic ability has caused them. You're not alone in having problems. I'm sorry I haven't been able to talk with you about yours before this; but there are a lot of volunteers, and we're only getting started."

"Well, what do you care about my problems? The techs already told me they don't matter. You just like to get personal?"

He looked at me like I'd just spit in his face. "You mean you still don't understand what you've been doing here?"

I looked down at the floor between my sandals. "How am I supposed to know anything? All I ever see are those damn techs. They're all alike and they don't tell me nothing, they don't even speak to me. Jeezu! What am I supposed to know—that this is a prison? Where the hell are all these other psions they keep talking about? I never see any of 'em, and I've been here forever!"

"You've barely been here two weeks. You'll see them when you're ready to work with them. And you are a prisoner—not ours, but Corporate Security's. Until I'm sure you'll work out for our research, you'll go on being their prisoner, and go on being carefully watched." He took a deep breath. "I am Dr. Ardan Siebeling. I am a medical researcher; I am also a psiopsychologist—I specialize in the treatment of emotional and behavioral problems relating to psionics. As a part of this research I'm trying to give all my volunteers—even you—what counseling I can. The whole point of this is to help you control your talents and learn to live with them. Does that answer your questions?"

I nodded, keeping my head down—wishing I could leave, and wondering why everything I said just made me sound stupider, and made him angrier.

"Then let's talk about what's bothering you. Goba said you'd experienced some shock early in life that was so painful you totally rejected your ability to read minds."

"I know. But he wouldn't tell me what it was."

"Apparently he can't. Even under hypnoprobing you never say anything about it. The human mind is full of unknowns; you can take a memory and throw it down a pit somewhere and never see it in your conscious mind again. But it's still there, somewhere, festering. The mind never really forgets anything—it only forgets how to reach that thing, sometimes." He looked down at the glass ball. He covered it with his hands, and closed his eyes for a second. When he took his hands away again, the picture had changed. I stopped listening and just stared; wonder caught in my chest. "You don't remember anything at all about what might have happened? Can you even remember a time when you knew what people were thinking?"

I blinked, and looked back at him. I shook my head.

"Has anything strange begun happening since you've been involved here? Have any peculiar memories surfaced—anything at all? Dreams?"

I nodded. "Dreams. I have a lot of bad dreams. . . ."

"What are they about?" He leaned forward across the desk.

"I don't remember."

He sat back again. "Something. There must be something—a setting, a feeling?"

"Oldcity. They're always in Oldcity." He raised his eyebrows. I shrugged. "Where else would they be?"

"Anything else, then? Close your eyes, remember how you feel just as you're waking."

I shut my eyes, trying to bring it back. . . . "Afraid," I whispered. I wiped my hands on the knees of my pants. "Somebody's s-screaming. . . ."

"What?"

"S-screams!" I opened my eyes, glaring at him.

"Whose? Your own?"

"Yes. N-no!" I pushed up out of my chair. "I d-don't want to do this."

"Sit down," he said, almost gently. I sat down again. "Do you stutter much?"

"I don't stutter!" I remembered what I'd just heard come out of my mouth.

"All right." He nodded, looking up through the skylight. "Let's try something else. How old are you?"

I took a deep breath. "Your guess is as good as mine."

"You must have some idea—sixteen, seventeen?"

"I guess so."

"Have you ever lived anywhere besides Oldcity?"

"No."

"Are you sure? You could have come to Ardattee when you were too young to remember. Did your family—"

"What family?" My mouth twisted.

"You're an orphan, then." He looked like he was apologizing for it, but there was something almost eager in the words that made me uneasy.

"I guess so." I made a sound that wasn't really a laugh. "And I remember living in Oldcity way back. I wish I could forget it, but I remember."

"Before you were, say . . . four years old?" The question wasn't quite casual. His hands closed over the picture ball; the picture changed again. He looked up, watching me watch it.

"Yeah," I said, remembering to answer him. "I got a good memory."

"How did your survive, if you were that young, and alone?"

"I lived off other people's garbage and junk." I felt him pushing me, a pressure I could almost see growing in my head. I twisted the hem of my smock between my hands, not understanding why it was happening. "I been a slip, and a beggar, and sometimes I was even—" I broke off. "What do you want from me!"

His face caught somewhere between disgust and pain. "Just—the answers to a few questions." It was a lie. He kept his voice even, but one question was burning inside him, stronger and deeper than any professional curiosity. I couldn't read him, but I couldn't stop feeling it, either. "What happened to your parents?" That wasn't the one.

"They're dead." I hoped they were; because if they weren't I wished they were, for what they'd done to me.

"Do you know which one was Hydran?"

"What?" I frowned. "What do you mean?"

"Your eyes and the bone structure of your face look Hydran. Your psionic ability makes it even more likely. . . . Do you know about the Hydrans?" he asked finally, when I just kept staring at him.

"They're the aliens." The word was hard to get out. "They come from Beta Hydrae system. I know some jokes. . . . Are you trying to make a joke outa me? It's bad enough bein' a freak. I'm human, I ain't some kind of monster!" I stood up again.

He stood up too, and leaned across the desk top, upsetting the picture ball. It rolled toward me. "You don't understand. My wife was Hydran. I had a son—"

"I don't care if your whole lousy family was alien, you devel I ain't, I ain't Hydran! And I ain't answering any more questions."

He pulled back, straightening away from me. I saw his face harden over with anger, felt his anger sink into my bones. He turned his back on me, as if even the sight of me was more than he could stand.

I looked down from the back of his head at the picture ball lying on the desk in front of me. I picked it up with shaky hands, and put it into my pocket. And then I got out of that room fast.

He didn't try to question me again. That was the last time he interviewed me, and Goba complained louder than ever when they got me back.

But then a couple of days later Goba came into the

lab with a stranger: someone who looked like he'd probably come sealed in plastic—everything about him was so neat, so plain, so mass-produced. The stranger looked me over and said, "So you're the shadow walker who beat up three Contract Labor recruiters?" I stood and glared at him. He smiled at me; it made his face look human. (Think you can take me too, telepath?) I heard it, but this time he hadn't opened his mouth: the words formed inside my head—his thought, not mine, and I wasn't even trying to read his mind. He was a telepath.

"God's teeth!" I held my head, looking back at Goba. Goba just smiled like a sadist and left us alone.

I put a table between the stranger and me, and wove my thoughts into a shield. No human had ever been inside my mind like this before—it was like a tumor of thought growing in my brain. The feeling made my stomach turn over. "You keep out of my mind, freak, or I'll show you what I can do." I held up a fist.

"Take it easy." He spoke it normally, this time. He looked nervous, which made me feel better. "Pull in your claws, Cat. I'm not here to—"

"I ain't an animal, you piece of meat!" I brought my fist down on the table. "I'm a human, even if they don't treat me like it around here."

His face changed. "My apologies." He nodded, glancing down. He looked soft, like somebody who didn't get any exercise. His dark hair was pulled back and fastened at the base of his neck, the way half a million other people wore it. It was like he'd done everything he could to make himself ordinary. His eyebrows were dark and smooth, like feathers; his eyes were a gold-

flecked green when he looked up again. "I didn't mean
to patronize you, and I guess I did. I'm sure they've
made your life more unpleasant than you had any right
to expect when you came here. Just between us, it was
meant to be that way. It's all a part of the . . . uh,
research. It helps to know those things; it puts it all in
perspective. Doesn't it?"

I stared at him, trying to figure out what he'd just
told me, and what the hell he was doing here. "Who
are you?"

"My name is Derezady Cortelyou. I work for Seleusid
Interstellar as a corporate telepath. I'm also a volunteer
in psionic research, like you. I'm here to help you work
on your own telepathy."

I sat down at the table and rested my head in my
hands. It hurt, as usual. "Jeezu. That's all I need."

He sat down across from me, picked up the stack of
cards with symbols on them that I was always having
to "see," and shuffled through them. But he didn't
start playing head games; he didn't even talk about
telepathy. He talked about the weather—about everything but psi. I didn't say anything. Finally, as if he'd
run out of ideas, he pulled out a pack of camphs and
put one of them into his mouth. I felt my own mouth
start to water. My fingers twitched.

He glanced at me, but he didn't offer me one. He
just sighed, and I could *feel* how good it felt. . . .

"Gimme one of those?" I tried to make it sound
casual.

He smiled and flipped one across the table.

I stuck it into my mouth and bit down on the end
of it. The bitterness numbed my tongue. I swallowed,

letting it deaden my throat, knowing that soon enough it would ease the tension all through my body. I sighed, like he had.

"Been a while since you've had one?" His voice prodded me, but only a little.

I didn't care. I nodded. "Seems like forever." Knowing there was no way I could get out of it, I finally began to relax and let the conversation happen. He held his mind loose and unprotected all the while—I could have walked right into it and read everything he was thinking if I'd wanted to. I didn't want to. I kept my own mind as tight as a fist, but he didn't try to reach me that way again. It was a laying down of weapons, and even I could understand that much. Which maybe was why I let myself answer his questions, and after a while even talked about psionics.

He knew more than I ever wanted to know about telepathy, and when he found out that I didn't know anything, he made me sit through it all. The only thing that kept me listening was the camph slowly dissolving in my mouth, and more where that one came from. But by the time the lights of Quarro were a net of stars in nebula outside the window, I knew all about the different degrees of telepathic ability. I had what should be the greatest, the most flexible: "wide spectrum," the ability to read everything from conscious thoughts lying on the surface of another person's mind to buried memory fragments and even pure emotion.

I'd learned that the mind was a net of electric fire— nerve fibers reacting to every sensation and image, every thought and feeling that let human beings interact with life. In most humans the input and reactions were woven into a snarl that even biofeedback training could barely begin to unravel. Psions were born with something more—a set of self-controls that let them weave the snarl into patterns and, more than that, to tap and use a kind of energy normal humans were blind to. Psions had a sixth sense—and their minds were both more open to it and more protected against it.

Some of them had two or more talents at the same time, different ways of manipulating an energy as universal as life-force, and as much of a mystery. Not all psions had the same level of control over their talents, the way not all artists had the same amount of skill. There were psions who were born with multiple talents like a crown of semiprecious stones, and ones born with a single talent like a perfect diamond. . . .

"A 'diamond in the rough.' " I repeated the words, finally understanding them. "That's what Goba called me." A flawed, ugly stone that needed cutting, he'd said, but that resisted every tool except the hardest. . . .

"He's right," Cortelyou said. "You have a level of control that would make anyone who wanted to be a psion green-eyed with envy." He laughed like that was a joke, but I didn't get it. "Except you've twisted it back on itself. You've used it to weave the fibers of your mind into a barrier, a wall of defense. They've been doing their best to fracture it—"

" 'And they don't much care if I break clean or shatter.' " I finished Goba's speech for him.

His mouth quirked. "I can imagine. I know the type." He sounded tired, suddenly.

I wondered again about what he was, and did. This

time I asked, "What's a corporate telepath do, anyhow?"

"I screen clients for Seleusid executives, and sometimes do security checks at their headquarters."

"You mean you're a croach."

"A what?"

"A backstabber. A paid snitch." I shrugged.

His mouth thinned, but if he was angry or insulted, he didn't let it show. "Some people have said that, yes." The words sounded used, like he'd said them too often before. But then he told me that he was also a precog—that he made predictions about the economic and political future of the combine's holdings. I asked if he'd do it for me, but he only said that you couldn't predict when you'd get a prediction, and that they weren't always accurate, anyway. "Besides, we're here to work on telepathy, not precognition."

That was only the first time he came to work with me, and it wasn't long before a part of me looked forward to seeing him. He was a new face, and he didn't treat me like I was a pain in the ass—another change from Goba and the rest. But besides that he was more interesting than he looked. He told me that he had total recall, he remembered anything he saw or heard perfectly; that it was a skill any psion could develop, even me, if I wanted to work at it. I told him I had enough problems. But he must have read nearly everything ever written, and almost anything I asked about he'd explain: stardrives or computer memories or just what my pants were made of. . . .

". . . and telhassium is the thing that ties them all

together. It makes the data processing detailed enough and the transportation economical enough so that it's worth someone's while to make cheap denim clothing on Earth and ship it all the way to Ardattee."

"Yeah?" I rubbed the knee of my jeans. "These really came all the way from Earth? Hell, they've seen more of the galaxy than I have." I laughed.

"They have a longer history, too. The original denim cloth . . ." And he was off again. Half the time what he told me was so technical I didn't know what he was talking about, but I tried not to let it show. Sometimes I wondered whether he really understood what he said himself.

But he seemed to enjoy having an audience. Not the way a performer did, or not exactly—it wasn't just that he liked to show off. But sometimes I caught flashes of a need that ran strong and deep inside him, felt him aching for acceptance. I was a challenge to him, and from the minute I'd taken that first camph and started answering him, I'd been feeding a little bit of that need. Knowing that, I used his need, because that was what life was all about—using and being used. I knew how to fake interest; and sometimes I didn't even have to fake it when I was listening to him. That just made it easier. "What's—telhassium, that makes things go?"

He smiled, blissed on the pure pleasure of knowledge. His eyes looked toward something beyond the pastel green laboratory walls. "Telhassium is element one-seventy. Its pure form is a blue-silver crystal used for information storage in computers. They lock data into the electron shells, and they can run a whole planet's information system on a crystal as big as your thumb. Telhassium makes starship travel easy, giving navigators the number-crunching computers that can set up a long jump in hours instead of weeks.

"Before they had telhassium, starships cost a fortune, and they couldn't even . . ." He went on into a wilderness of words, all of them longer than my arm. "And now even a fast ship like a patrol cruiser carries less than a cubic meter of telhassium crystals on board for its computations. The big cargo ships only carry a little more telhassium than an entire planet uses; and only in case of emergency, because they use the computers of mainline ports like Quarro to do their navigation. A major spaceport can compute a jump to any important system in the Federation, except in the Crab Colonies, in less than an hour."

"Whew." I rubbed my forehead. My mind was still stumbling in the undergrowth of words somewhere back along the trail. "I feel like I swallowed my brain."

"Then maybe we'd better get down to work." He glanced at his data bracelet, looking at the time.

"Hey, not yet. I got more questions. . . ." I never had enough questions, because once he'd answered all I could come up with, we had to work on my telepathy.

"You must lie awake nights thinking them up." His voice began to show an edge.

"I always work best after midnight." But it wasn't by choice any more. My eyes burned from the lack of sleep. I leaned back in my seat, waiting for him to start talking again. "Gimme another camph, will you?" I put a hand out on the cool white tabletop, palm up.

He didn't move, sitting across from me. (You'll have to work for it this time.)

I jerked and swore, unbalancing my chair. "Don't do that to me!"

(Why not? That's why we're here.)

"No!" I flinched as I heard it come out. "I mean, I know that. But I need more time. I just ain't—ready." I was pulling my thoughts in tighter and tighter, weaving defenses to keep him from getting at me again.

"When are you planning to be 'ready'? Tomorrow? Next week? A month from now, a year? You don't have that long, Cat!" Suddenly he was angry. "If you want to stay in this research program, you've got to show results. You have to be able to control your talent, not just 'feel' it—control it under pressure, in ways you never expected to. You have to learn when not to use it, and how to keep other psions from using it against you—" He broke off.

"Why?" I frowned, matching his own.

"Because those are the rules; and if you want to get along, you learn to obey the rules."

"Not where I come from." I pushed up out of my chair and moved away from him.

"You're not in Oldcity now. But you'll be back there in a hurry, Cityboy, if you can't learn to cooperate."

"What's eating you?" I turned to stare at him. He sounded like a Corpse. He'd never called me that before, or threatened me.

"Maybe that you don't even bother to hide how little

you care about all this, about what you're doing here,
or what I'm trying to do to help you." He got up,
following me but keeping out of my reach.

"What do you mean?" Knowing what he meant, that
he'd seen it in my thoughts. "I didn't—"

(The hell you didn't!) His anger and frustration
caught me from an unguarded angle, and hit me behind the eyes. (All right, shadow walker, you've been
using my patience like a wall to hide behind; but you've
finally used it up. No more camphs, no more questions,
no more games until you show me some return.)

"Lemme alone, you vermy bastard!"

(No more being left alone! You'll never be alone
again unless you *make* me leave your mind—)

"Get out, get out!" I pressed my hands against my
ears, like that would do any good. He was through
my defenses and on the inside, and I didn't know
what to do about it to get him out again.

(Make me.) His words echoed through the circuits
of my brain.

"Damn you, damn you—" I was half crazy with
the fear that he really meant it, that he'd never get
out of my head again. I groped for a weapon—not on
the counter beside me, because my body couldn't get
at him; but somewhere in my mind, where I could.
(Damn you! damn you!) Feeling the thought leap like
a spark across the gap between my mind and his. Suddenly making the connection, holding onto it, I com-
pleted the link of thought, (You slad, you son of a
bitch, get out of my mind before I burn you out!), with
a jolt of white-hot rage. (Break, break!)

He broke contact: in the same second my mind was suddenly all my own again, my eyes saw him sway and clutch at a chair for support.

I swayed too, reaching out for the counter edge behind me. I swore softly.

"Congratulations." His own voice was barely more than a whisper. "Psion."

"God." I gulped, and wiped my hand across my mouth. A few more words slipped out, more curses, as I stumbled back to the table and sat down.

Cortelyou sat down across from me again. This time he tossed me the whole pack of camphs. "Here."

I pushed one between my lips with shaking hands. Disconnected filaments pulsed behind my eyes—signposts, beacons, patterns that had lain waiting for me to turn my own eyes inward and see them. . . . We sat there for a long time, not saying anything; while I tried to make myself believe what had happened, while the camph calmed me down.

"How do you feel?" he said, finally. He was all solicitude, now.

"You should know." I glared at him.

He shook his head. "I'm not reading you now; you know that."

"Then how do you think I feel?" I looked away, wishing this room had a window.

"Proud . . . excited . . . like you've made a breakthrough?"

"No. Dirty, lousy—like a freak! That's how you're supposed to feel, ain't it?"

"Did Goba tell you that?" His smile disappeared.

"He didn't have to. Every time I get close to his

mind, or any of them, I can smell it." My hands tightened into fists on my knees.

Cortelyou grimaced. "Damn them, why can't they—"

"Why shouldn't they hate me? Who wants to have somebody else know everything you're thinking? I seen people get killed for less than that!"

"And that's why you're fighting this every step of the way." Half question, half answer.

I shrugged, letting him think he understood everything, when he only understood half of it.

"I'm sorry I was so hard on you." He bent his head. "I should have known . . ."

"Why should you be any different?" I wished he didn't apologize so much; it got on my nerves.

"Because we *are* different. We have to be—not just because of what we can do, but because of the responsibility it puts on us. We do things with our minds that most humans could never do, and that makes them afraid of us. 'In the country of the blind, the one-eyed man is stoned to death.' We have to live by a stricter code than the rest of humanity, to prove to them that they have nothing to fear from us. . . ." He leaned forward. "Do you want to know how I feel about my telepathy?"

No. But I didn't say it. I shifted in my seat, hung onto its hard, curving edges to keep from bolting as I felt him reach into my thoughts again. I held my mind loose, let the sparking strands link with his in the invisible space where our senses met. I was shaking with the effort, and I felt his mind cringe with the fear I couldn't damp out.

But he didn't push me away. Instead the weave of

his thoughts only loosened, like the first time, as he dropped all his defenses and drew me in. The impressions he wanted me to find shimmered on the surface of his awareness where I couldn't help seeing them: he was proud, glad, grateful for the Gift that he'd been born with. . . . Psionics could lead to a new future for humanity, filled with understanding and free of the fear that fed blind hatred. . . . He would never abuse his Gift, never do anything to make the blind ones think of his talent as a threat. . . . He would do *anything* to gain their trust, to make them understand.

But behind the images he held like banners for me to see, I felt the brand of a fresh wound laid on him by some psi-hating corporate lackey—heard the murmur of a thousand other ghosts and shadows. Fury raged in some deep part of his mind, held prisoner by his will. And I realized what it cost him to be a corporate telepath, a missionary in a world of hate-filled deadheads who didn't want to be saved. . . .

I broke contact. "How can you live with that?"

"What?" He looked totally confused.

"They spit on you, they don't give a damn about what you're trying to prove. It's eating your guts out; why don't you quit whoring for those bastards?"

His mouth fell open. "Where did you . . . ?" His face straightened out again. "I've lived with it for years. I'm barely aware of it anymore." It sounded like something he used to put himself to sleep at night. "I believe in what I'm trying to do. It isn't an easy thing, but it isn't impossible." One hand clung to the other. "Haven't you ever endured something unpleasant for something you believed in?" It was almost a challenge.

"Yeah. Staying alive—so I could stay alive." The words slid out, just another smart remark. But then my own mind showed me things I'd done, and let be done to me, that would probably make him say everything I'd just said to him. "I guess you get used to anything, if you have to." I looked down. "So long as you don't think about it too much." I thought about all his facts and figures, filling up his mind until there was no room for anything else to get in the way of his belief. And I understood suddenly why this research was important to him, why I was too, why he'd *had* to make that breakthrough today and force me to prove he was right. I thought about my being a telepath in spite of everything—seeing the lines of psi energy shining with life force. I thought about being born to use them: the Third Eye, the Sixth Sense, the Extra Ear . . . about a screaming thing locked in a cell somewhere in the pit of my mind . . . about thinking too much. I took out another camph.

"Do you know what a 'joining' is?"

I shook my head.

"It's a meeting of minds, between a telepath and another psion, so complete and unguarded that their minds become one—each open to the other totally, with nothing held back. Their psi powers are heightened, each one's by the other's; they do things they could never do alone. It's the ultimate form of giving, of belonging. It's like nothing else you can experience, and it can change the ones who join forever. . . ." His eyes were alive with longing.

"You ever do that?" I asked, because he expected something.

"Once." His clenched fists opened; I heard more joy and loss than I'd ever heard filling one word before. "A pure joining is very rare. It's almost impossible for more than two human psions. It's a combination of the highest ability and the deepest need. . . ." He looked up at me again, and his look told me I'd never experience it, unless somehow I could make my brain stop chasing its own tail.

"I can't imagine ever wanting to get that close to nobody." I leaned back, away from him.

He leaned back too, and sighed. "Well, a journey of a thousand miles starts with the first step."

After that the steps got longer. Now that I could actually make contact with him, he began trying to teach me all the things he'd said I had to learn about controlling my talent. I didn't see what was so important about most of what we did. But then, I didn't understand most of what was happening to me here, anyway. I hardly even knew when I was confused, half the time.

He told me I'd had it easy working with technicians who weren't psions themselves; their concentration and control was so poor that any telepath could keep them at bay. Working against another psion was going to be something else. He explained to me how trained telepaths could sort out the strands of image that patterned someone else's thoughts; how they could locate one particular pattern, follow it along all its branching ways to their scattered ends and back again. He also told me how another telepath could protect that pattern by weaving a shield—burying it behind and between tangles of other images and information—or by sensing the probe and sidetracking it, braiding the intruder's mind into a false strand, a lie. Most psions were better at protecting themselves from a mindread than normal humans, even if they weren't telepaths, just because they were more in control of their own minds.

I was supposed to be a stronger telepath than he was. It should have been easy to keep him out of my mind. But I hadn't been feeling my mind, exercising my talent—and he had. He told me that if one telepath knew the tricks of thought-tracking and the other one didn't, the greenhorn couldn't hide his deepest secret, no matter how much raw confusion he put up to save himself. Then to prove it, he'd make me nervous or angry. I'd forget what I was doing, and he'd walk right into my mind. He didn't usually go very deep, but he didn't need to. Using my telepathy never got any easier, and feeling him pry into me like that still drove me crazy. And then he'd jump on me anyway for letting him do it. For someone who looked so soft, he was as tough as steel when he was doing his job.

And no matter how hard I tried, I couldn't trick *him*, and that just made it worse.

But in spite of everything, working with Cortelyou I finally began to act like a real telepath. Or I thought I did, even if nobody else did. But Goba didn't have any time left to be fussy, he said, when he finally sent me to meet the rest of Siebeling's psions.

The psions were sitting in a circle of chairs, maybe a dozen of them, in a pearly-walled room with a floor of patterned tile. One wall looked out on the sky here, too; farther up in the building, and higher in the air, than I'd ever been before. Siebeling was at the head of the circle when I stopped in the doorway. He frowned at me like I was late and said, "This is Cat. He's a telepath."

They stopped talking. I spotted the red-haired woman from the day I'd first come here, staring at me. I didn't want to go into that room, and know what they were thinking, and be laughed at. What the hell were they staring at, anyhow—? But then I saw the woman with empty eyes who'd given me the scarf. She was watching me too, but her eyes weren't empty this time; and suddenly I saw myself from the outside, clean and neat in a fresh smock and pants, looking like anyone else. I wasn't dirty and dye-smeared now; they were all strangers here, too. A calmness came over me somehow, and suddenly everything was all right. She half smiled at me, and her eyes dropped. I went and sat down, at the end of the circle where all the seats were empty. I pulled a pack of camphs out of my pocket and stuck one into my mouth. Then I finally noticed Cortelyou sitting with the rest of them. He nodded at me.

Siebeling began to talk about how most psions felt afraid or ashamed because they didn't understand their abilities, and society didn't understand psions. Once they learned to control their minds the way they controlled their bodies, they'd see that they weren't freaks; that being a psion could be a good, valuable thing. He called psionic talent the Gift, and he said that it didn't have to hurt them, it was something to be proud of. Learning how to control the Gift was what we were doing here at the Institute. He was smiling all the while he spoke; pride and encouragement filled the words. I'd never seen him like that—it made him look like a different man. I watched other faces around the circle while he spoke, and some of them looked like they'd never smiled much at all, but they smiled now with him.

Afterward we started in on new exercises. Siebeling put a candle on the table behind him and said we were going to use our Gift to help us light it. He held a lighter up in the air and let it go; but it didn't drop. He was controlling it with his mind, by telekinesis. It drifted, past him through the air, and lit the candle. He blew the candle out again and tossed the lighter to the woman who'd smiled at me. "Jule?" I don't know why it surprised me to learn Siebeling was a psion too. A lot of things suddenly made more sense about him. I tried not to stare.

Jule stood up, and then she was standing next to the candle, and then she was back in her seat, before I'd

even blinked—she could teleport. The candle was burning, the lighter was on the table. Siebeling nodded; she
looked down.

Someone else made the lighter float again, telekinesis,
a little shaky; and then Siebeling was throwing it to me.
"What am I supposed to do with it? I ain't a teek."
But he didn't say anything. I sat there feeling stupid
and angry, and then suddenly words filled my mind.
(Fellow telepath. Ask me to light it.) I looked around
the circle until I saw somebody grin at me. It was
Cortelyou. I asked with my face but he shook his
head.

(Ask me.)

His mind was open to mine. I thought, (Will-you-
light-the-candle?) gritting my teeth.

He blinked. (Don't shout. I'll be glad to.)

I threw him the lighter. He reached over and lit the
candle. Siebeling nodded, and tossed the lighter out
again. It went on around the circle, and I started to
feel like maybe this wouldn't be so bad after all.

And when the lighter came to the red-haired woman,
she just got up and walked over to the candle to light
it, as if she couldn't find any other way to do it. That
made me smile, but she didn't look embarrassed. Siebeling saw me grinning. He said, to everyone, "Darra's
talent is precognition—predicting the future. Psionic
skills vary, just as artistic skills do. Sometimes your
skill will be the only one that can solve a problem;
sometimes it's the only one that won't. Don't feel self-
conscious if you have to do something the hard way—
like the rest of humanity." Everyone else laughed.

Later, when I couldn't move a chair, and neither could Cortelyou, Cortelyou shrugged and thought. (There's always the cards. We're the only ones who can cheat.) I laughed out loud then, so that everyone looked at me, and the woman named Jule smiled again. And I guess I'd learned more than a couple of psi tricks that afternoon.

But then Siebeling said something while I was thinking about that, and everyone got up to leave. I looked across at Cortelyou and thought, (What?)

(It's time for What to Do until Corporate Security Comes.)

I wondered what the hell that was supposed to mean, but I got up and followed everyone else.

It turned out to be another laboratory I'd never seen before. I sat down in a chair in front of a terminal and touchboard like everyone else, and someone at the end of the room began to talk to us about communications. He might as well have been talking backward for all the good it did me. I couldn't understand anything; I sat and felt bored, rolling a camph between my fingers, until he began saying, "Touch the segment labeled ON. Now spread your fingers across the area marked with . . ."

I stared down at the board in front of me, and put out my hand, and pulled it back. My skin started to itch. I can't . . . Cortelyou wasn't anywhere near me; I couldn't ask him for help. But Jule was sitting next to me, she looked like she knew what she was doing. I tried to reach into her mind. She gasped and her hand went up to her face; her mind drove me out with a bright flash of terror. Then her gray eyes were full of shadow and surprise, staring back at me. She was as afraid of intruders as I was.

I turned away, back to the terminal, my hands clenching. But it was already too late; Siebeling had seen it. He came up behind me, and I felt him look past me at Jule, and then down at the dark screen, before he said, "What's the matter?" I didn't say anything.

"Touch ON." Like he was trying to be patient.

I just sat there, feeling him get angry. "I can't."

"What?"

"He probably can't read, Ardan," the red-haired precog said, loud enough so that everyone in the room could hear it.

"Oh? Is that true?"

I nodded, barely moving my head, feeling like my neck would snap.

"Then I'm afraid you're not qualified to—"

I stood up. "Why do I have to do this? This's nothin' to do with being a telepath! The hell with—" I felt a touch, like a soft hand somewhere in mind, and then all of a sudden I shut up and sat down in my seat again, wondering. A voice said, "It isn't a crime. I'll help him, Ardan. Come on, Cat, it's easy, watch me. . . ."

And I watched Jule touch a corner of the grid, because I was too ashamed to look anywhere else. The screen brightened. She turned it off, and then I tried it. After a minute Siebeling said, "If you can learn to do it, I'll tell you why you have to," and he left us alone.

"You can do it," she said, not looking at me.

"What do you care if I can? Why should you help me?"

Her face changed; she looked up at me with those empty eyes and said, "I don't know." She shrugged. And she didn't know.

I felt stupid and confused again, I was going to tell her to mind her own, but I just said, "I'm sorry, about . . ." and I touched my head. She nodded. I didn't say anything more to her, but I let her help me.

Siebeling came back to watch me work after the others had gone for the day. He almost seemed disappointed to find me doing things right. "If you're going to have this much trouble with everything, I can't ask Jule . . ."

"But I don't mind, Ardan. He wants to stay; I'll help him." She got up. "I have nothing else but time."

"We could use another telepath," somebody said. "He did all right today."

I looked past Siebeling. I'd thought everyone else was gone, but Cortelyou was still standing across the room.

Siebeling frowned. "I just don't think he—"

"I want to stay here. I'll work."

He glanced back at me, hesitated. "All right, then. I suppose I . . . Jule? If you can wait, I'll . . . see you out." For just a second he looked like an embarrassed kid.

Jule had started fading away toward the door; she stopped and came back. I saw Cortelyou grin at nothing behind her, and then he followed her back to where I was sitting.

Siebeling looked annoyed, but he only said, "When

I told you what you were getting into, I didn't tell you everything; because I didn't know how you'd work out. Everyone else here already knows the full truth about what they're getting into. You should understand all of it too, before you make your final decision.

"We are psions working with our abilities; the FTA is 'sponsoring' it. Everything I told you about that part is true. But they hope it will be more than simply a research project. They're investigating a matter of Federation security that involves psionics; they think we may attract the attention of the criminal behind it—someone they call Quicksilver." The word seemed to burn his mouth. I saw Cortelyou's mouth turn down; lines of tension formed on Jule's face.

"Nice name," I said, raising my eyebrows. "You all got somethin' against it?"

"Quicksilver gives all psions a bad name," Cortelyou said, and Siebeling nodded.

"He's a renegade, he uses his psionic talents to commit crimes all over the galaxy."

"What kind of crimes?"

Siebeling started to frown again. Cortelyou answered the question: "Expensive ones. Impossible ones."

"Ugly ones," Jule said softly, and all of a sudden I didn't want to hear the details.

Cortelyou nodded. "He's rumored to have multiple psi talents, all of them perfectly controlled. Just take one, telekinesis, and let your mind play with the possibilities. . . . Combines hire him and use him against rival governments. He'll work for anyone who pays him enough. And he uses his psi to slip through Corporate Security nets like water. So far they haven't been able to touch him. They don't know his real identity—they don't even know what he looks like. But they want him stopped. That's why we're here."

"We're bait, in other words," Siebeling said, "and if Quicksilver takes the bait, we'll be expected to act as undercover agents. Nothing at all may happen; but if we do become involved with this Quicksilver, we'll be in considerable danger. Because of that I've arranged for everyone to be credited a substantial—"

"Everybody?" I said. He nodded, and told me how much; my arm slipped off the back of the chair. "Jeezu you mean . . . I'd have a rating, a data bracelet, the whole thing? Like a real human being?"

"I suppose so." He glanced at the clock in the lower corner of my terminal screen. "Is that acceptable to you?"

"Are you kidding?"

"Jule . . ." He turned to go.

"Hey, you gonna tell me any more about it?" Suddenly the strange questions the Corpses had asked me before I came here, and all the things Cortelyou had been showing me without telling me why, began to fit together in my mind.

"I thought you weren't interested in anything but avoiding Contract Labor."

The others looked at Siebeling, surprised, and then at me.

"Well . . . maybe I changed my mind."

"Do you know anything about the Crab Colonies?" That was Cortelyou, naturally.

"I heard the Crab Nebula is an exploded star. It's . . . out there, someplace." I waved at the window.

"It's forty-five hundred light-years from here," Cortelyou said. "But you're on the right track."

"What's a light-year?"

Siebeling sighed and dropped the folder he was carrying. "If you really want to know about this, you'll have to have more background than you do. I suppose we can give it to you. . . ." So the three of them told me about the Crab Colonies and the FTA and Earth, and what all that had to do with us being here at the Institute.

The Crab Nebula, Cortelyou said, was a cloud of gas and debris—what was left of a supernova, a star that blew itself up before humans ever left home. To astronomers on Ardattee it looked like a smoke ring; and like a smoke ring it was expanding through space. A light-year was the distance light could travel in a year—moving at around three hundred thousand kilometers a second. But even at speeds like that it took thousands of years for the light to reach us here; the real Nebula was even larger than the nearly five-thousand-year-old image they saw from observatories. Several star systems with inhabited planets were located near the Nebula in space; those were the Crab Colonies.

The Federation Transport Authority controlled the Colonies directly, and the rest of the Federation indirectly, because it regulated shipping. The FTA had grown out of something that had been set up long ago back on Earth, before the days of stardrives and space exploration. Its original purpose had been to oversee trade for the confederation of multinational corporations that finally took over Earth's old national governments. As the solar system was settled, making shipping and trade a thousand times more complicated, the FTA became more important. And it grew even more by taking over the distribution of resources during a handful of intrasystem wars. Finally it began to build its own ships and even weapons and hired more security forces than a lot of corporations did.

Then faster-than-light stardrive was invented, and suddenly humans could reach the nearest stars in weeks instead of years. Suddenly Earth's multinational corporate empires had the chance to become multiworld empires, and they started sharpening their knives to carve up the stars. The old toothless Worldgov mutated and survived; it set up guidelines for interstellar law, even though it didn't have the power to back them up. And the new Human Federation began expanding like a bubble outward from Earth. Finally the FTA set up an expedition to prospect in the Crab Nebula for telhassium. Cortelyou had told me about telhassium—an element so rare that it was almost impossible to find outside the heart of a star. The Federation needed it in large amounts to make its new faster-than-light stardrive cheap and simple.

The Transport Authority expedition found a piece of the exploded sun's corpse there, still orbiting the tiny neutron star that was all that was left of its mass after the supernova explosion. They called the thing Cinder, and it was the nearest anyone had ever seen to a solid piece of telhassium ore. Once they began mining it, the citizens of the Human Federation were free to travel between its settled worlds as easily as they'd traveled between continents on just one world.

But they hadn't counted on one thing: The FTA

took the telhassium for itself. Controlling the telhassium supply meant that the FTA no longer just oversaw the Federation's transportation, it controlled it. No matter how big any combine was—and especially if it wanted to get any bigger—it had to toe the FTA's line or it didn't get the telhassium it needed to move its ships and process its data. The original shipping empires suffered the most, because the FTA took just about all their independent control away and made them its tools. The FTA wasn't all that unreasonable in what it wanted—power and money—but it cut into the power and profits of everybody else. It also built up a big enough Special Forces arm to actually start enforcing some of the Federation's laws. It kept the combines from the kind of throat-cutting competition they were used to, and they didn't much like that. But they lived with it.

So an isolated Colony of the Federation grew up out around the Crab, controlled by the FTA and independent from everything else. And the rest of the Federation, even though it was still only a few hundred light-years across, wasn't a bubble shape expanding evenly into space anymore. It started to stretch out toward the Colonies. Earth lost its economic influence, and Quarro became an independent Federal District, the new center of power and money and everything worth having.

All of that was why Quarro's District Corporate Security, the FTA's own soldiercops, had gotten involved in something going on way out in the Crab Colonies. The FTA had learned through its spies and informers that some sort of dirty business was taking shape out there, and they figured some combine or alliance of combines was backing it. But they couldn't get any closer to the heart of it; all their leads just kept slipping through their fingers. They were sure Quicksilver was behind the plot, whatever it was. That made them real nervous, because the telhassium supply was out there in the Colonies. But eventually they learned that Quicksilver had contacts here in Quarro—and that he was looking for recruits.

So we were here to work undercover, to find the real source of the trouble and make sure it was stopped before it knocked the Federation on its ass. Siebeling made it sound like making history, like poor psions saving the galaxy. I thought about that, and about me as a big hero. . . .

Siebeling said, "Keep that smirk off your face. This isn't a joke. If you can't take it seriously, I'll send you back—you aren't being given the chance to slide out of anything here."

I sighed. "I'm glad you ain't a mind reader."

Cortelyou laughed and shook his head. Siebeling just turned away, looking toward Jule.

I watched them leave together, all of them going home when I couldn't. My head was crammed so full of information that I felt as if moving it would make everything overflow. I thought about psions plotting out in the Colonies, about going out there and stopping them, about being a hero and a part of history. I looked down at my hands, at my bare wrist that would be wearing a data bracelet in a few more weeks . . . at the

broken thumb that had healed crooked after I'd picked
the wrong pocket once. And I realized suddenly that I
was glad I wasn't going home.

The next day Goba and his techs used hypnosis on
me again, giving me a screen of half-true memories
that would protect the real truths I knew now from
anything but a direct telepathic probe. And beginning
the next day Dere Cortelyou worked me harder than
ever, forcing me to learn the mind tricks I needed to
handle a direct attack. It wasn't any easier; but at
least now I knew why I was doing it, so it was easier
to keep trying.

And then I really was a part of the research program,
playing psi games with the rest of the psions and
waiting for something to happen. Before long I began
to wish we'd be waiting there forever. Sometimes I
think that was the happiest time of my life.

It surprised me how fast I'd gotten used to the
Sakaffe Institute, because it was so different from—
everything, from before. I had decent clothes that fit
me. I could eat as much as I wanted to, any time I
felt like it. I even had my private room. They'd stopped
locking me in at night, but by now it didn't matter:
the bed was soft, clean, and mine, and that was all I
wanted. There were a dozen different projects going
on at the Institute besides ours, too; and once they'd
gotten used to seeing me, the lab workers let me hang
around and watch. Or just sit and stare at the threedy
in one of the lounges, if I felt like it. Nobody cared.
I was never bored. I didn't even miss the drugs; just
looking out any window was like some kind of an

alindith dream. I had to pinch myself sometimes to be sure it was all real.

I even liked to think about what I was supposed to be doing here: I'd seen a show on the threedy, *Nebula Pioneers*, about Colonists and miners out in the Crab Colonies making a home in the alien wilderness. Life was hard out on the frontier worlds, but it was exciting, and no one cared what you'd been before, only what you were trying to be now. It was a place where you were free to start again, and maybe make it all come out right this time. I thought maybe I'd like to try that; thought about using some of my money to go there when this was over. I was glad we were supposed to be helping them out.

But more than anything else I liked working with the rest of the psions—even if it meant being one myself. It was hard work, and Siebeling always seemed to make it harder; but I never wanted to quit. I was getting to be pretty good, too. I think I'd have been good even if I hadn't been trying to keep Siebeling off my back. I wanted to be good; I guess I wanted to prove something to somebody. Maybe to myself.

But even so, I wouldn't have been much good without Jule taMing. After that first day, whenever we had to work with any equipment she stayed around afterward, and went over everything we did with me until I knew it from memory. I'd half expected Cortelyou would take over teaching me, but he only laughed and said he knew where my attention was now—meaning on Jule—and I might as well follow it. I swore at him, blushing, and did.

Jule taught me how to use one machine after

another: she taught me letters and symbols that stood for the same thing on different boards; she worked with me until soon I could pick things up almost as fast as anyone else. . . .

". . . then that, and that—". I touched the wrong square and the comm panel lit up with red. "Damn!" I pulled back from the touchboard, shaking out my hands.

Jule leaned past me and cleared the panel for the tenth time, her dark hair brushing my shoulder. "Those two letters are almost the same; anyone could make that mistake. Try again," she said, still as patient and calm as she'd been an hour before. Somehow she never made me feel stupid.

But that doesn't mean I didn't feel stupid anyway. "Mother Earth, I ain't never gonna get them straight! They don't *mean* nothin'!"

She looked down at me directly for once. "You're tired. . . . Your body is screaming for sleep. Why do you stay awake all night, when you know you have to get up and work?" It wasn't critical, just curious.

I tensed; it still made me jumpy when she knew exactly what I was feeling. She was an empath besides being a 'port: she knew what everybody felt, whether she wanted to or not. I frowned at my hands. "I'm used to it." Back in Oldcity I'd stayed awake all night because that was when the crowds were out, and I lived off the crowds. Now I stayed awake because I was afraid to sleep.

Her face told me that she knew there was more,

but she looked away and didn't push it. She had her own fears. She shut off the comm's touchboard, murmuring. "They don't mean anything. . . ."

I followed her across the lab. Outside twilight was staining Quarro a deep violet-blue; lights were coming on. There was a roof garden a few stories down below us; trees moved in the cool air of dusk. Jule lit up another terminal and began to work with it. I stood beside her, looking out; close enough so that my hip brushed hers. And suddenly I couldn't help thinking about how close she was, touching me, the way her hair moved. . . . I felt a rush of heat rise through me, and wondered what she'd—

The thought that she knew everything I felt hit me like a bucket of cold water. I tied my mind into a knot, trapping the thought inside, and moved away from her.

She looked up, startled—either because she'd felt what I felt, or just because her awareness of me had been stopped dead. I looked out the window, taking out a camph, rocking on my heels.

"Cat?" She called me back. I couldn't tell what she was thinking, but for just a second the corners of her mouth turned up a little. She wasn't looking at me as I stopped beside her, but she said, "You move like a dancer. You're very quick and graceful."

"Me?" I laughed, embarrassed. "Comes from walkin' on eggs all the time." I pushed my hands into my pockets. It was the first time I could ever remember anybody noticing something good about me. "What's that?" I nodded at the terminal. It was just a plain bright screen with a couple of control buttons below it. There were three letters printed on the screen.

"That's your name."

I touched it with my hand. "My name?"

She nodded, tracing the symbols with a stylus, naming them, C-A-T spells *Cat*.

I said the sounds after her. "I seen all those letters before."

She nodded again.

But now they really mean something. I reached out, pulled back a little, finally took the stylus she was holding out to me. I touched its tip to the screen, leaving a bright smear.

Someone came into the room. I felt it before I saw them . . . Siebeling, and a Corpse with him. I jerked around, dropping the stylus, looking for another way out—

Jule's hand caught my sleeve. "It's all right. He's not here for you. It's me he wants to see."

"You?" But already I saw that he wasn't a Citicorpse, that he was wearing the insignia of some combine government. "Jule, you got a record?"

She didn't answer. Siebeling came over to us, leaving the Corpse waiting in the doorway. Jule usually started to glow all over whenever she saw Siebeling, but this time her face was set and pale, and her mind was full of darkness.

"Jule, there's someone here to see you," Siebeling said.

She nodded, keeping her head down. "I know. I don't want to talk to him, Ardan. Make him go away, please. . . ." She began to bite a fingernail.

"I think you should talk to him." Siebeling's voice was quiet, but it was almost an order. "Jule, you didn't tell me that you—"

She picked the stylus up and put it into my hand. "Here," she whispered. "Practice." Then she moved away from us, toward the Corpse, her arms folded in front of her and her hands clutching her elbows. She was trying to hold in her tension, but I could feel it like electricity in the air.

"What's he want? She ain't bein' arrested, is she?"

Siebeling glared at me like I'd insulted her. "Of course not. He brought a message from her family."

"Her family?" There was something so solitary about Jule that I'd always thought she must be as alone as I was. Siebeling was the only other person she ever really talked to besides me. The two of them had had a thing going almost from the start; everybody knew it even though they pretended not to. It wasn't easy to keep a secret from a bunch of psions, and Jule was only just learning how to keep her feelings hidden at all. She might as well have shouted it. If she wanted to get involved with Siebeling that was her business . . . even though I couldn't see what she saw in him, myself. "They sent a Corpse to tell her? Whose colors is he wearing?"

"Centauri Transport. It's a shipping combine; the biggest and one of the oldest." And the taMing family controlled its holdings. *Her* family . . . the thought was lying on the surface of his mind, bright with his own surprise.

"You mean she's rich?"

"Does she look rich?" He bit off the words.

I shrugged. "Not from here." She was talking to the Corpse, still hugging herself, still broadcasting resentment. "Don't worry. I ain't planning to mug her." I turned back to the screen, annoyed, and started trying to copy my name.

"What are you doing?" Siebeling said it like he'd caught me defacing property.

"Doin' what she told me to do." C . . . A . . . T. My hand shook; I was holding the stylus like it would jump out of my fist, and the letters looked like pieces of string. I made myself relax. C-A-T. C-A-T. CAT. CAT. CAT. The picture of my name. It got easier and easier. A feeling I'd never known before took hold of me. Maybe it was pride.

"A waste." Siebeling let the words slip out and squash it. His mind showed me an ignorant criminal, a green-eyed Oldcity hoodlum who was wasting everybody's time.

I looked up, smarting with anger, ready to do something we were both going to regret. But a burst of fresh feeling from Jule cut between us—a kind of startled triumph, and then echoes of the same feeling that had started inside me. She was walking toward us again; the Corpse was gone from the doorway. She didn't seem to notice our tension, for once. Her own mind was clenched around the irony that her family only interfered in her life when it was going right. But her gray eyes were shining and alive as she said, "I'm staying."

Siebeling's tight face relaxed into a sudden smile, his relief was almost as loud as hers was. But he said, "Are you sure that—?"

"Yes." She nodded, ending it. She started to look back at me.

Siebeling caught her hand, trying to pull her away; but she broke free. "Wait." Siebeling shot me a dark glance past her. I didn't say anything. Jule looked at what I'd done on the screen. She grinned at me for a second like we'd both had a triumph, and pride filled me again. Siebeling put an arm around her then, the first time he'd ever done that in front of me, and this time she went with him.

I went back to the comm console and switched it on, and went through the sequence she'd been trying to teach me. I did it a few more times, perfectly, and then I went back and wrote my name some more. I thought about asking Jule to show me some other words tomorrow: *maybe I could get an instruction tape, or something. . . .*

But after that there wasn't any more equipment I had to learn, and somehow Siebeling always seemed to have something better for Jule to do than waste her time on me. Without her pulling me, I went back to watching the threedy like the ignorant hood I was, and just forgot about learning anything else.

But that didn't change how I felt about being at the Institute. Being a psion, working with the other psions, was still like nothing I'd ever known. Even if some of them called me "the mental pickpocket" in the back of their minds, when we worked together there was still a bond between us. Because then we were all the same, and nothing else counted. If the psi talent made me angry, I knew that most of them knew how it felt.

Only they'd lived with it, and maybe hated it, a lot longer than I had. I knew I'd been lucky in burying it all my life, and that made living with it now easier for me.

I guess it was making it easier for all of us, sharing the changes. I thought some of them even began to like me a little—Dere Cortelyou, for one. And Jule. Back in Oldcity the closest I'd ever come to having a friend was sleeping in the same room with somebody. I'd never even run with a gang. This was the first time I'd ever belonged to anything; I never figured it would feel so right. I finally had something to lose. Sometimes I was afraid I'd pinch myself once too often, and wake up for good.

4

"Here!"

(Behind you—)

"Got it!" (Thanks.)

"Keep it moving. Again!"

"All right, all right. . . ."

"Here!"

"No, *there!*" Laughter.

We were working together, caught up in what Siebeling called "juggling." Each of us used our psi talents any way we could, to take the others by surprise or warn each other, in a free-flowing, shapeless game. We tossed things and moved things and moved ourselves, reached out with our bodies and minds; making our control surer and more fluid, training ourselves to respond without losing focus or dropping guard—

"Damn!" Or dropping a block, or a bowl.

(Gotcha!) "Gotcha!" More laughter.

"Twenty-three! Time?"

"Catch!"

"Over and under—"

(Cat, *warning.*)

Jule's sending lit my mind a second too late, as the stool that had been sitting clear across the room materialized right behind me. I stepped back into it before I could stop myself; my feet tangled and I landed on the hard ripple-rings of the tile floor. Siebeling had done it to me again. He was good, real good. Too good. I lay on the floor and thought things at him that I didn't have the breath to say out loud, but his mind was woven solid and he didn't feel a thing. *Didn't feel anything, the stinking—* Jule did; I saw her wincing, at my anger or at my pain. Guilt pinched me, and I tried to get control of my feelings, for her sake.

The others stood shifting from foot to foot. I shut my own mind against their muttering thoughts.

"Come on," Siebeling said, and you couldn't tell from his voice how much he must be enjoying it. "Get up, you're breaking the rhythm."

"You're breaking my neck! Why is it always me?"

"Because you're the least experienced," he said quietly.

"No—because you're always on my back, that's why!" I started to pick myself up, piece by piece.

"If I give you more attention, it's because you need it. You obviously need it or you wouldn't have fallen. Stop making excuses."

I got up, rubbing my bruises, and kicked the stool toward him. He watched me with that look I'd gotten to know too well, one dark with something I couldn't ever reach; as if maybe even he didn't know why he hated the sight of me. Then suddenly he looked away from me toward Jule, and the thread of tension snapped. He looked down. He shrugged and said, "That's enough for today. We'll work on this again tomorrow." He gestured toward the doorway at the far end of the hall, making a point of not looking at me now. As he turned, I heard Cortelyou mutter to him, "Quit picking on the kid, Ardan. It's not what he needs from you. You just make him expect to fail. . . ." I moved away from them, straight for the door; wondering if seeing me fail wasn't just what Siebeling wanted.

When I was almost to the doorway, I had a sudden dizzy flash, my mind's eye saw *me*, like a mirror picking up the image from some other psion's mind. But the image came from outside the room, not through the eyes of anyone here . . . not from the mind of anyone I knew. I stopped, touching my head. We were being watched; someone was waiting in the hall. But when I got outside, no stranger whose mind burned with cold fire was waiting for me. The hall was empty. I went on to the lifts; I got into the first one that came and sent it up before anyone else could follow me.

When it couldn't go any higher, it let me out into the quiet lounge at the top of one of the Institute's peaks. There were a handful of lounges spread through the building's ice-sculpture sprawl; this lounge was one not many people bothered with, because you couldn't see the ocean. Today the sky was weeping, lidded with clouds, wrapping the towers of Quarro in dirty gauze; no one else at all was up here. That suited me fine. I settled down into the formless pile of seat in the center of the room, letting it ease my stiffness as I took out another camph. I leaned back, watching the billowing rain slide down the transparent ripples of the dome. I'd never seen rain before I came here, except once, in Godshouse Circle. It was warm and brown. I'd felt like Quarro was pissing on me, and I didn't like it. I remem-

bered how for a long time I hadn't even known what
the sky was.

I'd thought I'd come up here to be angry, but somehow now I didn't have the strength for it. I just felt
tired. My mind lay open, gray and empty like the sky.
I closed my eyes, listening to the patter and drip of
water; but the space behind my eyes filled up with
images of Oldcity, like tears, and I blinked them open
again. "Damn!" pinching myself one more time, just to
be sure.

"Cat. Come in out of the rain."

It was Jule: I knew her voice; I knew the quick, shy
whisper of her mind. I hadn't heard the lift come up;
but she didn't need the lift. I turned on the couch and
she was standing there half smiling in her dark,
shroud-soft clothes, with her black hair in a heavy
braid hanging to her waist. The room seemed warmer
and lighter suddenly, now that I was sharing it with
her. "You still here?"

She shrugged, glancing down at herself. "The world's
a prison, and we are all our own jailers. . . . I was still
here the last time I looked." Jule was a poet—poetry
was like psi, she said, like thought, a thing that com-
pressed images to essence. Sometimes she talked like a
poet; she made a little joke of it, so that you wouldn't
mind. I didn't mind, anyway. She came over and sat
down beside me, not too close. She was like a shadow,
somehow too insubstantial to be an intruder. She always seemed to know what was happening inside me—
sometimes better than I did myself—and whether she
should stay or go away again.

I'd asked her once, early on, what it was like to be

able to teleport. She said, "It's good when you want to get away from it all," not looking at me. The image that slipped out of her mind then was such a surprise that I didn't believe it. But I knew it had to be true, so after a while I'd asked the only question I could: "Jule, what made you come here?" And knowing she'd already shown me half the answer, she said, "One night I tried to drown myself." She told me about it like she was telling a story about someone else; how a Corpse who was a telepath had pulled her out of the lake in the park. He'd spent hours talking to her about why she hated her life, and in the end he'd told her about this research program, how they were looking for psions who needed help. He'd made her promise to look into it, so that she'd have something to hold onto again. She kept the promise.

I'd told her then why I was here—my side of it. Everyone already knew Corporate Security's side. And it was being able to tell that mattered, letting it out; what we were telling didn't make any difference, as if there was an understanding that no judgments would be made. But she never told me why she'd wanted to drown. She only said, "It happens when you've forgotten all your excuses for not doing it. I've remembered some of them again, now."

Now she sat beside me looking out at the rain. I looked at the smooth profile of her face; I wondered again about questions without answers. But I didn't go after the answers in her mind. Not because I was afraid she'd catch me, but because I knew how she felt about intruders. I knew how I'd feel. Even now she was so shy that she barely spoke to any of the others, except for Siebeling. I didn't know why she still liked to share space with me, but somehow I was glad she did. I didn't want to do anything to make it end.

"Your mind was all gray," she said. "Where was it taking you?" She still watched the rain. It was hard for her to look at anyone for long, she'd said: the eyes were a window to our minds.

"Oldcity." I shrugged, working my twisted thumb, watching the rain.

"Oldcity . . ." She murmured the word, closing her eyes. "Here in Quarro they call it the Tank. Why is that; do you know?"

"No." I glanced back. "Maybe because once you're tossed down there, you can't ever get out."

"Fish tank," she sighed. "Feeder tank." She looked at her own hands; her nails were bitten down to nothing. "When I was a little girl, my father took me to a pet shop. There were hundreds of creatures there, all crying, yearning at me with their hearts; I couldn't choose. Then I saw the fish—two walls full of them, beautiful living jewels, and another tank, half hidden away. The sides of that one were green with slime, and the fish were gasping on the surface for air, or lying stunned and still in the water, waiting for death. I asked why, and they told me that was the feeder tank, it didn't matter how they lived. I could feel them suffering, and no one cared! I started to cry and hold my head. 'Let me have them, Daddy, they're sad, they hurt. . . .' All the animals and all the people in the store began to moan and cry, because I projected it. My father was mortified." Her voice roughened. She folded her fingers under; one hand hugged the other. "His changeling daughter had humiliated the family in public again. He took me away without buying me anything, and never let me have another pet." She looked back at me, finally. "That's what I know about tanks. . . . I've always thought, If they could only feel what I felt, if they could only *know*, they'd never—" She broke off, and her eyes were looking somewhere else, desperately.

I sank further into the couch, hunching my shoulders, and didn't say anything. The spicy end of the camph smarted on my tongue.

We both jerked upright at the chime of the lift arriving, and turned to watch as the door slid open. A man stepped out—tall, middle-aged, rich. He had a neat dark beard, an expensive hairstyle to go with the expensive hand-cast gold at his throat. He wore a summer suit draped with watercolor silk; his clothes were so simple, and fit so perfectly, that they had to have been made for him alone. He was almost as thin as I was, but his face was handsome, in a way that looked like it would last all his life.

And he was dead. I heard Jule suck in her breath beside me, feeling the same thing with her mind: nothing. No . . . *not dead. He was Death.*

"I hope I'm not intruding." He spoke, and even smiled as he came toward us. "My name is Rubiy." He bowed to Jule and made a series of gestures with his hands—something that would've fitted two people meeting in a palace. He didn't even glance at me; I was glad.

"You're a psion," Jule said faintly, more to herself than to him. Her own hands were motionless in her lap.

He nodded. "Yes, I am. Something we have in common." Suddenly the deadness in my mind made perfect sense. He didn't let anything out. But what he had wasn't like my own blind defense; his was the kind of talent that Siebeling had told us about, the kind that none of us could ever hope to reach.

"Are you joining the research?" Jule asked, with a kind of awe.

"No." He smiled politely, but it was just something he did with his mouth. He controlled his body as perfectly as he controlled his mind. I'd seen men with that kind of arrogance in Oldcity. I knew enough to keep out of their way.

"What do you want from us?" I said, finally, because someone like him didn't do things like this for no reason.

"Direct and to the point." He was still smiling. He settled smoothly on the cushioned window ledge, keeping his distance. "I heard about what Dr. Siebeling was doing here, and came to see it for myself. And to offer you a job. I've been more fortunate than most psions, obviously. . . ." He gestured with a ring-covered hand. There was something strange about the way he spoke: not an accent, but just the opposite. The words were all too perfectly shaped, like he was afraid of making a mistake. "My psionic ability has given me everything I could want. But I've never forgotten the suffering that psions endure in this society. And so I've come to offer you the chance to work for me—with me—in a project that could give you all the wealth, all the independence, all the power you ever dreamed of."

I swallowed a laugh. "You're not too sure of yourself, are you? What do you do with your psi, rob vaults long-distance? Heart attacks for hire?" I thought about the rumors and horror stories I'd heard, all the reasons why people should hate psions.

"Telekinesis has its uses." His ice-green eyes narrowed. Suddenly I was afraid—afraid I might be right, afraid of him. "But neither of those possibilities falls particularly close to the mark. My venture is on an entirely different scale."

I glanced at Jule, my skin prickling. Her look said that she was there way ahead of me. I drowned the realization in mind-static before it could form into conscious thought: that this was what we'd been waiting for. The messenger from Quicksilver, the psion who could make the whole Federation afraid of his shadow. I tried to make all my sudden jangling excitement feel like it belonged to what Rubiy had just said; not sure if he was trying to read us, or even whether we'd know it if he did.

"Isn't this happening too fast?" Jule sat forward, surprising me. "You don't even know us."

"On the contrary." He shook his head. "I've been observing you all, privately, for days—studying your talents and your resources, making inquiries . . . deciding who would fit in, and who would simply be a ¹' bility. I've already narrowed my list."

I wondered how much more he would have narrowed it if he'd dropped in on us a few weeks earlier, and overheard one of the "special sessions" we'd been put through. . . . I pushed it out of my thoughts again as fast as I could. I was realizing suddenly what it would mean to try to spy on a whole gang of psions. The thought made me sweat. But if Rubiy hadn't seen the truth in my mind or somebody's by now, it couldn't be that simple, even for someone like him. The false images that we'd had put into our memories must be working; and besides, it wasn't that easy to walk into another psion's mind. I ought to know that, if anybody did. I began to relax, just a little.

"You have both telepathy and telekinesis?" Jule was saying.

Rubiy nodded. "As well as teleportation. I am something of a genetic freak, even among 'freaks.'. . ."

I'd thought no human could do all that. Rubiy went on asking Jule questions, answering her own. Her voice was so small that it was hard to hear. I wondered why he'd choose somebody like her, someone so nervous that he could hardly count on her under pressure. . . .

". . . And you are, of course, one of the illustrious taMings," he was saying. It wasn't a question. "Your family controls Centauri Transport. It's rare to find a psion of such distinguished lineage."

Jule frowned. "Most of them are strangled at birth." The bitter sarcasm of it startled a laugh out of Rubiy. I looked at Jule, not really believing those words had come out of her mouth. Her hands twisted the worn black cloth of her shirt. "I'm only a country cousin."

But doors shut in her mind; even I knew she was lying. Rubiy had to know it, too; just like he had to know that whatever she'd been once, she was nothing and nobody now.

But he said, "Nonetheless, for what we'll be doing, it's an excellent qualification."

She didn't ask why. I did.

Rubiy only smiled at me, gently.

"Okay, then." I pulled my feet up under me. "Why me? If you've really been watching what we do, you know I ain't worth spitting on as a 'path. I might as well be dead for all the good I'd be to you." I wasn't sure if I was just asking, or trying to talk him out of something.

"You may want to think you're the psionic idiot of this group, but believe me, your potential is greater than anything you'll ever see here." Suddenly his eyes were like spotlights, and my own were like window glass.

No. I looked down and away, shaking my head. "That ain't—that ain't what Siebeling thinks."

"What Dr. Siebeling thinks, and what he really understands, are two different things."

Jule stiffened beside me; a tiny line formed between her brows. I said, "You ought to tell him that."

"I intend to. Because he is a doctor—and for other skills—he is also one of my 'chosen.'" Rubiy nodded, dark humor twisting his face. His foot tapped a silent tattoo on the carpet.

"What makes you sure I'm so good?"

"The obvious: Your shield ability. Your eyes. That

clumsy trauma-barrier you've built can be broken down. These incompetents have hardly breached it. And then your mind will shine like a star."

My eyes. . . . I rubbed the scar above my left eye, feeling my body tense again.

His face changed, and so did the subject. "You're currently on probation of sorts, from Corporate Security: you didn't welcome the attention of Contract Labor's recruiters. Would it really have been so bad, compared to Oldcity? They say 'Contract Labor builds worlds.' That it teaches you skills, and gives you a stake. That it's a chance to escape from a place like Oldcity, a choice—"

"They say you're better off dead than living in Oldcity, too. But that don't mean I want to find out the hard way. At least in Oldcity I knew what to expect."

"I see." He—understood, somehow I knew it. I could feel it. "And what did you do there?"

"Steal things, mostly; I was a slip. But now I'm just the mental pickpocket around here." My mouth twitched.

And then for the first time I felt his mind make contact—not to intrude on me, not to take anything, but only to give: pictures slipped loose somewhere in his memory and he showed me why he understood. . . . I caught images of a ragged, hungry kid with psi burning inside his head like fire, cursed by the Gift, like too many other psions in too many slums, in too many cities on too many worlds. But not like all the rest— not a loser, not a weakling; selling what he could do with his psi to anyone who'd pay, for anything they wanted. Anything. And they always paid, plenty, or they were sorry they didn't. Until before long he was out of the slum and rich, he didn't need to sell his talent anymore. But he still hired out, on his own terms, if the offer was right; because he was the best and he enjoyed proving it.

And he was sitting there across from me, with his arrogance licking at us like a colorless flame, the sky weeping behind his back: *Quicksilver*. This was Quicksilver himself—suddenly I knew it couldn't be anyone else. He'd come here to choose us personally, not even hiding his face or name, making fools of Corporate Security without even realizing it. He was that sure of himself.

His cold green eyes held me, and I wondered what he could see in my face; but I didn't feel him touch my mind again. "Are you interested in what I have to offer?"

"Yeah." My voice hardly carried to my own ears, but I let him read it in my thoughts. Jule nodded too, but she was only answering the question he'd spoken out loud.

"Good." Rubiy stood up. The audience was over, and somehow it was more like he was dismissing us than leaving. "I'll be in touch with you again." And then he disappeared. A sigh of air rushed in to fill the space where he'd been.

We sat looking at the emptiness and at each other for a long time before either of us said anything. Finally I said, "Quicksilver. That was him, Jule. Right here."

"Quicksilver himself? You mean he—" Jule broke off, glancing from side to side, groping with her mind.

"You might as well finish it, even if he's listening. If he's gonna find out what we're really doing here, it's better if he finds out now," almost wishing that he would. "Before it's too late—for us." I pulled a finger across my throat.

She grimaced. "He . . . he could kill without a thought, couldn't he?"

I nodded. *Or with one.* But the memory of what I'd seen in his mind made the words stick in my throat. He was an iceman; he could do anything to anybody and never feel a twinge. Maybe he'd had feelings once— too many feelings: I'd seen his kind snap under Old-city's weight and turn into something that wasn't even human. *Alike . . .* were we really so alike?

"I think I've met a truly inhuman being for the first time." Jule wrapped her arms around her like she felt cold.

"Then you've been real lucky," I muttered. *Inhuman, nonhuman, alien. My eyes . . . what about my eyes?*

"We should find Ardan." Jule started to get up. "Tell him. . . ."

I shrugged. "Rubiy's probably doing it for you, right now."

"We'd never be able to hold him here, anyway." She shook her head. "But he won't tell Ardan he's Quicksilver; Ardan won't know who he's really dealing with. He doesn't have the talent for reading—"

"He'll be all right. Rubiy won't try anything here, either. Besides, Siebeling's got a good nose for scum." I folded my own arms, looking away. "At least that's what he's always telling me."

She settled back onto the seat again. "Don't." The

tiny frown line came back between her eyes as she read my feelings. "Not now. If we can't hold together now—"

I didn't try to shield it. (It ain't my fault!) "Siebeling's the one who's always making it hard. You know it ain't me"—I realized suddenly what I was saying— "you *know* it, Jule. Don't you . . . ?" I leaned toward her.

She nodded, pressing her mouth together. "Yes, I know." Her voice almost disappeared again. "But try . . . try not to hate him, Cat. He's bleeding inside, there's something so sad, so terribly deep. . . ." She reached up like she could pull it out of the air. "I don't know what it is yet, it's too broken, too buried. But something about you . . ." She shook her head, not meeting my eyes. "He doesn't mean to."

"That's supposed to make a difference? That's supposed to give him the right to make me bleed?" *Something about me. Something about my eyes, Rubiy said.* Siebeling had said it too, trying to tell me what I didn't want to hear. . . . "Jule." I took a deep breath. "What did he mean about my eyes?"

"Who?" She reached mentally, trying to follow the change of my thoughts.

"Rubiy. And Siebeling. Both of them said it, about my eyes. My eyes are green. But 'all psions have green eyes,'" remembering Rubiy's, like sea ice. "Don't they?"

She looked up at me, and hers were gray, with round, normal pupils; but I wouldn't let my gaze break. She said, "Oh." Her fingers wove through the fringe on her shawl. "I know, there's that saying. . . . But most of them don't anymore. Not green as grass, not like yours.

It's been a long time; most of them are hazel, green diluted with other colors."

"What about you?"

She smiled; the flash of metal was in it again, gone again. "A curiosity. No one in the family dreamed . . . my parents were certain there was no tainting of their bloodline. They wanted to forget the early days, when Centauri Transport . . . But psions don't always have green eyes," changing the subject almost angrily. "Not anymore. It's been a long time."

"Since what?"

"Since we met the Hydrans."

My hands tightened on the cushions.

"You know the history—?" she asked, like Siebeling had, when I didn't answer.

"Not much." My voice was barely louder than hers. "What's to know?"

"Well . . . that when humanity got a stardrive and began to expand outward from our home system, they found a humanoid people on Beta Hydrae III, and on several other inhabitable worlds in the same general region of space. They were colony worlds of a stellar union that had begun to pass its peak long before the coming of the humans. At first we were overjoyed to discover another intelligent species, proof that we weren't alone in the universe—and to find they were a gentle, nonaggressive people; no possible threat to the Human Federation. But they happened to be psions, too. At first that was just another marvel—their societies functioned on totally different dynamics and sources of energy from our own. We learned a lot about them . . . and in the process we destroyed them. But in the be-

ginning there was a period of peaceful contact, inter-
marriage, and sometimes even children born of it. The
children tended to inherit the Hydran psi, and also
eyes that were as green as grass."

"How could they have kids? That's . . . I mean,
Hydrans ain't even human. No human marries an
alien now. Ain't it illegal or something?" I frowned.

She didn't see it; she was still looking out at the rain.
"Some people still do. Ardan did. It's not illegal; it's
just not easy. Things have changed over the centuries—
attitudes. And the Hydrans have suffered because of it.
But the aliens must be 'human,' Cat, or there wouldn't
be any saying about green-eyed psions. . . . Or else
humans are 'alien.' There have been some people who
say that humans are a world of defective Hydrans,
mutant—mute. That our psionic blindness has made us
lose our true humanity."

"Crap," I said, flexing my hands.

She shrugged a little. "But there are still a lot of
hazel-eyed human psions; even if green-eyed ones like
you are very rare."

"Because nobody in their right mind would want
a half-breed freak for a son."

I felt her look at me. *She always knows, she can't
help it—why didn't she understand?* I looked back at
her, with my green stranger's eyes. And her mind
flooded with shame and grief, reflected pain, confusion,
apology. (Sorry, sorry, *sorry!*) . . . Tears were starting.
"Please don't *feel* like that!"

I tightened my mind, wove it together—to keep from
feeling her, to stop her from feeling me.

She drew a long, shaky breath, pressing her mouth

with her hand. "You didn't know that you had Hydran blood? I thought. . . . How could you not know?" The words wavered. "Didn't anyone ever—?"

I shook my head and said bitterly, "Just lucky, I guess." But the bits and pieces were fitting together in my memory: the joke, the insult, the senseless beating—the truth that I wouldn't let myself understand. I'd never figured it out. Maybe because I didn't dare, because I couldn't carry one more weight, one more stone dragging me down. Maybe that was the real thing I'd spent my life hiding from, in dark corners, endless days alone, drug dreams . . . the thing that all the hunters sensed, that marked me as a victim.

Jule's eyes held the nowhere look they got when her mind was on things meant only for her. So I sat staring out at the rain, and thought about being a— No. It only figures, with your luck. And maybe it explained my luck, all the way back. Always bad. Maybe it even explained Siebeling—a man who'd had a Hydran wife, who had a half-breed son somewhere in the galaxy. A man who had to be ashamed of his perversion, who hated that secret locked in the closet of his past. Because who wouldn't hate a thing like that? Or somebody who reminded him of it? He'd even told me so. And I'd tried to ignore it, again. But this time there was no escape.

The lift chimed again, and I turned, looking toward it. Jule stirred and turned too, her face stiff. The doors opened and Siebeling was standing there. I didn't have to be anybody's mind reader to know he was upset about something. He came toward us without a word. Jule's face brightened and came alive; I caught a pang of bittersweet from her mind that had nothing to do with anything but the sight of him.

But Siebeling was looking at me, and suddenly I knew we had unfinished business.

"Ardan," Jule said, "he came. Rubiy, the one we've been waiting for. He came here; he told us about his—offer. And Cat thinks he's—"

"Both of you?"

She nodded. "Both of us. I—he was—"

"It has to wait, then." He shook his head. "Until we discuss something more personal." He had something in his hand, and he put it down on the low table between us. It was a clear ball that looked like crystal but wasn't, with a gold and green insect caught in flight inside it. "This is a nice little toy. Where did you get it?"

And then I knew what I'd done wrong. I'd forgotten about that ball. "It . . . ain't mine."

"I believe that." His voice was sour.

I shook my head. "I mean, I never seen it before." I couldn't keep my eyes off of it. I never could.

"Then I suppose it was just in your jacket by accident."

"Look, if you want to call me a thief, then do it. That's what you're thinking." I wondered why I'd bothered to get up this morning.

"That's what I'm saying, then."

"I didn't steal it! I—I borrowed it. I just wanted to . . . see how it worked." I wondered why the truth always sounded more like a lie than a lie did. Probably because it was only half the truth. I'd taken it, all right, off the desk the second time he interviewed me.

I'd picked it up for spite, almost without thinking, never meaning to keep it. But I never gave it back. . . . I couldn't. When you held it in your hands, it made pictures, things like I'd never seen—images of some other world. When you were tired of one it made another, and if you wanted one again it came back. I'd never seen anything like it. I just couldn't give it up. So I kept it. I knew I'd be in trouble if anyone found out, so I'd just blocked it out of my mind. The perfect crime. I felt my face getting red.

He put his hand on the ball, gently, and there was a new image inside it. "Why?" His voice strained.

"What?"

"Why did you take it?" That wasn't what he'd meant. His mind was a tangle of burning thoughts I couldn't read, most of them not about me. . . . And suddenly I understood: that it was an alien thing, a Hydran thing. A thing that had belonged to his half-breed son. And I'd taken it. *You gork, you stupid damn fool!* I grimaced.

"Why did you take it?"

"I . . . I . . ." How could I tell him how warm it felt in my hands; how could I tell him about the pictures? How was I supposed to tell him something I didn't understand myself? "It . . . was pretty; I liked it."

"You liked it."

"Yeah, you—" I bit my tongue, trying to keep from saying the rest of it. "All right. I took it, and I kept it. I knew it was wrong. I'm sorry. I won't take nothing again, I swear. All right?" It had to be all right. I was even admitting I was wrong. What else could he want?

He whispered a name—an alien's name. His wife's name. And his wife was dead. Pain filled the memory. He was looking down at the ball, and I don't think he knew he'd said anything out loud. I was sure he hadn't meant for me to hear it. He glanced up at me again. "It shouldn't respond for you, you couldn't even understand. . . .". Like he was blaming me for something.

But he was going to take the ball. I reached out, my fingers touched it. The picture changed.

He grabbed my wrist. "Keep your hands off that, you cheap gutter thief! Maybe you think a fast apology is all you need to save you every time you 'like' something. Well, not with me. If that's the best behavior you can manage, then maybe you're not good enough to go on working here." *(And you won't ever be—)*

"You got no right to think that." I jerked free. "I'm as good as you are. And I'm sick of getting treated like I ain't!"

He picked up the ball. "Then consider yourself dismissed. Get out, I don't want to see you again."

I blinked. "What?"

"You heard me."

"But . . ." Somehow I stood up, numb all over. "I guess we both know why you're doin' this, don't we?" He didn't answer. I looked back at Jule. Her face was pale and her eyes were wet; she was staring down at her hands with the bitten-off nails, and they were twitching. "Jule." I said it quietly; she didn't look up. "It's gonna be all right. You'll see." I put my hand out over hers, the only time I'd ever really touched her. Her fingers curled around mine in a kind of spasm;

she clung to my hand for a second. I knew her tears weren't about anything going on between any of us here. "Look, I'm going now. I'll . . . see you later, huh?" She didn't answer me. I didn't figure she would.

When I straightened up again, Siebeling moved between us, forcing me to back off. He leaned over, murmuring something to her. I went to the waiting lift and took it down.

5

The lift stopped at the usual floor, because I'd said the number without thinking. I almost stepped out, almost went back to my room; thinking there was nothing else I could do except go there and wait.

But I stood looking down the empty hallway, looking at another world: one I didn't belong to anymore. Siebeling had cut me loose, and soon enough Corporate Security would come for me and make it official. . . . I'd known all along this was too good to last, like any other dream. My fists tightened, the numbness that had me by the throat suddenly let me go. It was over, and I'd been screwed. I owed nothing to nobody. And I was damned if I was going to stay here like a loser and make it easy for them to take me back. The doors slipped shut again, and I went on down.

I got out at the main reception lobby. Its three-story vault was draped with wall hangings that turned every sound into a whisper. I tried to walk like I had a right to be there; but even if I didn't, no one seemed to care. I moved through the changing dance of bodies, trying to believe I looked as normal as everyone else seemed to think I did, until I reached the building entrance. There were no guards waiting, not even a solid door to fill the arching space. A soft tingling, a breath of forced air, and I was through—standing free in the open in the wide fountain square that I'd seen from high above.

It was all so easy. I stood where I was, just letting myself breathe, wondering why I'd never done this before. I could have walked out of here any time I'd wanted to these past weeks, if I'd only tried. I turned back, glancing in through the open entrance. I looked up and up along the smooth mirroring face of the Sakaffe Research Institute, and wondered where my room was inside it. I looked down again, suddenly feeling dizzy, empty, and alone. Knowing why I'd never tried to leave, now that it was too late.

I turned away and started out into the square. The rain had stopped, but the air was still dim and heavy. The fountain was doing things I'd never seen water do before; as I passed it, a drift of spray blew into my path. I moved through it, blinking. The wet heat was suffocating after the coolness of the Institute. I'd forgotten how summer felt, and how much I hated it—almost as much as I hated winter. At least there wasn't the summertime stench that made Oldcity smell like a dead body.

I entered a canyon between two towers. The street was brighter than any street I'd ever known—and quieter, smoother, cleaner. There were only a handful of other people around me, most of them taking the moving walkways or drifting in and out of building entrances. Far up above my head were aircab balconies and passageways threading the building faces together like chunks of jewel; single mods and multimods jostled in the space between them. Looking up as I walked, I couldn't see the tops of the towers, couldn't even guess

how high they had to be. . . . I began to think about
falling upward into the fog. I looked down, and didn't
look up again.

I went on walking for a long time, with my thoughts
wandering as aimlessly as my feet. I was caught in a
silence that wasn't all in my mind—everything seemed
to be happening far up in the air. As the hours passed,
the fog melted away and the sky began to clear. Sunlight winked and sparkled between mirroring walls, off
them, through them; falling on me in bright showers.
Display floaters advertising upside goods caught my
eyes and ears, pulled me everywhere, left me standing
in my tracks staring at things I didn't believe even when
I saw them. Sometimes somebody else would put a
hand through the shimmering, transparent security
screen and touch something. I wasn't the only one
who couldn't believe what I saw.

But when I reached out, my hand felt the screen,
soft and yielding—it wouldn't let me past to touch what
was inside. I jerked back, afraid that somehow it knew
me for what I was. I stood still again for a long minute, with my heart beating too hard. But nothing more
happened, and finally I realized that nothing was going
to. I started to believe that there was only one thing
different about me that it could have known: I didn't
have a data bracelet. Not guilt, just *Insufficient Credit*.
I noticed that somebody had scrawled something with
a marker on the base below the display; a single, simple
word. I knew all the letters. I sounded them out, and
when I heard what it said, I laughed. I thought about
the walls in Oldcity, covered with words like that. I'd
put some of them there myself, but I'd never known

what I was copying; I never even cared. I just wanted
to make my mark somehow, some way, on a world that
didn't know I was alive. It was strange to realize there
were really people up here who felt the same way. For
a second I thought about Jule.

I moved on, with my hands in my pockets, searching
for a credit marker or a camph, for anything; knowing
in that same sick moment just how empty they were.
Then my fingers closed on something solid. I pulled
it out into my hand: candy. I'd stuffed my pockets full
of the damned things whenever I could, in the cafeteria
at the Institute. One piece left. I closed my fingers over
it, opened them again. I put it into my mouth, felt it
dissolve and the dark, oily sweetness cover my tongue.

It didn't last long. After it was gone, I began to taste
the smells in the air around me. There were places to
eat here, just like in Oldcity. Even the gods had to eat.
Most of it smelled better than anything I remembered—maybe because there wasn't Oldcity's stink
mixed into it, or maybe just because it was here and I
was hungry. *Hungry.* My throat ached with the thought.
It was too easy to forget how it felt to be . . . No. It
was too easy to remember. But without a data bracelet
I was scared even to try a lift or a doorway and feel it
turn me back again.

The day was closing in on evening; there were more
people on foot now, children as well as adults. I wondered where they went all day. Maybe just someplace
cool. It was getting loud and confusing and hard to
move; my mind started to buzz with the feedback of
too many other minds. I wove a defense and held it

so hard that I couldn't feel a thing, until I could forget that I'd ever even been a psion.

Lights were beginning to show, and I tried to feel like I was back in Oldcity night. But there was no music. Music was the only thing I'd really missed about Oldcity. Sometimes there'd been songs coming out of the walls at the Institute, but they were thin and gutless; listening to them was like drinking water when you wanted hard brew. . . . I wondered whether I was walking on solid ground now, or whether Oldcity, with its noise and smells and darkness, was somewhere just below my feet.

And I wondered if maybe I couldn't pick a data bracelet off someone in this crowd. . . . But I wasn't in Oldcity, I didn't know which way to run; and even if I did, there was no freedrop waiting to take it off me for a handful of markers. And I'd never be able to break the code on someone else's bracelet before they missed it and had it killed. I was lost in this world, I was a ghost—I didn't belong here, I belonged in Oldcity. And if I wanted to go on walking free I'd better start thinking again, about how to get back there before it was too late.

There were signs everywhere, but I couldn't read them. Trying to act like just another tourist, I went up to the closest stranger in the street and said, " 'Scuse me. Can . . . uh, how do I get to Oldcity?"

He looked at me, squinting a little, and I felt the prickle of his surprise, but no suspicion. "Why, just take an aircab. . . ." He waved a pudgy hand at a nearby call stand.

I shook my head. "I don't—I mean, I want to walk there."

"Walk there?" The squint turned wide-eyed. "But you can't. That's impossible." He shrugged.

I opened my mouth, shut it again, and pushed on past, frowning.

"Take a cab!" He yelled it after me.

I went on down the street, asking other people, always getting the same damn answer; until I believed that they all believed it, and started to hate them: *Lousy, selfish bloodsuckers*— But I had to keep trying. I had to believe that if I could just make it to the Hanging Gardens, then . . . " 'Scuse me," bumping into an old woman, putting out a hand to steady her. She murmured something, fumbling and flustered. "What?" I said.

"Are you all right, dear?" She patted my arm.

"Me?" I almost laughed. "Sure. I—I'm looking for the Hanging Gardens."

"The Hanging Gardens?" She smoothed the silken drape across her shoulders with ringed fingers. She glittered with jewels, but most of them were fake, and the cloth looked worn. "Oh. Why, they're very far away." She stretched out a hand, pointing to my left. "Why don't you take a cab?"

I held the frown back, and said, "I want to walk. I mean . . ." Suddenly I was reading into the look she gave me, seeing the suspicious sympathy lying open behind her eyes, "Yeah, I—I'm a little short on credit. If you got some spare markers . . .?" I held out a hand, forced it to stay steady.

The sympathy didn't disappear the way it always did

in Oldcity; it only furrowed deeper into her face. "Oh,
you poor thing. No, I never carry markers. But here,
open your account,"—she reached for my wrist—"and
I'll transfer you a little sum."

"No." I pulled away. "Forget it. . . . It's all right,
I'll walk." I pretended to lean down and pick something up. "Here. I think you dropped this." I gave her
back the jeweled pin I'd stolen when I bumped into
her, the only thing she was wearing that looked like it
was worth anything.

"Oh. Thank you. Thank you! I. . . . But, wait!"

I went on, almost running to get out of reach of her
gratitude.

I tried to follow the snaking streets in the direction
she'd pointed, asking people again and again for the
Hanging Gardens. I got farther away almost as often
as I got closer, and it was the middle of the night by
the time I finally found them. By then my feet were
blistered on the blisters, and I felt like I'd walked halfway to the nearest star. The Gardens flowed uphill
and down on every side of me, tier on tier of eerie,
rustling life from a hundred different worlds, gathered
here at the heart of the Federation. But there wasn't
much to see that wasn't hung with night shadows
even for my eyes, along the dim-lit walkways that I
followed up and down through the air between tiers.
Not that I cared, by then. By then all I wanted was to
be back where I belonged and forget I'd ever even
seen Quarro. Finally I reached the lowest tier, the one
that ringed the lip of the well above Godshouse Circle.
I walked it around and around, looking for a hidden
stairway, for a ladder, footholds—anything that would

let me down past the sheer supporting rim wall and the impossible stretch of air below it. But there was nothing. There was no way down; no way back.

Hanging out over the fragile fence and looking down, I could see the spire of the Godshouse gleaming dimly far down below, and people moving through the open space around it. A lone aircab and then another rose like bubbles while I watched, rising past me where I stood and drifting on into the night. I could hear the sound of a thousand voices crying and music playing; I could even smell the stench rising on the heated air to make my empty stomach turn. I leaned out farther, going a little crazy, shouting, "Help! Help! Up here—!" like I thought somebody could hear me. Like I thought somebody would care. But my voice was lost in the space between. I was a ghost to all of them down there as much as I was up here, one more shadow among the garden shadows.

The fence swayed and gave under me. I pushed back onto solid ground; not ready yet to go home the hard way. I turned my back on the Tank . . . *fish tank, feeder tank* . . . a fish out of water, drowning in the open air. I threw myself down on the soft, matted grass of the hillside and lay staring up into the black height of the sky; at the stars, the stars, the stars. . . .

It was almost a relief when the patrolling Corpse woke me up just before dawn, and arrested me for vagrancy.

It didn't take long for the Corporate Security data-files to spit up my whole life story. And it didn't take much longer for them to get confirmation that Sie-

beling didn't want me back again . . . and Contract
Labor did. But it was late in the day before the black-
suited Labor Crows came to take me away: one more
flight above Quarro, looking down at the crest of the
city on fire with the colors of the setting sun. Then
the mod flashed across the green waters of the bay to
the spaceport complex, and buried us alive in the dark
sprawl of Contract Labor's holding pens.

Then it was more corridors, worse than the Corporate Security station, with walls the color of grease and
cement. I wondered why all government buildings
looked like prisons. Maybe because they were. The
guards threw me into a cell, and took turns working
me over a little. As they left, one of them said, "We
got a special treat for you, Cityboy, for all the trouble
you gave us. We're going to let you see what you're in
for. Enjoy the show." They went off grinning.

"You know what you can do with it, Crows!" I
yelled. "I don't care. It's only ten years!" My voice
shook a little. Ten years was more than half my life. . . .

"It'll seem like forever." They laughed; the laughter
echoed after they were gone.

I wiped my bloody nose, shaking myself out. They
hadn't broken anything; lucky for me they didn't want
damaged goods. I looked around. The cell was about
the size of a closet, and empty except for a foam sleep
mat, a toilet, and a sink. At least I was alone. I stumbled
to the sink and drank water from my cupped hands.
Then I sat down against the wall and thought about
when they were going to feed me, to keep from thinking about Jule and Cortelyou and everything I'd lost. . . .

But then the room went dark, and the wall across

from me lit up like a threedy screen. A bored voice was droning: ". . . planet number five of a blue-white sun, spectral type B-three-V, listed Survey One-three-nine-six S-One-three-nine-six-dash–five hasn't got a name, because they couldn't think of one that fit. Climate in habitable zone fluctuates . . ."

The voice kept on but I was only half listening. Suddenly the room was steaming hot, and it stank of rotting plants. I felt bugs crawling on me, biting me, and I leaped up—

In front of me a string of dirty, sweating images of men struggled up an oozing path cut through jungle brush, going ankle-deep in steaming mud with every step. Most of them had some kind of heavy mesh baskets slung on their backs, weighing them down; a couple had stun rifles instead. Then one of the laborers stumbled. A guard moved in on him, and something that looked like a load of yellow slime dropped out of a dead tree and landed on the guard's head. There was a shower of sparks, the thing slid off his back. I shouted as it landed on the one on his knees in the mud. He didn't have any protection. I pressed my hands against my ears, but I could still hear him scream.

The scene changed. Someone else was being dragged under in a mud-colored river by something with suckers. A red stain spread on the brown water. Another laborer tried to go after him; one of the guards clubbed him with a rifle. He fell, more red running down his face, over his hands . . . splattering on me. I started yelling for someone to shut it off, but it went on and on, until I thought it would never end; horror after horror happening in front of me and around me and even through me, until I was crouched in the corner, hitting my head against the wall, trying to go deaf and blind. . . .

After a long time I realized that it was light and quiet and cool again in the room. But I stayed where I was. It didn't matter that what I'd seen wasn't real—because it had all been real where it happened, and that was where I was going. *Damn Siebeling! Damn all of them!* Yesterday I was sharing with them and laughing with them, and today I was going to hell and it didn't even matter to them.

The lights went out again and then I was at the door, beating my hands on it, yelling, "Let me out! You bastards, lemme out of here—"

But there was no one to hear it. And there was nothing else, this time, only the darkness—maybe it was night already. I rested against the cool surface of the wall, and then I went back to my corner and sat down, and said, "I wish I was dead." But there was no one to hear that, either.

By the next morning I was more than ready to get out of that room. The guard who came for me grinned and said, "You don't look like you slept too much." I didn't answer, and he thought that was funny, too. He kept trying to get a reaction out of me as he led me down one hall and then another, and finally into a big room full of data storage.

"The kid here's ready for a little vacation. S-One-three-nine-six." The guard flipped a tape bobbin onto the counter. "Lucky boy."

"Go to hell, scumsucker," I said, finally, just to shut him up. He grinned again and twisted my arm.

The narrow-faced woman behind the counter put a readout on her screen and said, "Are you sure? It's not on any direct line from here—it's hardly cost-efficient." She looked down her nose at him.

The guard glared. I figured it was my turn to grin.

"But, if you want to press your point—"

I changed my mind.

"—you could send him through, say, Tillit Sector. You can bond him here and they'll handle the transfers."

"Tillit Sector?" The guard looked surprised. But he nodded. "Do it."

The clerk smiled a strange smile, and I wondered. But then she lit the counter top with an image showing a lot of tiny print. "Sign here." She pointed to a line at the bottom of it. "This is your formal contract, stating your agreement to work. At the end of ten years indenture you get five thousand credits. If you want to buy out your contract before that time, you owe that much to us."

"Like hell! I ain't signing that piece of—"

The guard picked a writing stylus up off the counter and stuck it into my fist. "Sign it or I'll break your hand."

I signed it. But only with an X.

The clerk nodded, but then she caught my thumb and pressed it down on the readout. I looked, and saw

my thumbprint there in blue. "Just for insurance."
Then she fed the assignment tape to a stamper on the
counter. She caught my arm and stuck that in, too. I
tried to pull back but her grip was like iron. I felt a
hot slash of pain, and thought I'd lost my hand for
sure, but all I'd lost was my freedom. What I got for it
was a bright red bracelet about two fingers wide. I
touched it, wiggling my fingers. It was hard and still a
little warm; and bonded to the smarting flesh of my
wrist. I thought about how this wasn't the kind of
bracelet I'd been expecting to get, up until yesterday. . . . "Thanks for the jewelry."

"He's ready. Take him to Processing."

I got processed. They took away my good clothes and
handed me a worn-out jumpsuit. I wondered if somebody else had died in it. Then they asked me whether
I was blind or deaf or dead. . . . I said I was, but the
examiner said the question was purely rhetorical anyway, whatever that meant. He sent me on again, to
more insults, vaccinations, humiliations, until finally I
was back in a cell again and this time I didn't have any
trouble sleeping. The next day, or maybe the one
after, I was taken out and sent onto the spaceport
field, jammed into a carrier with a load of other dazed
human cargo.

I'd never seen the spaceport before, and I didn't get
much chance to see it now. But still a strange kind of
excitement tightened inside me at the flashing glimpses
I got of energized grids and silhouetted pylons, out-
buildings, gantries . . . *ships*. I tried to shake off the
choking mind-cloud of everyone else's despair and let
myself feel the sight: these were ships that went to the

stars, that weren't tied to one place or even one world,
that had the freedom to cross hundreds and thousands
of light-years from sun to sun. . . . Ships like the gleaming disk with the Centauri Transport insignia on its
side, that lay waiting up ahead to take me away from
the prison of Oldcity and Quarro and Ardattee—to
something a whole lot worse than any of them.

On board I was sedated and strapped into an accel-
eration sling so I couldn't move. For hours I lay waiting, not knowing what would happen next. Then at
last the ship came alive around me and began to lift.
I didn't know what to expect when it finally happened.
Maybe I was lucky, because they didn't bother to make
our free ride easy or soft. I felt my body tense and
fight and scream as the ship tore itself out of gravity's
fist, pushing upward and outward into clear vacuum
with a will that was stronger than universal law.

I never even saw what it looked like to go up from
Ardattee, leaving my life behind, or what my homeworld looked like from out in space. But by then it
hardly mattered, to me or anyone else, because it was
too late anyway, for all of us.

And then there was nothing to do but go on waiting.

I never knew where Tillit Sector was, or even what
it stood for. The FTA used Contract Labor to fill its
needs for nontech workers, and it used them all over the
Federation. There wasn't even a planetside Colony in
the system where the ship came out of its final hyperlight jump: only an orbiting way station chained by
gravity to a lifeless, lonely world. Not that that mat-

tered, either. All that really mattered was what happened when I got there.

For days I waited in a gray stale room, with a bunch of others who lay staring at the ceiling, mainly, because there wasn't anything else—hope, or even sorrow. One end of the room looked out on the scarred, angry face of the nameless world staring up at us from below. I sat on the floor in front of the port for hours, staring back. My mind was as bleak and empty as the view, and all I could think about was the red bond tag on my wrist; how there was no way to hide it, no hope for me either, now.

Until finally a guard came into the room and picked me out, glanced at my bond ring and said, "Okay, bondie, you're it. Up." He pointed with his thumb.

"N-now?" My voice shook.

He laughed. "What do you think?" He took me out into the hall.

There was another Crow waiting there; but this one looked like an official, and he said, "Your name is Cat?"

I nodded. *They know about it* here? I wondered if they went to this much trouble to make everyone suffer who'd ever slugged a recruiter.

"All right. We've got a special request on you, bondie."

I touched the bond tag, feeling insects crawl across my mind; seeing something yellow and slimy drop out of a tree. . . .

He cleared his throat. "I understand you can drive a snow vehicle?"

"What?" I stared at him.

"We have a priority request for a snow vehicle driver, from one of our agents. Our records show that you're qualified—?" (*Somebody had paid him to ask me this. He expected me to answer yes.*)

I didn't disappoint him. "Been driving them all my life. Sure." Sure that he could feel the lie seeping out around the edges of my thoughts, like water through a sieve. But why should he care?

"You're already assigned, though." He looked at the bond ring, surprised or confused; that wasn't in the plan. I held my breath. "I'll put through a transfer."

I started to breathe again. We were walking. *Orders on me:* Who had the contacts to bribe the FTA and fix its records . . . and knew about me? *Siebeling*— maybe he'd changed his mind? But Siebeling wouldn't go to that kind of trouble; he wouldn't need to. I tried to pick the official's thoughts, but he didn't know anything about why he'd been sent here to collect me— only that somebody up the line had made it worth his while.

And the one who was waiting for us was nobody I'd ever seen before. His name was Kielhosa, he was an agent for Federation Mining—which meant nothing to me. I looked him in the eye but there was no sign, no sort of recognition—and none lying secretly on the surface of his mind, either. He was as real as the tag on my wrist. I wondered if it could be some sort of crazy mistake after all. I wondered where the other bondie was whose name was Cat. And I hoped they didn't send the poor slad to S1396 instead of me.

Kielhosa had a jaw like a steel trap and hair as gray

as an Oldcity morning. And he thought I looked like a street rat; he didn't believe I could drive a snowtrack. He threw a couple of questions at me about how they worked; the Crow started to look uneasy. But I read the answers that lay waiting in his mind and gave them back to him perfectly. For once, I was glad to be a telepath. I tried to find out where I was going, then— but his mind was choked with schedules and delays, deadlines to meet, and the scum of Earth that he was stuck with picking over.

Finally he nodded and signaled to the guard. "I guess this one will have to do. Get him ready."

The guard led me away. I wished I'd had time to find a clear answer; but in Oldcity they always said, "Asking questions is asking for trouble." Wherever I was going, it couldn't be any worse than S1396. So I kept my mouth shut and let it happen.

PART II

CRAB

6

There were stars everywhere. I'd been lost in the
stars as long as I could remember, beautiful stars and
night. I moved in the cold darkness—and cracked my
fingers on something slick. The ceiling, about half a
meter above my face. My eyes blurred, and when they
cleared again, I could see that the stars were only a
projection on the wall across the room. And I remembered that I was on a ship again, and where we were
going. I felt in the dark for the restamped bond tag;
and tried to smile but my face was numb.

They'd given me some kind of drug that had knocked
me out back at the way station; getting me ready for
a long trip this time, turning me into freight. I didn't
remember coming onto this ship and I didn't figure I
was supposed to be awake now; none of the others were,
lying below me in tiers of bunks like bodies in a
morgue. But I'd been awake before. I remembered
watching the stars for hours, unchanging, while the
ship sat in space and the crew computed the next
hyperlight jump. Somewhere back in another life, Dere
Cortelyou had told me how the length of a jump de-
pended on knowing the shape of space—and if you got
the wrong solution, it was anyone's guess where you'd
come out on the other side. One time I saw us take
the jump, saw the stars go blank and come back

changed before you could hold your breath. I wondered if we'd made the right one; and then I remembered that any jump we made only meant that I was more light-years away from home and everything I knew.

I wondered how far we were going, and how long it had been. One of my arms was strapped down, and something was dripping into a vein. I never felt hungry, or even thirsty; I didn't feel much of anything. I just lay in a bunk in a long dark room and looked at the stars—or their image on the ship's hull: my mind was never clear enough to wonder why they were there. I could hear the crew sometimes, and once one of them came through to check up on us. As he passed my bunk, I let my free arm slip off and hit him in the face. He nearly leaped through the wall. But most of the time I lay alone in the quiet night counting stars, until I lost track of my fingers.

I was starting to count again, when all at once the stars blinked out and changed. And this time I was looking at a world; a new world. But I stared at the image on the wall for a long time before I understood what I was seeing. Inhabitable worlds were always in blues, like Earth on the Federation Seal. I'd seen Ardattee in pictures—soft-edged, smooth, blue and white—and the way station world's sterile reds and browns from orbit. But this was different from either one, and somehow I knew it was all wrong. There was no blue at all. And it was . . . lumpy. Between swirls of pale cloud the mountains rose up too far, like the skin of a shriveled piece of fruit. We were far enough out to see the planet's curve, but over the mountains I looked down into deep valleys of twisting golden green. The atmosphere shivered and glowed with light, and between the mountains the plains were silver, catching fire on the day side, as if the whole world was a piece of gem; until I wondered whether I was really seeing any of this. And I wondered what they needed me for. . . .

When it was over, they couldn't wake me up. I didn't remember a thing about the landing, or how I got to the bed I woke up in, in what turned out to be the tiny port hospital. It was an improvement over the ship's floating morgue, but I wasn't awake enough of the time to appreciate it. The hospital med techs claimed that my internal organs were peculiar, that the drug didn't react predictably but that it would probably wear off in time.

They were right. There comes a time when you can't even sleep any more, and when I woke up for good, Kielhosa was still waiting. I opened my eyes, and the first thing I saw was his face: I remembered then why I'd wanted to sleep forever. I'd come to the end of my journey and my choices, and now I was stuck with the consequences.

I was the only one of Kielhosa's new recruits who hadn't made it to the mines right after we landed; it didn't make him real happy. But when he led me out of the starport at last, I got enough of a shock to make me forget all my problems. The port town was cheap duraplast on one muddy street, but the world around it was . . . beautiful. The mountains rose up on every side in wild fingers with the town lying in their palm, like something out of *Nebula Pioneers* on the threedy. But this was real; I was real, standing with the planet pressing against my feet, breathing in the fresh, sweet air. I felt weak and clumsy, I was shivering, and my eyesight seemed dim somehow. But none of that mattered. I turned around and around, and started to laugh because I couldn't believe it. The sound startled me; I hadn't laughed for a long time.

"What's so funny?"

"It's beautiful!"

"Hunh. This poisonous hole? That is funny. You didn't come here for the scenery, bondie. You're a working boy, remember? It was an inconvenience, letting you sleep it off in that hospital. You'd better be worth it." He started on again. I followed him, hardly listening. "Watch your step, you're moving in one and a half gravities. It makes you awkward until you get used to it."

"Uh, why do you need somebody to drive a snow-track here?" Maybe it was only for the winter; it was cold here, but I didn't see any snow. It was crazy to hope my luck had changed, but . . .

"You'll see."

I didn't say anything more.

We walked out past the edge of town. A whitish, sandy track ran through a field of rust-colored grass spotted with yellow flowers—and craters, spitting steam, and pale blots of mud. The biggest of them wasn't more than a meter across, and some of them were only dried mud pits; but up ahead the track swerved around a fresh break in the earth, where white mud crusted the dying grass. The scent of flowers and the stink of sulphur mixed in the sharp wind.

On the far side of the field was a blue stone building. Out beyond it the land dropped off like the end of the world. The view as we reached it made me ache. *All of it real*: green hills folding into long, green-golden valleys, bright water spilling over slate-blue rocks all the way down to . . . I shut my eyes and looked again. "What the—" The hills ended, and beyond them the land lay flat clear to the horizon. Endlessly flat and silver, and the sun's reflected light burned your eyes, like sunlight on metal. "Is that—?"

"Snow," Kielhosa said, behind me.

Disappointment caught in my chest. I swore under my breath. Kielhosa frowned and rubbed his head; I'd projected it without meaning to. I shut my mind tight, looking back at the mountains again. They were still green. "But . . . how?" Even I knew that what I saw just didn't make sense.

"Steam heat, in a manner of speaking—lot of volcanic activity in those mountains." He pointed past me, and following his hand I saw plumes of smoke hanging in the sky over a couple of the highest peaks. "Cinder is a piece of star, it was the companion to that sun up there until it blew itself up. The fragment's still hot enough to melt rock at its core. Where the heat leaks up to the surface it keeps the ground warm, makes hot springs and geysers, that sort of thing. That stream down there would scald you. Water freezes solid out past the foothills, though. Temperature never gets up to freezing."

I ignored everything he'd said past: " 'A piece of star' . . . you mean, *Cinder*? Is this the Crab Nebula?"

"Where did you think you were, kid? What do you think all that garbage is up in the sky?"

I glanced up, into a sky the color of sapphires. Shining across it like cobweb was the end of the star that was Cinder. The sun made me squint, but I couldn't see its circle, just a starpoint of light that flickered, cold and pale, like a strobe. It was only six miles wide—that was why everything seemed dim—and they called it a pulsar. I heard Cortelyou's voice in my mind: *Forty-five hundred light-years from home.*

So I'd made it to the Crab Colonies, after all. I looked down again, at the bond ring on my wrist, and down the green-gold valley at the snow.

"Nice view," Kielhosa said. He was laughing at me. I spat.

We went back to the stone house. It was covered on the outside with the slate-blue rock I'd seen pushing out of the hillside; someone's strange idea of decoration, I supposed. I couldn't see why they were showing off a pile of stones. The inside of the building was wooden; it looked even stranger, with the computer console set into the board walls. We put on thermal clothes from a locker, and then went on through to an outside loading area. "What's that?"

Kielhosa walked over to the transparent room-size bubble hanging from a steel wire. "A cable car. It's the cheapest thing here for moving ore up the hill." He nodded at me. "Get in."

I came up beside him and caught hold of the waiting entrance. The whole bubble moved under my hand, as fragile as a crystal glass. I jerked my hand away and looked back. "Oh, no. I ain't getting into that—" Kielhosa's face said I'd better not give him any more trouble. I caught the doorway again and stepped inside. My feet didn't go through the floor, but the bubble rocked like a hammock and threw me forward; I staggered and fell onto a platform at one end. Kielhosa stepped in just like it was home, and we barely shifted. He sat down on a seat at the other end, balancing our weight. There was a clear square with lights on it; he pushed a button and the lights went green, from red.

The bubble bounced once, and then swung out away from the building . . . into the air. The ground dropped out from under us; I could see it far down below our feet. We were suspended up there between spidery towers in nothing, not even a mod; just a bubble, drifting down. . . .

"Where's your faith in modern plastics, bondie?" Kielhosa thought it was funny.

I stuck my hands into my pockets and tried not to weigh anything.

It was almost a relief to stand in the trampled slush at the bottom of the hill. Someone was waiting with a snow vehicle, though; and out beyond him the snow was waiting for us all.

The other man said, "Get what you came for?"

"I got him, Joraleman." Kielhosa nodded. He treated Joraleman like an equal, not like a bondie. I wondered who he was. "Supplies loaded?"

"Right. Check the list if you want." Joraleman looked over at me. "The new driver taking us back? I've had it up to here with double duty."

I shook my head but Kielhosa said, "That's what he's here for. You're lucky I got you a replacement so fast. Not many 'track drivers end up in the labor pens."

I looked for a way to change the subject. "Uh, why don't you use some kind of mod for moving your stuff? Wouldn't it be faster—"

"The air currents are too erratic, and the gravity's too high. It would take a magician with psi to keep anything flying out there." Joraleman shrugged. He was a big man, tall and heavyset, still young. He had a beard, and his hair was nearly as blond as mine; but his skin was pale and freckled. I couldn't see his eyes behind his opaqued goggles, but when he smiled it wasn't like he thought I was the joke. "We tried it."

"Oh," I said, knowing I couldn't fly a mod either, even with psi. Right then I didn't feel like anybody's magician. "Well, I . . ."

"Let's go." Kielhosa nodded.

"I still feel a little sick. You mind if I don't drive?"

"You've had a week already," he said. "A person might get the idea you were stalling for time."

I started toward the snowtrack. It looked like an orange egg lying on its side on balloons. That didn't help much. It was a lot bigger than I'd thought by the time I reached it. I climbed up into the cab and looked at the instrument panel. Kielhosa sat beside me, and Joraleman slid into the narrow seat behind us. I tried to pick their minds for something to help me; but my own tension got in the way and I couldn't pull out a clear thought to save my life. There was a touch-board with letters on it, but I couldn't tell what most of them stood for. I made a half guess on one and got the power started. It made me feel braver and I touched another. It didn't work. The snowtrack gave a god-awful screech and leaped about a meter. Kielhosa pushed me out of the seat and got it stopped. Then he kicked me out into the snow and called me some things I'd never been called before, and a lot more things I had been called.

When he ran out of ideas, he told me to get up, and Joraleman asked me if I'd ever driven a snow vehicle before. There wasn't any reason to lie now, so I didn't. Kielhosa looked at me funny and I knew he'd finally figured things out. By now it wouldn't take any brains.

"Take them off." He meant my mittens.

I took them off. The cold made my hands smart.

He looked at my bond tag. "It's been stamped over."

Joraleman frowned. He pushed back his goggles and looked at the bond tag, too; then up at me. He said, "Did you decide to gamble?"

I just shrugged.

Kielhosa caught me by the front of my jacket and brought up his fist. "You little whoreson, you're going to be sorry you were ever—"

"Let him be, Kielhosa." Joraleman pulled Kielhosa's arm down. He looked tired, and disgusted. "He'll have plenty of time to regret it when he gets to the mines."

Kielhosa let go of me, grimacing. "If it's one thing I don't need, it's a goddamn godlover standing on my conscience when I have to deal with these animals!" But he only shook his head, and Joraleman smiled just a little.

I backed away from them, looking at Joraleman. "I

could learn to drive a snowtrack! Just show me how. I learn fast."

Kielhosa unlocked the doors at the back of the van.

"Sorry, bondie. You didn't learn fast enough." Joraleman gave me a shove. "Get in."

I climbed into the back. All I could tell was that it was dark and full of crates, until my eyes adjusted. Then I saw two other bondies sprawled on the crates. I figured they must be there to do the loading. One of them was asleep; he didn't wake up even when the doors slammed behind me. The other one stared at me with flat black eyes. Both of them had blue skin. I'd never seen anybody with blue skin before. The first thing I said, before I even thought, was, "Where you from?"

He said, "Hell," softly, and shut his eyes. I wondered if that was an answer.

The snowtrack started up with a jerk, dumping me back against the door. I slid down to the floor and stayed there, folding my legs up, since there wasn't anyplace more comfortable. It was a long ride. But not long enough.

I knew from things Cortelyou had told me that Cinder was only a hundred twenty kilometers in diameter; its surface area was hardly equal to a good-size island back on Ardattee. But the gravity was one and a half times heavier than standard, because Cinder was made up of impossible things: compounds with inert elements, superdense rocks with incredible crystalline structures, super-heavy elements that were never supposed to occur outside a lab. Things that would only form naturally in the heart of a supernova—like telhassium. They could mine the rest, but it would barely be worth the trouble by the time they'd shipped them back to the heart of the Federation. The tel-hassium made everything worth it.

Telhassium ore was the blue stone I'd seen on the building side; maybe half the planet was made of it, and perfectly formed crystals lay all through the matrix of the rock. Federation Mining could go on picking them out forever. Or the bondies could do it for them. Till hell froze over . . . the bondies said it already had. They cursed the day the FTA ever set down on this godforsaken star corpse, and it didn't take me very long to learn why.

I was already wondering, riding stiff and cramped in the freezing hold of the snowtrack; thinking about the faces of the two bondies lying a couple of meters away from me. It was night by then; night and day didn't last long on a world the size of Cinder. The domed mines compound blazed against the darkness like a sun half-buried in the snowfields as we closed the final distance. . . .

I jerked out of dark daydreaming, wondering where I'd gotten that image, when the sealed blackness around me was total now. Then I realized it had come out of Joraleman's mind, falling into my own drifting thoughts like a warm spark. He wasn't a psion, but something about his mind was both looser and more focused than Kielhosa's.

I breathed on the image spark, let it grow and warm my thoughts for a while, until the snowtrack stopped again. The doors banged open; guards shouted us out into the spotlit compound yard. The bondie who'd been asleep from the start didn't get up. A couple of the guards dragged him away. I tried to reach into his mind as they took him past me, hating myself for trying. . . . He wasn't dead, but his mind wasn't anywhere I could reach, either. I shivered.

And then I was in his place, following the other blueskin, unloading crates of supplies. The guard who stayed with us had an electrified prod—a soft, glowing switch with a bite like acid. He liked using it. Joraleman stood watching us work for a couple of minutes, before he turned suddenly and walked away across the yard. Kielhosa stayed, smirking, until we were finished.

I could hardly pick up my own feet by then. My arms twitched and my knees trembled from working in gravity half again as heavy as what I was used to; the backs of my legs smarted with small burns where the guard had used the tip of the prod on them. When he started us away finally to whatever came next, I did my best to stay ahead of him. On every side of us were towers winking with lights, endless black bulks of refinery buildings, cranes and gantries; a grim, dark city grown out of the frozen desert . . . my new home. Finally I began to see low white-lit buildings up ahead—anonymous, silent, expensive-looking. We were heading toward one of them, but the sight of it didn't feel right to me, not with my legs smarting and my breath coming in heavy gulps. Those buildings were only a mask. This wasn't what came next; not for us. . . .

Burial alive was what came next. We went inside one of the buildings that stood away from the rest, and the guard herded us into a freight elevator. It dropped down a vertical shaft that could have gone straight to Cinder's core before it finally stopped and we got off again, somewhere deep in the heart of the stone. The controls were print-idented; no one could operate the lift who wasn't meant to. It was the only way down, the only way out.

The guard left us in a long room lit up nearly as bright as day, full of mats, most with bodies lying on them. I just stood and stared, not understanding, until the bondie who'd worked with me went to the nearest empty mat and collapsed onto it. A couple of the others raised their heads, let them drop back again; all of the faces had blue skin. I began to understand.

This was where we slept, or tried to. The small red points of light at the corners of the ceiling were monitor cameras. There was no privacy, no peace, nowhere to hide here, except in sleep. . . . I found a mat and lay down, feeling the light prying through my eyelids. *Ten years.* . . . I flopped onto my stomach and buried my face in my arms, waiting for oblivion. It didn't keep me waiting long. I dreamed about the Sakaffe Institute, about soft beds and good food and laughter, and about touching Jule taMing.

A kick woke me up again, after what seemed like only a couple of hours. I staggered out to the mess hall with a hundred others, and gulped down the plate of slop that was breakfast. And then we went on down the black hole, and I started to learn how long a day in hell could be.

At the bottom of the shaft was a huge vault cut from the stone, fogged with dust, the fog glowing yellow under banks of lights. Someone handed me a helmet with a lamp on it and something heavy that turned out to be a cutter. I followed the rest of the shift through the sulphur-colored haze like a blind man, up ladders on the far wall of the vault into a shadowy gallery half-eaten into the blue-gray rock.

They started in to work, nobody saying a word to me or each other while the guards were watching. The sound of their cutters was almost too high and too low to hear, drilling into my head, echoing and reechoing against the sound of half a thousand other cutters all through the underground. I stood where I was, watching, trying to figure out how to start. A guard came toward me; the light on my helmet filled in his silhouette as I looked up at him. He didn't look human—until I realized he was wearing a mask against the dust. We didn't have masks. "Get to work." The words were only a mumble, but I didn't have to guess what he was telling me.

I shook my head. "I don't know—" His prod jabbed me in the ribs and I finished it with a yelp, backing into the wall and dropping my cutter. "Wait, listen, will you"—starting to panic as his arm came up again—"just tell me what to do!"

The bondie working next to me reached out for my shoulder and jerked me around. "Shut up and take this." He pushed a clear, silvery tube into my hands. I held it while he dropped a blue crystal the size of his fist into it and sealed the lid. "Stick it into my shoulder bag." I did. The guard watched us, the prod glowing in his fist; and then he moved on.

"Thanks," I said, feeling weak.

The bondie shrugged, pushing stringy blue-black hair

back from his blue-stained face. "For what? I need a new partner, you're it. Do everything I tell you, do it fast and right, or I'll beat the crap out of you myself." He broke off, coughing deep in his chest, and spat. "Understand?" He was bigger than I was, and older, and he might still be stronger. His fingers tangled in my hair.

I nodded, too tired to fight or even to resent it. "Anything you say." He let me go. When he didn't say anything more, I asked, "What're you called?"

He almost looked surprised. "Mikah."

He didn't ask back. Finally I said, "Cat. I'm Cat."

"Shut up. Pick up that cutter and do what I tell you with it."

I picked up the cutter and did what he told me.

And every day after that was the same; until I didn't know day from night, buried alive in a blue stone tomb. Day after day we peeled off layers of ore and dumped it, looking for blue lumps of crystal, and everything weighed too much, even your feet felt like lead. Break the stone. Find the crystal and drop it into a tube, before its structure shattered and the matrix fell apart around it. . . . They used human beings because it was a delicate, dirty job; machinery broke down too easily, and was too hard to replace out here in the middle of nowhere. Warm bodies were cheaper than cold machines—when a pair of hands couldn't hold a cutter or pry out a crystal anymore there was always another pair to replace it, or ten, or a hundred: it didn't matter to Federation Mining whether you lived or died. After a while it hardly even mattered to me. Everything that had ever had any meaning shrank down to the simple effort of living through a few more hours of breaking stone.

Then, you tried to get the same plate full of slop into your mouth while your hands shook. You stumbled back to your dormitory and fell onto a mat still hungry, to sleep like the dead under the endless daylight of the spotlights. You tried to do it all over again, at the new shift; a few more hours, one more day. . . . The blue dust from the mines got into your eyes and nose and mouth, into every pore; it made you cough, it stained your skin blue, but nobody cared if you were too tired to scrub it off.

I kept thinking I'd get used to it, the work would get easier after a while. But it never did. I just got more and more tired; too tired to think straight about anything, or even to remember. . . . But over and over I dreamed about the Sakaffe Institute, about the psions and belonging to something good. And always the dream changed, and I was a slave, crawling through mud, digging my own grave out of blue stone, while Dr. Ardan Siebeling stood over me with a whip. I'd wake up coughing and full of hate, and wonder why I'd ever thought I was saving myself from anything by coming to this place.

But I didn't want to be a slave, I wanted out—there had to be a way out. I knew that to get away you had to get back to the spaceport; there was nothing else on Cinder. On a clear day you could see the Green Mountains from the mines compound, if you were lucky enough to be on the surface. Sticking up at a freaky angle, like the ragged edge of spring calling me out of winter—across fifty kilometers of wasteland, where the temperature never got up to freezing and the snow turned to acid when it touched your skin.

I'd heard strange stories about things happening outside, too, that no one could explain away by "snow accidents." The bondies claimed that there were "others" here who hated the mines, but no one would admit it. But they also claimed that Cinder was haunted, that it could drive you crazy, that it tried to get you lost outside so you'd freeze . . . until I didn't know whether to believe anything I heard.

And a blue-stained face wouldn't get me out of that hellhole anyway, so what was the use?

But there was a way—an easy way. Whenever they shipped the telhassium to the spaceport and brought back supplies, they used a couple of the bondies to do the heavy work, the way they'd done on my trip out. It was a free ride all the way to town, and they picked newer men because they were in better shape.

I'd figured Kielhosa would stop any chance I had of getting a break; I guess it was stupid to think he cared that much. But I couldn't believe my luck when one day they called me out for the trip.

Mikah and I loaded crates of crystals and bars of half-refined ores, our bloodshot eyes half-blind in the glaring daylight of the yard, while a guard leaned against the snowtrack and yawned. Mikah was coughing all the time—he was spitting red, something I'd never noticed down in the darkness. I did my own work and half of his, to keep the guard off our backs. Even so, I felt stronger than I had since I'd gotten here; almost human again.

We were nearly finished when the driver came up— the official named Joraleman. He stared at me for a minute, before he grinned and said, "Sainted Sarro, it is you! You've made me a lot of extra work, bondie. We haven't been able to find anyone else that handles a snowtrack like you do." He laughed; I stood blinking at him for a minute before I realized he was making a joke. "Kielhosa's sharp, kid. Nobody's outmaneuvered him like that in a long time." He stopped smiling. "Sorry it didn't do you more good."

I just shrugged, moving my tongue inside my dust-dry mouth, wondering if he expected me to answer. Afraid to try, but afraid to guess wrong, I did something I hadn't even thought of for months: I probed his mind. Lying on its surface I saw his relief at finding me still alive. And below it was something I almost thought was guilt. He was the one who'd gotten me this ride. He'd asked them specifically to find me. I wondered why the hell he should care what happened to me. But I squinted past him at the mountains, wiping my face, and I almost smiled.

The guard gave Mikah and me thermal jackets, shoved us in on top of the crates, and locked the doors. I felt the snowtrack start up, and felt us go through the dome airlock.

After a while I found a check window and got it open. It wasn't big enough to squeeze through, but at least there was light, and something to do. The cold air stung my nose and numbed my face; but once I began to watch, I couldn't look away. The endless blue-and-whiteness burned away the exhaustion that fogged my mind.

I swallowed and swallowed again; my mouth was always dry, no matter how much I drank. "Look"—trying again—"look out there, Mikah. All that snow and sky. The real world—" My voice broke. I coughed up blue phlegm and wiped my mouth. "It makes you remember you're still alive." He didn't say anything. "You want to look?"

"Nah. Somebody could go blind staring at all that snow. What makes you such a poet?" He frowned, scratching inside his jacket.

I flexed my hands, feeling the calluses on my palms. "I ain't digging ore."

"Crap. You think you're going to take off when we reach the port."

"What makes you figure that?" I stared out the window, feeling the snowtrack's hold close around us again.

"They all think it at first. Even me, once."

"How long you been here, anyhow?" trying to change the subject.

"I don't know. What year is it?"

I looked back at him. "Twenty-four seventeen, I guess."

"God," he mumbled. "Is that all? Five stinking years?" I wondered why I hadn't seen anybody down in the mines who was even close to the end of his ten years. Mikah's voice hardened. "Listen to me. Don't try to make a break. Joraleman doesn't come on as strong as some of the others, but he'll stun you as quick as the next if you do. And when you get back to the mines . . . ever see what they do to runaways?"

"What if I did make it?" I remembered how Joraleman had asked for me.

"You wouldn't. But even if you did, you'd never get offworld. They check for the bond tags. It just ain't no use. Look, anything you do this trip reflects on me, too. So don't try anything stupid." He broke off, coughing again. "Damn . . . damn it! Shut that thing, for God's sake. We could freeze in here." He stretched out on the bars of ore and shut his eyes. "I'm going to sleep. . . ." He was asleep almost before he finished saying it.

I reached over to pull the window shut. And then suddenly the world tilted and fell out from under us.

7

Cold . . . so cold. My hands were stiff with the cold, stretched above my head; my whole body was numb. All except my head—somebody must have kicked me in the head, but I couldn't remember the fight, couldn't even remember. . . . But then I remembered that I hadn't been in Oldcity, or even on Ardattee, for a long time. I opened my eyes.

I was lying head down in a pile of crates, and far up above me was sky, a deep twilight purple. I watched aurora move silently in the gap of the snowtrack's sprung doors, watched the fog of my own breath blur and combine with it. I sighed, enjoying the peace of the sky.

Somebody moaned. I raised my head, remembering Mikah and then finally everything else up to the end of the world. "Mikah . . . ?" I struggled, kicking broken boxes away, feeling a kind of sweet pain at the sound of muffled shattering as crystals decomposed inside them. I pulled myself up, buried to my knees in the jumble of crates and ore bars. Mikah lay on his back close to me, mostly clear of the ore. I moved what I had to to get him free, glad after all that we'd had to load the snowtrack as full as we did. The front wall was the closest thing it had to a floor, now; if there'd been less of a load, we would have been buried under the ore.

Mikah was out cold, but he was breathing easy, and when I reached into his mind he wasn't far below the surface. I left him alone and stood still for a minute. There was nothing to hear except the sound of his breathing and mine. Nothing. I wondered what had happened to Joraleman . . . what had happened to us all. It looked like we'd fallen into a ditch.

I put a hand up to the knot on the back of my head. My eyes weren't working just right, and I couldn't seem to think about more than one thing at a time. I decided to think about getting up front to Joraleman. Getting help. He must have a radio, or something. . . . The doors were sprung, and I knew I ought to feel happier about that than I did. I started to climb up and out.

As I reached the doorway, the whole snowtrack shifted and dropped a few centimeters under me. I froze, swallowing my heart again as the 'track didn't slide any farther, and pulled myself through into the snow. The snow lay in a wide fan around me, against a long concave wall of ice; snow that had given way and dumped us into this. . . .

I looked past the doors and down. And down. And then I sat back slowly in the snow, pulling my knees up to my chest, and hugged myself against a fit of shuddering. The snowtrack was resting on a ledge, barely. And below it translucent walls of green fluted ice fell away for a hundred meters or more into caverns of shadow. One slip, one shifting, even the tiniest wrong move . . .

After a while my body began to let itself go, too cold and beaten to sit there huddled in a knot forever. My mind eased out of its blind terror the same way. I started to inch forward finally, crawling, trembling, to look down again into the crevasse. Holding my breath, I saw the cab of the 'track hanging over the edge, resting on air. There was no way I could reach it, or Joraleman, or the radio without killing us all. I backed up again, wondering about Mikah. As long as he stayed unconscious, he'd be better off where he was than he'd be if I tried to move him. If he woke up . . .

But I couldn't make myself climb back into the snowtrack's hold, couldn't even make myself touch it. And I couldn't stay where I was, either, waiting for all of us to fall or freeze. So I started to climb, floundering up the face of the broken snow.

I made it to the surface, panting, covered by clinging white powder. Before I brushed it off, I wadded a handful in the palm of my glove and looked at it. I'd never seen more than a few flakes of snow at once before. Frozen water. . . . I put the handful into my mouth. I spat it out again as my mouth started to burn, remembering too late that this snow had some kind of acid in it.

I got to my feet. Up ahead I could see the Green Mountains, but they were on the other side of the crevasse from where I stood. They might as well have been on another planet. My throat tightened as I thought about how close. . . . I turned and looked back the way we'd come, shielding my eyes against the bloody glare of sunset. The snowtrack's trail disappeared in the distance. There was no sign of the mines compound at all. The wind moaned and cried, sucking up whorls of dry snow, letting them sift down again as its voice fell away into sighs. The snowfields glittered like broken glass. I'd never seen so much open space before. I'd never been lost all alone in so much space; cold, bleak, and empty . . . so *empty*. I stumbled back and covered my eyes.

But I couldn't panic; *I couldn't*. I brought my hands down. Because the shaking that had hold of me now wasn't just fear. I didn't know how cold it was, but it was colder than anything I'd ever known; and with the sun setting it wasn't going to get any better. I had to keep sane and keep moving or I'd freeze right here. I made myself start to walk back along the snowtrack's trail, the only thing I could think of to do. The crust held my weight, as long as I was careful. This was a small world, no matter how it looked to me. It couldn't be that far back to the dome, and warmth, and help. . . . I kept walking, shivering harder.

Something caught my eye as I reached the first long curve of the trail, coming out of blue shadow below the foot of a buckled sheet of ice. I stopped, glancing up the sunlit slope; stood still, with the freezing air catching in my throat. The wind stirred. Sweet chiming music broke the silence, and a shower of rainbow sparks danced on the snow. *Not real*. I shook my head. My eyes weren't seeing this: not a garden of glass fracturing the sunset, a fantasy forest spun out of ice crystal, thorn and teardrop and gossamer. . . . "Not real." I whispered it, remembering the stories the bondies told, wondering if this world was haunted after all.

I picked up a chunk of fractured snow crust, ready

to throw it—and then I dropped it again. I stepped out of the rut and started up the open hillside, breaking through the snow crust, staggering and sinking, but always getting closer. I reached the trees at last, plunged into rainbow as I fell down on my knees below their glistening fingers. They laughed and chimed and sang to me. I got up slowly, reaching out to the final proof of my sanity. . . .

And as I reached out, I saw the other, standing like my own reflection beyond the fragile garden of crystal spines. My hand jerked, hitting the branch. It burst open with a sound like shattering windowpanes. Splinters of burning ice flew into my eyes. I cried out, losing the stranger and everything else in a haze of fire. I dug at my eyes. Suddenly a hand was on my arm, solid and real, turning me, pulling my hands away from my face. I looked up but I couldn't see anything, only a fiery blur.

An alien thought probed deep into the core of my mind. Suddenly all my senses burst open—and then I was wrenched into blackness.

I was sitting on my knees on a floor of rough stone; my mind was still trying to settle back into my skull. I wiped at my oozing eyes, swearing.

Mikah was lying on his side staring at me, when my eyes finally cleared. I hoped I didn't look as scared as he did. "You"—he gulped—"you alive?"

"I am if you are." My voice didn't sound very sure of it. I felt the lump on the back of my head again, glancing past him. Joraleman was lying beside him. We were in a blue stone room with no windows. "How . . .

how long've I . . . we been like this?" *Trees—where were the trees?*

"I just woke up. Where the hell are we? I can't see anything." There wasn't anything to see, but I didn't bother to mention it. He pushed himself up and started to run his hands over his body, wincing and cursing at the bruises.

"Not the mines." For one sick minute after my eyes cleared I'd thought we were back where we'd started. Now I was sure it was somewhere else. But where? "How's Joraleman?"

"I don't know. He's bleeding. Maybe he's dead."

"Well, hell, why didn't you check?"

"Because I was out cold, jerk."

I crawled over to where Joraleman lay. His pale hair was covered with blood from a cut across his forehead, but it looked like the cold had stopped the bleeding. He groaned when I shook him. "He's alive." I noticed that his stungun was gone.

"Tough luck." Mikah rubbed his hands together.

"Shut up," I said, feeling guilty somehow. "He's the only one who might know what happened to us. You better hope he stays alive till he tells us that much." Mikah shrugged. I shook Joraleman and he groaned again. There was a first-aid kit on his belt. I got it open, but I didn't know what to do with the things I found inside it. There was a wet cloth sealed in plastic; I pulled that out and wiped off his face.

Mikah leaned past my shoulder. "Sure is a lot of blood."

"Too bad it ain't yours," I said, disgusted.

He pulled back, starting to cough again. When it was

over, he said, "You know, at first I thought we were all dead, and the real hell was a lousy snowball just like Cinder. Damn, I don't ever want to die, if . . ." He didn't finish it. "Did you see anything? About what happened to us? I don't remember a thing till I woke up here."

I sat back on my heels while everything I'd seen played through my senses again.

"Well?" He gave my arm a poke.

I pulled away from him. "Yeah. We—" I pressed my lips together. "We fell into a big hole. Somebody must've got us out. I don't know how." *Or who.* Who else was there? Who had I seen, in that last second before . . .

Joraleman's blue eyes opened, and for a second there was pure terror in them. He'd been conscious before, for long enough: the view through the windshield of the snowtrack was burned into his memory like a brand. "It's okay," I whispered, touching him. "You're safe." He stared at me, and at Mikah, for a long minute before he tried to push himself up. He fell back again, running his hand over his face. "Hell and devils. . . ."

"Yeah, maybe so," I said. "You hurt bad?"

He didn't answer me at first. "My—ribs. I think something's broken. Feel dizzy." His voice slurred.

"There's a cut on your head."

"Aid kit. Get out the large white pills—two of them."

I handed them to him. He chewed them up and swallowed with an effort. He started to breathe more easily then, and he sat up, staring at the walls just like we had.

I leaned back on my hands. "Where are we? What's happening to us?"

"I don't know." He looked back at me, annoyed. "How would I know if you don't?"

I shrugged, and got up. He stuck out his hand, so I helped him stand. He peered around like it was too dark to see clearly. I suppose it was, for them. My cat eyes didn't have any trouble. He went over and ran his hand along a wall. The room was long and high, but rough around the edges, like a hole, and nothing but blue rock. I saw a telhassium crystal glitter as I glanced past. There were no windows, and now I realized there were no doorways, either. There were no openings at all. . . . I let my mind skid on past that without stopping; trying not to think about suffocating, trying to believe that if we'd gotten in, there was a way out, somewhere. Nobody else said anything about doors, either. A couple of lamps that burned with a shimmering blue glow were set into holes in the wall; otherwise the room was empty. "All the comforts of home," I said.

Mikah grimaced. "Where did you grow up?"

"Spooks. It has to be," Joraleman muttered.

"What?" I looked back at him; so did Mikah. "You feeling all right? Maybe you ought to sit down."

He shook his head. "I'll hold for now." Then he frowned at us; his hand went looking for his stungun, and tightened when he didn't find it.

"You—uh, figured out where we are?" I wondered if that crack he'd taken on the head had made him a little gorked.

"I think so." He leaned against the wall and sighed.

"We're 'guests' of the Spooks. The snowtrack didn't just drop into a crevasse by accident. Something happened to the instruments. . . ."

"You think ghosts did all this to us?" Mikah said sourly.

Joraleman laughed once. "The sort of 'Spook' I had in mind would be one of Cinder's natives."

"I never heard of any natives," I said.

"I know you haven't." He shrugged. "We don't exactly advertise it while we're mining here. Squatter's rights aren't legally supposed to apply when there's a native culture. But the Federation needs telhassium—and the Spooks weren't about to leave. The FTA did its best to get rid of them. The problem is that they're psionic—they read minds, they can teleport. And they live underground. It makes them hard to back into a corner." He was staring at the solid walls, and he smiled; but he didn't think it was funny. "By the Seven Saints, I don't know why I'm telling all this to you. The point is that the Spooks won't even deal with us on a normal level. In the beginning they pulled some ineffectual sabotage, but it was barely even an inconvenience; I guess they didn't have much to work with. After that they dropped out of sight, literally. And now . . ."

"Why shouldn't they fight?" I said. "It's their snowball." I wondered why that even mattered to me.

"I know that! But why now? That's why we needed a new driver, kid: the last one didn't come back from a trip to town. Neither did the snowtrack. . . ." His voice faded. For a second the terror was back in his eyes.

I rubbed my arms. Green ice, falling away into the shadows. . . . "Why do they call them Spooks?" I remembered the figure I'd half seen waiting for me—and the sense-twisting wrench that had pulled me from the crystal garden to this freezing hole with no exits.

"I suppose 'Spook' was the first thing that came into somebody's head. Nobody has seen one in years; I've only seen a holograph, but you could say there's a resemblance: dead white and spindly-looking. They appear and disappear. And they don't speak—apparently they communicate only by telepathy, although as far as we know they can't or won't link minds with a human."

"Look, what good is all this talk doing!" Mikah wiped his face on his sleeve. "We're just wasting time —we have to get out of here before those things come and kill us!" His voice wavered.

Joraleman pointed a hand at the walls, his face set and gray. I felt his tension rising. "If you've got suggestions on how to get out, bondie, I'd like to hear them. Otherwise, you might as well just shut up and wait." He didn't know how bad he was hurt, and he was keeping his own voice calm with nothing but willpower. He folded his arms against his ribs and slid down carefully to the floor.

I sat down too and rubbed my cold-aching hands, wishing I had a camph. *Psions . . . telepaths.* I wondered. I shut the room out of my mind and stretched my thoughts. It seemed like forever since I'd even tried to use my psi. It was hard to concentrate; it hurt to search, hunting a doorway in the dark and falling over things I couldn't see. I didn't want to do it, I'd never wanted to, I hated it. But somewhere . . . somewhere . . . *there.*

"Hey, you, what're you doing?"

Something snapped and I was looking at Mikah. "Jeezu! You stupid—"

"You look dead, sitting there with your eyes unfocused."

"What do you want me to do about it? I'm thinking." I looked over at Joraleman. His eyes were shut. He wasn't asleep; he was praying. He wanted to be out of this so much that it was almost a physical pain, merging into the pain of his broken body.

"Then think of how to get us out of here, smartass." Mikah got up and started to cough. His own fear crackled like static.

I blocked them out of my mind. I'd done it; for a second I'd found someone, something. I loosened my mind, let it reach out again; this time knowing where to start, spinning out an invisible thread, casting into the dark waters . . . and then suddenly *contact*, feeling, sound, vision, everything: blinding, alien sensory feedback, twisting and warping my mind's sight like crazy mirrors, roaring and ringing, shocking every nerve ending in my body.

I broke contact. I sat with my eyes shut tight, more grateful right then for the emptiness in my mind than I'd ever been for anything; not even wanting to face the real world. But I'd done it. And knowing that I had, that I could, I had to go back again. . . .

This time it was almost easy; I knew the way through

the dark. But I took it slowly, keeping control, making the sudden explosion of images and impressions filter through blocks and byways to reach my mind's eye. And I understood this time that I hadn't contacted just one of the aliens. Somehow I'd contacted them all, more minds than I could ever comprehend, all at once. I was looking through hundreds of eyes at once, breaking in on a hundred different lives, plugged into the circuits of enough energy to burn out all my senses if I lost control again. I could barely touch the wild electricity of living a hundred lives at once. My own thoughts began to tangle helplessly. I started to struggle, to pull my mind free. . . . And then suddenly I knew that they knew about me.

I broke contact and tried to disappear. But they followed me back across the broken connections, and my defenses fell apart until nothing lay in their way. I was drowning in image—

I was back in the stone-walled room; Mikah and Joraleman were standing over me. My face hurt, and after a minute I knew someone had slapped me.

"He just went crazy. Dumb twist sits there staring like he's seeing things and says he's 'thinking,' then he starts—"

Joraleman said, "What's the matter with you, kid? Can you hear me?"

I nodded. "Yeah. I made contact—with the Spooks."

"What did I tell you? He's crazy," Mikah said.

"I ain't crazy! I'm a telepath. I got into their minds, and they found out."

"Is that the truth, bondie? You can read minds? Did you find out anything?"

"Yeah, it's the truth. But there was too much, it all ran together." I shook my head. "I'm still trying to get it. . . ." I looked up and away from him.

Two of them were standing there in the room with us. Spooks: a woman with hair like a cloud, whose moon-white skin was netted with age lines; and a man who looked almost human, I thought—I wanted to laugh but I didn't. They wore heavy clothes, like our own but rougher-looking. I felt them searching us with their mind. I tried to deaden my own mind, not even thinking. . . .

"It's him. He's the one you want!" Mikah pointed at me.

B

The aliens were startled; I could feel their surprise. They moved toward us. I got up and backed away from Joraleman and Mikah, toward the far end of the room. The old woman stayed where she was, watching them; the man followed me. I looked back at the others and said, "Do something," but they just stood gaping like none of it was real.

The man stopped in front of me, and I couldn't look away from his eyes. They were green, all green like a cat's. And when they met mine, the world stopped. Suddenly I couldn't move. I couldn't even think; my mind was paralyzed like my body. There was only the wall, behind me, holding me up—the wall, the only thing that wasn't a part of an anger that didn't belong to me, a thousand bright fluttering rags of image choking my mind . . . a sudden knife of focused thought sinking home behind my eyes, searching for my soul—

(Wait, stop, what do you *want*?) I felt my memories separating and coming loose, my mind being torn open. He was searching for the answers to a question I didn't even know; and I couldn't stop him, I couldn't reach him—I couldn't even remember how. I couldn't remember my own name . . . I was disappearing, disintegrating, feeling my mind flowing out of me layer after layer. . . .

Until he tore away the last of my defenses, so deep in my mind that I hadn't even known it was there. And the secret walled up behind it burst out: a nightmare of blood and screaming and agony. His own mind reeled back from it. Just for a second he lost control, giving me time to fuse the defenses he'd torn loose and choke off the horror before my mind had to put a name to it. And then I held him away; I let my own rage against what he was doing feed, and focused a thought from somewhere, (C-A-T spells *Cat*.) I built on it, strand on strand, to thicken a shield and force him out: *He didn't have the right, nobody had the right to do this to me.* . . . I felt surprise, but it wasn't my surprise. He shook my mind and I slipped, but (I'm Cat . . . Cat . . . and I won't . . .)

And then he twisted my mind back on itself and made me see what I was facing: see that all their strength held me—not just his mind, but his mind multiplied a hundred times over. I'd trespassed against them all. They were all there inside his mind, reaching through his eyes, holding me . . . his eyes burning my mind like emeralds burning, green fire, green ice, green as grass—green as mine. (No! Don't hurt me, I'm like you! Look at my eyes, look at my eyes, they're green!)

I stopped disappearing. One frozen moment went on and on, and then the scattered puzzle pieces of my memory came spinning back together, making me gasp, and I was whole again. But before I could do anything else, he—they—reached back through my eyes. I became a link forged into a chain, while they opened up my thoughts again, all of them together reaching into my head, shattering the walls that I'd built for my fears to hide behind—my shields, my armor, my safety, my sanity. Making me stand naked in the circle of their minds with no protection; making me feel every instant of their own lives. My mind was burning out, but I couldn't make a sound, even inside my head; couldn't do anything but help them. . . .

And then, just when I thought I couldn't stand it any longer, all of it was gone. I was alone again: the deep and total bond was broken, and instead there were quiet messages forming on the surface of my mind— the only kind of contact I'd ever known before. But this time it wasn't in a way I'd ever known it. One voice was made up of all voices, impressions formed instead of words. (And it was true . . . they knew my eyes, they had seen through them now; it was true,) with feeling shifts inside it I didn't understand. (They found a mirror in my mind, saw their own eyes trapped in an alien face. I was the one who had been twice-promised, whose coming would begin the righting of all wrongs. . . .)

But I didn't understand it, I didn't want to; I only wanted them out of my mind. All I could think was, (God damn you, for what you did to me!), and I threw it at them. (Everybody thinks they can use me like a garbage can. But I'm human, for God's sake; I got a right to keep some part of me to myself!)

Their mind touched me again, gently, weaving its hundred voices into harmony with mine—healing, fusing, comforting. Showing me that my shame was meaningless, that with them I had no need for shame. My shame melted away; my anger went with it, even though I didn't want it to. And then I realized that

all the clumsy barriers were gone that anger and fear
had thrown in the way of the Gift I'd been born with.
My mind's vision was as clear as open sky. . . .

(Through ignorance they had trespassed in my—
self. Now they tried to make amends. . . . But none of
the other desecrators, and none of their blue-skinned
slaves, had the gift of true sharing. I was the one who
had been promised, but they had not realized that I
would walk between worlds; not human, not one of
them. They wanted to know why I was different. How
had I been made this way?)

I shook my head, because it was all I could do. I
thought, (I—I don't understand. I don't know. It just
happened, I guess. But, we're not different, really; we're
all the same) remembering what Jule had told me.
(Your people and mine. That's why I'm the way I am.)
It came so easily, I didn't know what was happening to
me.

I felt the strange surprise fill my mind again, and a
flicker of disgust, a wave of disbelief. (All the same, a
unity? Not the mindless ones, the destroyers, the slave-
keepers, the savages. They were less than animals. It
was the will of the One that those who mined the
sacred stone be stopped . . . made to do no further
harm. . . .) The image blurred behind my eyes; not
death, but a nothingness, like everything I knew disappearing. (I was the one they had been told about.
It had been promised long ago that one day their own
would return from the stars and end their suffering
exile. The outsiders would be swallowed up, would
disappear, and all wrongs would be righted. It had
been promised, and promised again. I was proof that

the promise had been kept, and the time had come at last.) The aliens broke contact then, setting my mind free—and leaving it filled.

I stood staring at the alien's human/inhuman face in front of me, into it, through it. Because I'd been half blind all my life, and now I could see. I was in control again, but my mind still absorbed sights and thoughts and feelings that weren't my own, without even trying. Alien, human, everywhere—I sank into them. My mind dissolved like sea foam, until I could hardly breathe. And then the aliens disappeared, both of them winking out as if they'd never been there. After they were gone, my knees buckled and I slid down the wall.

When I finally felt like getting up again, Joraleman and Mikah were still standing where they'd stood all along. I hit Mikah and knocked him down, even though I knew it hadn't made any difference that he'd told the aliens who I was. "Croach."

"I'm sorry, kid," Joraleman said. He looked dazed. "There—wasn't anything we could do."

"Don't make much difference if you're sorry now." I shook out my hand.

Mikah got up and started to come after me, but Joraleman stopped him. "What did they do to you? What happened?"

I tried to tell him what they'd done to me, but it was too personal. I looked away, and only told him what they'd said. When I finished, Mikah said, "You hear that? They're gonna kill us! And not him." He glared at me. "Why should you get off? You vermy rat, you're not special. These aren't civilized aliens, you're not kin to them. You're just a half-breed freak and a lying son of a bitch." He started toward me again.

I looked at Joraleman. He didn't say a thing, trying not to feel the same way Mikah did. I started to back away from them.

Joraleman said, "Stop it!" suddenly. Mikah shut up then, but I kept on backing away. I went to a corner and sat down, watching them. Joraleman put an arm across his ribs and sat down, too. He swallowed more pills from the aid kit. Mikah just stood staring at me, his breath wheezing in his chest.

My mind was still lit up like I was doing dreamtime, although it was fading some since the aliens had gone away. I could still feel everything Joraleman and Mikah were thinking, their fear and anger—more of it than I wanted to. I kept trying to believe it didn't matter; I didn't care what happened to them. But . . . "Look, I'll try to find out what they're planning for us. Maybe it'll help."

Joraleman glanced up, startled, from across the room. He almost smiled.

I closed my eyes and let my mind slide back into alien water, easily now, trying to find the things I had to know, and trying not to drown. These were Hydrans; they had to be, even if I didn't know what they were doing out here so far from the rest of their kind. They were my own kind—my mind fought it—they knew me, had *expected* me. A feeling of cold wonder burst inside me. *Why? How? And the answer came:* (Because they existed to protect the blue stone of this world.) *Telhassium ore.* (They/their ancestors/their god, was/were the

One, and the ore was sacred to them, giving life and light to them on this frozen piece of star. The Ancestors, the wellspring of their spirit, had gone from here long ago, but would return; it had been promised. And meanwhile they kept a sacred trust, and preserved the sacred stone.)

They remembered their ancestors' going; they remembered everything. Their memories pooled age on age—every mind among them was bound to every other, present and past, through hundreds of years; totally, freely, holding nothing back . . . in a joining, the ultimate sharing of mind and soul. They were a whole people who joined and were never separate; each individual was no individual but an outlet for the whole. Every image that any of them, living or dead, had ever shared was woven into the cloth of their group mind. But the wearing of years, hardship, and change had faded and torn the oldest images, until they no longer knew the true meanings, but laid new meanings over the old.

And so I saw the truth, although I didn't understand all of it then. That the Hydrans had come to the Crab long before the supernova's shining dust ever showed in Ardattee's sky. That they'd come here from a stellar empire that had passed its peak and was slipping down; looking for telhassium on a cooling piece of star. They'd set up a Colony of their own here, and then the civilization slipped down even more and the Hydrans on Cinder had lost contact with the rest of their people— with the Ancestors. Cinder grew colder and colder, the humans came; time and hardship shrank the lost Colony until the people no longer understood who they really were, or even why they'd come. But they still understood some things. And so they called the telhassium sacred, and the humans desecrators, and they waited, and waited. . . .

And they were a whole people who joined. Because once, at its height, a whole civilization had been able to join. The thing that for even two human psions was a wonder had been the soul of every Hydran, had been their strength, their world, their One. . . . And when I touched the truth in their mind, I felt fear in a way I'd never known, of things I would never understand. Because it was something that had almost destroyed me; and yet some part of me *wanted* it. . . . My mind broke away, but I forced it back again.

(Now the time had come at last; their waiting, their exile, were coming to an end. The key to the place of evil and its destruction had been sent to them, as they had known he would be.) *Me, they meant me.* (Now he would be taken to the holy place, to touch the spirit of the One, who would give them a sign.) And inside the matrix of the thought I saw flame. . . .

I fell back into the real world, and the others were still watching me.

"What is it—?"

"They're gonna burn me!"

Mikah laughed. "That's a switch!"

"Shut up, we don't have time—" Joraleman turned on him, his voice sharp. "Tell me what you found out," he said, looking back at me.

I told him all that I understood of what I'd seen.

"And there's a place filled with fire, I saw it, blue fire; it's a holy place. They think I'm sent by their ancestors, they want me to go there and give them a sign. The hell I will. I'm not gonna be burned alive!"

"What's going to happen to you if you won't? What's going to happen to us?"

I looked down. "I didn't stop to find out. But it ain't no happy ending, I guess. Humans are 'desecrators.'"

Joraleman sighed. "Damn. . . . You said the flames were 'blue'? You saw them? Give me some details."

"They were coming right out of the walls, out of the floor. . . . Wait. I saw crystals, like telhassium crystals, everywhere—hundreds of them."

"Like the lamp over there?" He pointed. I remembered thinking that it looked peculiar. Now I finally saw why. The lamp was a bowl shielding a piece of crystal, and it was the crystal that burned.

He went over and brought it down; he moved slowly, like moving was getting to be an effort. "That's a telhassium crystal they're 'burning.' Their 'sacred stone' . . . wouldn't you know they're religious fanatics. Putting a concentration of the crystals together causes a spontaneous deterioration. That's why you put them in shielded containers when you dig them out. If that's what makes this holy place shine, then maybe you've got a chance. What do you think? Is this it?"

"Yeah, it looks the same. But what difference does it make? It's still fire."

He held out the lamp. "Put your hand into it."

"What do you think I am?" I jerked back.

He passed his own hand through the shimmering light. "Ever heard of 'cold fire'? Most of its radiation

isn't released as heat. It won't burn you. Here." He
held it out again.

I held my breath, pulled off a mitten, and stuck out
my hand. I jerked it back again; but I hadn't felt it
beginning to burn, so I reached out one more time.
After about half a minute my fingers started to go
numb. I pulled my hand out of the fire and shook it
hard.

Joraleman said, "What's wrong?"

"My hand, it feels like it's dead." I put my mitten
back on to warm my hand.

"How long have you been at the mines?" He was
thinking, (*Too long; my skin was blue, he didn't know
if I could take that much poison . . .*)

"What do you mean, 'poison'?" I said. "What's going
to happen to me?"

He looked at me, startled. "Oh. All right, then; since
you already know. . . ." He looked away. "Telhassium
ore is radioactive. The level of radiation is extremely low;
but it builds up in the human body, like any cumulative
poison, like mercury or arsenic. Exposure to dust poisons you slowly. But contact with this 'cold fire' poisons
you fast, the radiation level is much higher. So what
happens to you depends on how long you have to make
the exposure. If you can cut it short, you should be all
right. If you take too long it could kill you." Joraleman
wiped his face; he was sweating now in spite of the
cold. I turned away from him, from the pressure of his
tension and his pain, from the blue crystal shimmering
in his hands.

"Hey." Mikah caught at Joraleman's jacket.

Joraleman winced and dropped the lamp. The crystal

imploded, throwing blue embers across the floor. He put a hand over his ribs. "What is it?"

"What good is all this doing for us? You've been figuring out how the freak's gonna save his neck, but he didn't say anything about how it's going to help us. How about it?"

Joraleman looked at me. "He's got a point."

"Yeah." I turned back to them, feeling the window-less walls closing in on me. I pulled my mittens off and started to rub my fingers. They'd been frostbitten a couple of times back in Oldcity, and they ached when they got cold. "Well, they think I'm gonna work mira-cles. If they're right, I'll work one for all of us." I pushed the corners of my mouth up.

Joraleman was getting one of the white pills out of the first-aid kit, and suddenly he reached in and pulled out something else. He caught my hand and slapped the thing down on it.

It stung. "Ow. . . . What was it?"

"A stimulant. If anything will help you, that should."

I hadn't even said I could save him. "Thanks."

"What about us, freak?" Mikah grabbed my wrist and one of my mittens dropped.

But I only looked away, feeling *something*—

The Hydrans were back.

"Never mind," Joraleman said, staring at them. "Do what you can."

I nodded. I turned again toward the door, and the two aliens were waiting for me. They put their hands on my arms. My mind started to flow into the sea of image, and I dropped the other mitten. My hands were cold. I felt a smile start to form on my mouth.

I heard Mikah say, "He wants to go with them," but I didn't, I didn't. . . . I did.

All I could see was flame, blue into blue, burning. But I saw the Hydrans too, dozens of them. . . . Or maybe I only felt them, drifting, whispering against my mind; like dust against a wall, or sand, or snow, or wind. Or flame. . . .

And then I knew where I was, and why, and my mind was my own again. I stood inside the place that I'd seen in my mind, a shelter inside a greater cave of darkness. Its space was lined with blue crystals, piled with them, alive with their shivering light. I knew what it was I had to remember: that this wasn't a place of ancestor spirits, that their god-self was superstitious garbage. That all I had to do was talk to nothing, make it good, and get it over with.

But maybe I'd been wrong. Because now the things I'd seen in the mind of the Hydrans came back to me, and somewhere in my own mind there was a . . . presence stirring. The thing that had hungered for the wholeness of their shared lives, that knew their loss for its own; that said they were right to welcome me, to have waited for me to come home. Because I was Hydran, this was my real heritage, and I should give thanks for my returning at last. . . . I went down on my knees and bowed my head, answering the stranger awake in my mind; and under my knees in the floor was the silver metal of a thing that had been placed there longer ago than anything I knew of. . . .

But as I kneeled there I felt the deadness creeping up my arms and legs, and I knew that if I stayed much longer I wouldn't get up again. I pushed myself to my feet and took a step, and another. It felt like someone else was doing it. But I left the holy place, and my people were waiting for me. Only two of them were physically there with me, the man and the woman; the rest were watching me through their eyes. This time my mind didn't lose its shape. (I did what you asked—) I thought, not knowing where to begin. My stomach knotted in a sudden cramp; I put my hands over it.

(A sign. The cold fire. . . .) It formed in my mind with a kind of awful joy.

I thought they meant the pain, but then something caught my eyes. I looked down, and my hands were glowing blue. So was my face. I rubbed my hands on my pants; but then I remembered the dust from the mines and how it stained your skin. They'd been answered. I let my hands drop and wondered how long it would last. Maybe too long. (What happens now?), wondering what their answer would mean for me.

The answer came: (You are the promised. You are the key, you will begin to unlock the future.)

I licked my lips. My tongue felt thick inside my mouth. I thought, carefully, (What about the others?), picturing, *(Joraleman and Mikah.)*

(It was my wish that the outsiders be returned to their settlement?)

(Yes! Don't hurt them. Let them go.) I was surprised that they actually cared about what I wanted.

(It would be as I asked.)

(And me?) Feeling a giddy rush of power, wondering how much I could ask of them. (I—)

They broke into my thought, (My guardians were waiting for me. I would be taken to them.)

I swallowed hard. (My guardians? Who? What—?)

But there was no answer. I let them lead me away from the shrine. There was a wide stair worn into the rock, as if they humbled themselves by coming to this place on foot. Behind us the blue glow leaped up the walls and was swallowed by the darkness. The stair spread out and down, to a ledge along the cavern wall, and the walls from there dropped away forever. There were things etched into the stone of the wall, strange symbols. I wondered what they said. The blue-silver glow behind and above us lit a path along the cliff face, along night's edge. The thought of walking it made me feel sick. There was nothing below us but darkness, and a few sparks of blue light, far away, like stars. I was shivering with cold, and I wondered if even the Hydrans knew what was out there in the night. And then I felt myself sucked down again into the whirlpool of their mind. . . .

". . . come on, kid, can you hear me? Try to concentrate."

I was shaking; somebody was shaking me. Joraleman. Mikah. "Damn, d-don't shake me!" And I was sitting against the wall of the blue stone room. The shock of being human, and with humans again, left me numb.

"He's glowing," Mikah said.

I looked at my hands. "They think it's a sign. . . . You're free. They said they'll take you back to town. It's all right."

"You mean that? We're really free?"

I nodded.

The lines of fear and strain eased on Joraleman's pale face. "Thank God." He thought his prayers had been answered.

Let him think it if he wanted to. A wave of cramps hit me again, and I held my breath. "They'll . . . be coming back for us."

"How do you feel?" He was worried. He figured I was in bad shape; but I didn't care. Right then nothing mattered, I felt too lousy.

"Hey, freak." Mikah pulled at my arm; I turned my face away. "God, you look like hell." Something about his voice sounded almost ashamed.

"I'm all right; I'm just tired. Don't call me that."

The Hydrans were back again; I didn't have to look up to know it. I got up slowly and moved away from the others until I stood between them and the Hydrans. (Is—it time?)

I thought the woman nodded; but she hadn't moved. She was expecting me to come with them, promising me (the others would be returned to their settlement as I had asked.)

I glanced at Mikah and Joraleman. "They'll take you back now."

Joraleman said, "Wait a minute. Where are you going?"

I didn't turn around. "With them."

"You can't do that! . . . You need medical treatment."

"I said I'm all right."

"Are they getting you free from the mines? Let me go with you, please. I . . . I can't take it there much longer. I don't want to die in that hole!" Mikah's face was tense and blue; he was remembering what Joraleman had said about the ore.

"They're not getting me free." I shook my head. "They just said I've got to go with them. I got no choice. They said somebody wants me. I don't know who, or—or what. Or even why." I was afraid even to guess.

Mikah looked at my face and then he shut his eyes; his hands balled up into fists.

"If I knew I was going free, I'd let you come." I raised my hands and made the truth-swearing oath.

"Sure." He nodded. "What the hell, it was worth a try." He glanced at Joraleman.

Joraleman didn't look angry, like I'd thought he would. He said quietly, "What's your name, bondie?"

"Cat."

He put out his hand, and at first I didn't understand. Then I wiped mine on my pants, but it was still glowing. He shook it anyway.

"Thanks. Good luck, Cat."

I nodded. I could feel the Hydrans waiting restlessly, their mind pulling at me. I started toward them, just wanting to get it over with.

"Hey."

I looked back one last time. Mikah made a funny motion. "Good luck, Cat."

"Sure." I nodded. "The same to you."

We were standing in another cavern, one that the Hydrans saw as a meeting place, even though there were no openings in these walls, either. I felt dizzy and confused; the pain in my gut was getting worse. But still I was able to see things in this room that didn't belong in a cave; alien things, but things the human side of me half recognized as high tech. And then I saw someone appear at the other end of the room. My eyes wouldn't focus, and at first I thought I was seeing things. They looked like humans.

I dug my hands into my eyes and looked up again. They were still real, standing at the far end of the hall. Another Hydran was with them, but I knew they weren't prisoners: maybe three of them, staring back at me. Murmuring and pointing. I looked at my hands. I tried to yell, "I'm human!" but I wasn't sure anyone had heard it except me.

The Hydrans beside me were telling them, (Here was the one they had been waiting for, the promised, the key. I had the true gift, and the sign had been laid upon me. I was being delivered safely to them. Now at last they could keep their own promises—) The thought had a sudden sharpness behind it.

I felt someone else reach into my mind then; a human probe. I didn't try to block it, and it was gone again as quickly as it had come.

(He is the one. We thank you. Now everything will happen as we promised.) It was one of the humans, answering the Hydrans; the one who'd probed me.

Pain drove into my stomach and I doubled over; I felt one of the Hydrans catch hold of my arms. The fingers felt like steel.

(I'm all right . . . let go of me.)

The hold loosened and I straightened up with my arms pressed against my stomach. I could feel the one who'd traded thoughts before with the Hydrans ask what was wrong. The humans came toward us across the room.

My eyes cleared again and I could see their faces at last. But I saw only one face. Siebeling's. Then suddenly it all came clear to me. The contact at the Sakaffe Institute, from the psions who were making trouble out here in the Crab Colonies. . . . They were here, now. And Siebeling, who'd done this to me, was here with them. I wanted to tell them who he was, to pay him back for it. But I couldn't shape the words anymore, or even the thoughts. Then all I remembered was falling into his arms.

G

After that I was lost for a long time, doing dreamtime
without end while my body paid the price. My mind
sealed itself off from the sickness of the hurting, helpless flesh that held it prisoner. But inside the formless
walls of my brain, some part of my consciousness still
wandered, restless, afraid to surrender to what might
be the final sleep of all.

And so I drifted through a strange dark universe,
startling awake images and memories, seeing them flare
up like embers from a long-hidden fire. I saw my life
flicker past me, in bits and pieces, like they say you do
when you're dying. And I felt the nerve circuits open
and close, the currents flow, the messages being sent
and the changing chemistry and pressures of life inside
my brain. . . . I was those things, sensing needs, tending
to them, taking a part in my own healing in a way I'd
never imagined I could do.

Or maybe that was all a dream, or maybe the dreams
were only a part of a greater rhythm, carried on the
tide of a universal sea. I had drowned in that sea when
the Hydrans took my mind—and been reborn. I'd felt
the beauty of their oneness and their sharing, of barriers
and walls broken down to let in the healing strength
of shared lives. And alone in its own darkness my mind
ached to feel that sharing again. I ranged further and

deeper, searching the past for a sign, a guide—crying into the unknown with a voice I could barely control.

And I was answered. Reliving my life, I found memories tangled up with my own that had never been mine before—like drawn to like from the other side, cracking the shell of solitude, giving refuge to my dreams and escape from my nightmares. . . .

Hands, thin child's hands—my hands, smeared with rotting fruit, pulling apart compacted wads of garbage, cramming slimy bits into my mouth; swallowing, gagging. . . . Scarred, bloody hands—my hands, my fists beating some nameless punk senseless with terrified bloodlust for calling me *freak*, because if I didn't the rest of his gang would close in and take me apart. Daring to steal the jacket off his back where he lay, because I needed one. Daring to turn my back on the rest of them and stagger away, because feeling him break and bleed made me sick, and all I wanted from them was to be left alone. . . . Beating my bruised fists against the wall in some icicle-hung alley, cursing with the pain of it, cursing because it didn't help; because the weight of my own life was too heavy, and sometimes I wished, *I wished* . . .

. . . Wishing I could fly away. Standing on a silver balcony under the night sky, jewel-covered hands clinging to the vine-covered railing: white-knuckled, slender, woman's hands (not my hands, not my body, not even my own memory, *fusion, confusion*). Strands of gleaming black hair slithered free from the coils at the back of my head, clinging to my tear-wet cheeks. The agony of half a thousand blind emotions at once tortured my helpless mind; but there was no escape from the reception in the embassy at my back, drunken lecherous selfish greedy pitying hating *screaming*. . . . Biting my red-stained lips, to keep from screaming to drown them all out. *No escape, no escape, help me, God, help me, please please someone.* . . . Staring up into the empty sky filled with stars (strange stars, stars in patterns someone named Cat had never seen). Losing myself in the glory of stars— And feeling a poem-seed take root in my soul, until I forgot everything, even tears, in the sudden need to give the poem life. . . .

. . . Alive, dancing through a sweltering Oldcity night to the heartbeat rhythm of endless music, giddy from a jolt of glissen, swept up in the arms of a party that had spilled into the streets and didn't care who joined in. . . .

. . . *Dead.* Staring and staring at the transcript of the 'cast handed to me in the sterile hall of a med center, reading the words over and over that couldn't be true. (*Fusion, confusion*; not my eyes, green cat eyes that could barely read my own name; not my memory, not my life.) My life coming to an end with the end of someone else's, my wife butchered, my child gone, all gone. . . . My eyes blurring out of focus, the walls falling away, the world crumbling, dropping out from under me . . . lost, lost. . . .

. . . Lost, in endless fields of whiteness under a rippling sky. . . . Lost, drowning in an ocean of bodies twice my size, nighttime in Godshouse Circle. Running, falling, crying, crazy with the fires exploding in my head. Shrieking my loss to the world until I lost my voice, until the holocaust of horror burned itself out at last and left my mind in ashes. Whimpering in the lap of a sagging old woman I never saw again as she held me, held me, murmuring slurry booze-soaked words, not the right words, not the right voice; my world, my past, even my name lying in ashes, smothered, dead. . . . Lying at peace in someone else's arms, long years after: the soft, sweet-scented arms of a girl named Gallena. Breathless with discovery, feeling all my senses heavy with joy—trying not to see the emptiness in her eyes when I told her how she'd made me feel. "Where's the stuff?" she said, looking away. "You promised." I got out my handful of escape and shared it with her. We lay there together talking about our dreams; until her pimp walked in on us and threw me down the stairs. . . .

. . . Crossing the rain-gray Latai Range with a woman I loved, on a Colony world called Timb'rellet, to reach an outland settlement that had once been my home (but not *my* home, *fusion*). . . .

. . . Oldcity, my home. A necklace slipping loose, into my palm; a blade clipping the strings of a brocade pouch. An angry hand closing over my wrist, twisting my arm, bending my thumb back and back—pain-stars. . . .

. . . Leaving home: moving, unresisting, swallowed up into the heart of a starship, seeing the insignia of Centauri Transport everywhere. Surrendering and striking back—leaving behind the family and the life I'd always known (but not *my* life, *confusion*) and the heartbreaking, mindbreaking indifference, the disgust, the fear. Knowing all the while that there was no escape, that it followed even now, wearing new faces, new

minds, eating away my soul; always with me, until
death. . . .

. . . Lying on a mat in the back room of an abandoned building that was shelter for a dozen other
thieves and boytoys. Hearing voices drift in from another world; shaking with fever, wondering if I was
going to die, and how long it would be before anybody
noticed. . . .

. . . Looking out through the walls of a corporate
tower, the gleaming transparent walls as clear, as hard,
as unfeeling and unyielding as the minds of the ones I
served (but not *mine*, not my memories or minds).
Crumbling under the weight of their derision, trying to
pity their fear, trying to win by surrendering, to earn a
respect that would never exist in minds as dead as
carrion. . . .

. . . Looking out through the windows of my eyes
(but not *my* eyes) at empty faces, treating an endless
stream of wounded minds, life's work that had lost
all meaning because the ones who meant everything
to me were gone, and had taken all meaning with them,
turning all my windows into walls. . . .

. . . Looking down into the midnight waters of the
lake, as dark as the darkness in my soul (but not *my*
soul)—softly lapping, whispering peace, oblivion, an
end. . . .

. . . Shocked out of oblivion by the press gang closing
in. . . . Aching for oblivion as a stranger's heavy hand,
with sharp heavy rings, closed over my arm. . . . Small
trembling hands, my hands, lifted, begging. . . . Hunger
aching in my belly . . . blue dust glowing on my skin
. . . music playing . . . green ice walls . . . blue stone

tombs . . . wormhole alleys boring into the endless
darkness of the underworld. . . .

. . . The sudden brilliance of the Street of Dreams,
music and life and showers of gold. . . . The bright rush
of a thousand living minds into the space of my own,
the input of alien senses bursting apart the walls of my
prison and filling me with light, more light than I'd
ever seen, growing brighter and brighter, burning away
the darkness. A transformation, another world. . . .

Daylight. I opened my eyes and the sun filled them,
blinding, beautiful, its warmth lying across my face. I
shut my eyes, opened them again, not believing. . . .
and it was dusk, with long blue shadows stretched out
on the bed like mourners. I heard music, somewhere
far away, voices and laughter. All I could see were the
ceiling and walls where they met in the gray angle of
a corner, my bare arms greasy with nutrient gel, a
monitor pad lying across my chest. I didn't know where
I was, but I felt peaceful and proud to be waking up
there, as if it was a place I'd reached after a long journey.
I sighed and slept; not afraid to, now.

Sunlight, prying at my eyes. I drifted up into the
new day, felt its warm touch moving over my face. . . .
Human touch, my mind said. I opened my eyes and
watched the room slide into focus, and with it the hand
moving away from my face, a face looking down at
mine—a face I'd never thought I'd see again. (Jule?)
I'd wanted to say the word, but I couldn't; my mind
said it for me. I saw Jule's face brighten with surprise.
She leaned forward, starting to smile.

My hand trembled in the air until she caught it,
completing the circuit of her reality and mine. (Yes,

Cat, yes!) Her sending dazzled my mind like a miracle
—not short-circuited anymore by defenses I couldn't
let down. And suddenly I knew how much I'd missed
her, and knew I'd never really missed anyone before.
My voice struggled in my throat, but nothing would
come. Feeling I couldn't put into words burst through
the link between us like an electric shock; her hand
tightened in a spasm and she pulled free. But her mind
didn't cut me off. It held me, calm and steady and
accepting, as she reached out to the table beside the
bed and brought a cup of water up to my mouth. She
helped me drink it; nothing had ever tasted half as
good. I sighed and drank again.

A portable hospital monitor sat on the other side of
the bed, scanning everything my body did and reading
out meaningless garbage on a screen; the pad still rested
across my chest. But we weren't in any hospital room,
and I heard music and voices again from somewhere,
things I hadn't heard since I'd left Quarro. *Quarro*. . . .
I let it rise up into my mind, let myself believe I could
be back in Quarro: safe, protected, cared for. That my
time in hell was over, and everything was really all right
at last.

Jule took the empty cup away from my mouth. I lay
back on the bed with a half-assed grin stretching my
cracked lips. Just watching her move was pure pleasure;
even seeing her dressed in heavy pants and boots, shirt
and shawl, my eyes were filled with her beauty and
grace. I flexed my fingers; my hands ached like the
hands of an old man. They were splotched with yellow
and purple, like I'd been bleeding inside. So were my
arms. But the marks were already fading; the worst was

past. I wondered how the rest of my body looked, but I didn't really want to know. At least I wasn't blue anymore. . . . I said, "God, I want a camph."

Jule looked back at me, the heavy black braid rolling on her shoulder. Her smile filled with gentle irony and crinkled the corners of her eyes. "Tough," she said, and I wasn't sure if she was talking about me, or my chances of getting what I wanted.

I laughed. It sounded like a death rattle. "'S good to be back."

"It's been over two weeks. For a while we weren't sure you were coming back." She didn't mean to Quarro. Her smile faded. I felt her remembering that I'd been in a hospital room before I'd been here; caught a memory of my body racked on a life-support system.

"A long trip." I remembered how I'd felt when I woke up the first time. "Over now." Contentment filled me up and overflowed.

Colors changed in the feeling that reached me from her. "Cat . . ." I saw the truth show in her face.

"We ain't—back on Ardattee?"

"No." She shook her head. "We're still on Cinder, in the port town."

I looked down, seeing the bond tag still locked into the flesh of my wrist. I shut my eyes. Her concern drowned in the dark rush of disappointment that came with the truth. Jule was here, on Cinder. There could only be one reason for it, and it wasn't because she'd come to get me out of anything. It was only to get me in deeper trouble. If she was here, then I really had seen Siebeling, in the underground with the Hydrans. And if he was here, then Rubiy must be too, and the target of his plan had to be the Federation's telhassium supply: the mines, where I'd been a slave—was still a slave—because of Siebeling. Siebeling, who must have known what I'd wanted to do to him. Siebeling, who hated me. . . .

"Cat—" I felt Jule's mind knot with tension.

"Lemme alone." I kept my face turned away until she left the room. And then, because it was easier than facing the truth, I slid down again into deeper blackness.

Siebeling was in the room with Jule when I woke up again; I sensed him before I ever opened my eyes. I left them shut and pretended to go on sleeping. If the monitors gave me away, he didn't notice. I lay still, listening to them talk.

Siebeling sighed. "Are people like us born with faulty circuitry, or are we what human beings *should* be? And how used to living with the Gift can any of us ever become, in a society where it isn't universal? The best we can ever hope for is to learn control, to 'fit in.' And there's never been a place psions can go for real help. It's what I wanted to do at the Institute—"

"If only everyone could be empathic, or telepathic. Then maybe we'd really learn to understand each other; we wouldn't have to see everything distorted by our own fears. But if we were given a choice, we wouldn't be. . . ." I felt the rueful smile in Jule's mind.

Siebeling laughed once, bitterly. "If there was any justice in this universe, there never would have been a stardrive. We weren't ready for a galaxy. Humanity is an infestation, not a civilization. We never learn. Never. . . ."

I found him with my mind: he was thinking about his wife. And then he was thinking about me, and the tension inside him was a pain. I opened my eyes just enough to watch him through my lashes.

"Damn it, sometimes I wish I'd never heard of the Sakaffe Institute!" He moved away from the window; sunlight made me squint. "It was a fraud, an exploitation . . . an insane risk."

Jule got up from where she'd been sitting at the foot of the bed. "It helped us all more than you can know, Ardan. . . . It saved my life." Her voice was calm and even, but her thoughts were too full.

"And what did it get you, or any of us? It got us here, trapped inside a conspiracy with time running out— waiting for *him* to find the strength to betray us all." He meant me. "And the 'lucky' volunteers are simply back where they started, barely surviving in their own lives. I was wrong to think I could do anything to make a difference, anything that would last. I was a fool, letting myself believe it. We're not professional spies; we never could be. Corporate Security must have known it was impossible—just like they knew we were expendable. I should have known it. . . . God, I'm sorry I got you involved in this." He put his hands gently on her shoulders.

"You didn't. It was my choice. And I'm not sorry." She met his gaze, held it, her own eyes shining too brightly.

He looked down, shaking his head. "I'm not, either . . . I am and I'm not. Because simply by being here you help me to remember that there are human beings who aren't—like I am, in the galaxy. And then I believe that stopping Rubiy could still make a difference. But I cherish you, Jule. You're the only one, since . . . You mean too much to me, it makes me afraid. If anything happened to you . . ." He pulled her to him; her own arms closed around him. I felt their need, and the sharp edge of fear that sweetened every moment they held each other. Their kiss seemed to go on forever, burning itself into my brain, until I felt my body begin to answer it. . . . But then my own need curdled into envy, and I broke contact.

Jule broke away from Siebeling, murmuring, "It won't. Not now. I don't know what brought me to this place, but it was right."

Siebeling reached for her again, but a high-pitched beeping broke the silence of the room. Siebeling swore; his hand covered his data bracelet. "I've got to get back to the hospital."

She touched his cheek.

He nodded as if she'd spoken, and kissed her hand. Then he turned to check the monitor, and I shut my eyes again, forcing myself to relax. If he saw anything that surprised him, he didn't let on about it. "He's going to be all right." His voice hardened. "It's just a matter of time." He went out of the room. Jule stayed behind, but somehow I couldn't make myself say anything to her. I pretended to go on sleeping, and after a while she disappeared, with a soft inrush of air.

The next time I saw her, strain showed on her face, and I felt a stab of sudden doubt touch her mind as she looked at me. For a second I couldn't understand it. But then I remembered what Siebeling had said about me, *just waiting to betray them.* "Jule, you don't have to be afraid of me."

She started, but then her face relaxed and she began to smile. "I know," she said. And now she was sure. She sat down beside me, twining her fingers together, glancing at my face. "I missed you, Cat; I missed you a lot. After . . . after you were gone. I'm glad to see you again." Her mind touched me and let me know how glad she was. That made me smile; I guess she knew why.

From then on I saw her alone; I never saw Siebeling. She spent as much time as she could with me, when she could get away from the job she'd been assigned to. She fed me soup and wiped my skin with a cool cloth, always as gentle and patient as I'd remembered her; forcing me to admit I was going to live, whether I liked it or not. The first few days I didn't even ask questions, because I wasn't ready to face the answers. She seemed to understand that, or else for her own reasons she didn't try to tell me more than I wanted to know.

When I could sit up, after a couple of days, there was a view of the mountains out the single window. But there were heavy curtains at the window, closed half the time because Cinder's day and night were too short, nothing close to a standard day—most humans were built to sleep and wake up on Earth, and their bodies didn't change just because they lived on a new home-world. I couldn't even get to the window to open the curtains on my own; but Jule brought flowers into the room, and gentled me with promises of walking outside when I could get my feet under me again.

And one evening she read me some poems she'd

written, from a little notebook she had. As she read to me I felt doubt straining inside her, and I understood that she was sharing something very personal, not knowing whether I wanted it or could even accept it. But as she began to read, the images shimmered and burst open, letting me see into them. She'd told me once that poetry was like psi for her, distilling word and thought to their purest form; and as she read to me, the distance between her voice and the touch of her mind closed, word and thought flowed together into one bright song and then another. A lot of the poems were full of pain, but that only made them easier to understand. I don't suppose they meant the same things to her that they meant to me, in the end; but maybe that doesn't matter, anyway.

> I remember one last night,
> the darkness gathering around me,
> quietly knowing
> every stone and the tyranny
> of grief
> and all the vows that are made. . . .
> Or do I only know
> the blinding silence of the billion stars
> burning and burning;
> the glory of Orion striding up the sky—

Lost inside my own memories as she read, suddenly I saw her through the images, the filter of her feelings and my own: shivering alone on a balcony, her hands on a vine-covered railing, her eyes open to the night, transfixed by stars. Double vision stunned me as I knew

it for a memory of my own (but not my own, *fusion,
confusion*) swelling out of the dark underworld where
I'd been lost these past weeks.

Jule stopped reading, watching the changes on my
face, feeling the shift of my attention. "What is it?"

I didn't answer her at first. And then I only said, "It
means a lot to me." Afraid to tell her why—not only
because of the memories that had answered it already,
but because somehow in one of them I'd shared the
moment that poem was born inside her. I hadn't been
meant to know that secret moment, and I figured she'd
only resent it.

But she smiled, content. I asked her to read the poem
again and again, until I knew it by heart. And I wished
that I had something to give her in return, a poem,
anything; but anything I could think of seemed cheap
and ugly next to what she'd given me.

After she left me again, I lay looking at her memory
caught there in my mind, as much a part of me as my
own were. Other scenes that had never been a part of
my life began to surface, then—some that I knew or
guessed belonged to her, some that I couldn't put any
tag on. It scared me, not knowing what had been done
to me while I was sick—until I saw suddenly that I was
the one who'd done it to myself.

And then, finally, I began to understand everything—
that what had happened after the Hydrans had been
inside my head had gone on happening, as though
they'd found something caged and set it free. In sickness
my mind had wandered out of itself; it had found open
doors and gone through them, into the deepest parts
of other human minds; pain drawn to pain, hunger to

hunger. And from what I could tell no one had known it but me.

And now, whenever I was with Jule, it was easy to reach what lay on the surface of her thoughts—I could read her without trying, like I'd been doing it forever, like breathing. I was a real telepath at last. And I wondered whether the Hydrans really knew what they'd done. I thought about them sometimes, what they'd done to me and for me; and when I did I felt a kind of longing.

But in the long hours when I was alone, I began to work at controlling what they'd left me with; trying to stretch my waking mind to match what my unconscious had done. Because I'd been given a gift whether I wanted it or not; and whatever happened to me now, I figured I was going to need it. At first it was hard to handle; I didn't know how to control it. I was still weak and it was so strong—like the tail wagging the Cat. But day by day it got easier.

Jule had told me why I heard music: that this hidden room where I lay was somewhere in the starport town, over a bar that was about the only entertainment on Cinder. I couldn't reach very far with my mind, I didn't have the energy yet; so I spent a lot of my time watching the ones down below with my mind's eye: feeling them bored, frustrated, homesick, afraid. Feeling the emotions get loud or fade or blur, feeling them shift and the images run like a ruined painting as they drowned their sorrows in alcohol and drugs. Sometimes I followed them down to oblivion, because that was as close to pleasure as I'd been in a long time.

By now it was simple to tell a psion from a deadhead.

Normal human minds were an unfocused snarl, and my own was light and sharp enough now that I could wander into them like a thief, taking anything I wanted, and no one even knew I'd been there to steal their thoughts. If they'd had anything worth stealing.

Most of the deadheads were from the mines—guards, technicians, officials, who never knew they were sharing a table with a psion who'd come to Cinder to steal their world out from under them. Because most of the townspeople were psions by now. Jule had told me Rubiy had been replacing as many of them as he could with the psions he'd recruited. She and Siebeling had come here together—he worked at the port hospital and she had a job at the spaceport—after "disappearing" for a while out in the Crab Colonies. Her memories of that time turned private and warm, but edged with bright fear, as if she was almost afraid to think about what their time together had meant to her. I caught a wisp of image of a world I'd seen in false memory before, but not her memory. . . . Siebeling's homeworld. Seeing it again, in her mind, I felt alone and angry.

Dere Cortelyou had come in on the next ship. The turnover of workers on Cinder was high to start with because of the radiation levels—even with an energy shield projected around the planet to keep most of the pulsar's radiation out, the background levels on Cinder itself were still too high—and because of the boredom and isolation. Rubiy's people had been raising the turn- over even more by spooking the deadheads with psionic suggestion, playing on the negatives that were already lying in their minds.

I watched them do it, looking into their own minds—

some of them tight-woven and always shielded, so that
I had to use everything I'd learned and more to measure
their skill; some of them almost as tangled and sprawling
as any deadhead. Most of the psions weren't criminals,
not the types you'd expect to find plotting to take over
a world. But most of them were hungry, and angry, and
all of them were ready to take any chance to get what
they thought the Federation owed them.

And none of them had ever known anything to match
what I'd felt when my mind had been joined with the
Hydrans. I began to understand that no joining of
human psions ever did. None of the psions I probed
matched what I could do, either. No one even tried
to; I never felt anyone test my own shield, and by now
I was sure I'd know it if they did. Rubiy himself was
the only one I wasn't sure about—remembering how
afraid I'd felt the last time I'd seen him. Jule said that
he'd disappeared right after they'd found me; he'd gone
offworld, and she didn't know when he'd be back. She
was glad he was gone; so was I.

I could find Jule anywhere in town, any time; a part
of her mind was always open, listening for me, in case
I needed her. It made me rest easier to realize she was
always there, even when I didn't see her: someone
quiet and kind watching out for me, who wasn't just
waiting like death to catch me when I couldn't fight
back. I touched her thoughts a lot through the days,
without letting her know it. Making contact with her
wasn't like reaching a stranger, it was more like finding
another part of myself. But I never went deeper than
the surface of her thoughts, or tried to take anything

that wasn't my right. Just touching her with my mind was enough.

After a while my strength began to come back, and I finally began to face up to life again. And lying alone in a room with four blank pale walls, staring out the single window at the same view you can't ever reach, gets old. Jule was the only thing I had to look forward to; I couldn't help it if I began to wait for the sight of her, the sound of her voice, her touch, the soft sigh of air as she materialized at my bedside. And now that I was really a telepath, I couldn't help it if I began to wonder how it would feel to make love to someone while I was sharing her thoughts—sharing every desire, every pleasure, every secret hidden in our souls. . . .

10

(Cat?)

I turned around on the table where I was sitting, beside the wood-framed window, to see Jule appear in her usual spot—by the bed I was still supposed to be lying in.

"Here." The dim sunlight coming through the streaked panes barely warmed the back of my head.

The scattershot confusion of her thoughts collected into relief as she saw me. "What are you doing there?"

"Looking out." I shrugged like it was the simplest thing in the world. It had taken me five minutes just to get from the bed to the window, and the hospital tunic I was wearing was soaked with sweat.

Objections surfaced in her mind, half angry, half reluctant. She didn't bother to say any of it out loud; she didn't need to.

I got up, feeling my legs tremble under me. They carried me a whole couple of steps before they gave out. Jule caught me and helped me back to the bed. I held on to her a little harder than I needed to.

"You're sick," she said, like I needed reminding. She pushed me down; her hands were gentle and strong. I noticed that she wasn't biting her nails anymore.

"I'm sick of lying here like a corpse." My heartbeat

was so loud in my ears that I could hardly hear myself talk.

Her mouth tightened a little at the image. "There are worse things."

I glanced at the bond tag on my wrist. "Yeah." I covered it with my hand, remembering when a week in bed had seemed like all I could ask of heaven.

"I brought you lunch." She bent her head at the two plates on the bedside table, one for her and one for me.

I looked at it, but suddenly I wasn't hungry. "Jule . . ."

She raised her eyebrows, sitting down at the foot of the bed.

"What's gonna happen to me?" Asking it at last.

"I don't know." Her voice got faint. She pulled her shawl closer around her. "I don't know what's going to happen to any of us now. But Rubiy wants you back; that's why they're sheltering you. He's been searching for a way to get hold of you ever since you arrived on Cinder."

"Me? . . . The mines. It's what I know about the mines?"

She nodded. "It must be. His people have been on Cinder for nearly an earthyear, some of them, but they've never been able to get into the mines compound. They're beginning to get desperate. Whoever is backing them is losing patience, and the psions who've been here the longest can't stay much longer without suspicion. Our only hope has been that Rubiy would fail because of time—we've been watched all along, we haven't been able to do anything to stop him, or even to get a warning out. But now that he has you, everything's changed again." *(For the worse.)* But she didn't say it.

"When Rubiy gets back . . ." She didn't hide the disgust she felt when she thought about seeing him again. She remembered his dead man's eyes searching every centimeter of her body, peeling away even her skin, probing for her soul. . . . Humiliating her—not because he thought she was a spy, but just because her name was taMing. He knew that she'd been born into all the wealth and luxury anyone could claim; but she'd still been born a psion—and there wasn't enough money or power to make that stain on the taMing honor disappear. He hated everything she stood for and was heir to; he enjoyed the pain her Gift had caused her family. And he'd let her know that he'd brought her here because of all that, as a pawn in his private game with the Federation's mortal gods. But he wouldn't show her what the game was. . . .

I grimaced and looked down. But I only said, "Where's Rubiy now?"

She shook her mind out. "We think he's gone to meet with his backers again. There are several combines involved in this, but we don't know which ones. A woman named Galiess is in charge, but she doesn't give anything away. Dere can't read her."

"How come Dere ain't been to see me?" He hadn't even been into my head to say, (Hello). I wondered if he didn't trust me now, either.

"Ardan won't let him. He won't let anyone see you until you're stronger."

Strong enough to betray them. A prickle of anger

made my skin itch. I took a deep breath, and said, "What about Siebeling?"

She looked away, twisting dark shiny strands of hair between her fingers. Suddenly she was the woman I'd known in Quarro again, frightened and uncertain. I realized how much she'd changed in the time since then—the confidence she'd found, the control of her psi talent and her life. And at the same time I understood that Siebeling had been the one who'd made her reach out again—not just because of what he'd taught her about controlling her psi, but because of the thing I'd felt between the two of them, a sharing and a healing each gave to the other. . . . I touched it again in her mind, and pulled away like I'd been burned. That was why she couldn't answer me: because she couldn't make how she felt about me match up with what he felt about me, and what she felt about him.

I lay back, not knowing what to say; staring at her but thinking about Siebeling . . . until it didn't even seem like a surprise when I caught the pattern of Siebeling's thoughts, and realized that he was coming here. Someone else was with him, a psion—a telepath— a mind I'd never seen the inside of. . . . But I had seen it before. Just once, on the edge of consciousness there in the Hydrans' underground world. I sat up just before the door opened, and watched them come in.

"You aren't supposed to be up" was the first thing Siebeling said to me. He was wearing a medical coat under his parka.

"I'm not," I said, looking past him at the stranger. It was a woman.

"You were." Siebeling pointed at the hospital monitor. "That lets me know everything about your condition. You're recovering from radiation poisoning; your body can't take that kind of stress yet. Don't do it again unless you have my permission."

My mouth twitched, caught somewhere between anger and laughter, because this was nothing like the meeting I'd imagined. But then the stranger caught my eyes. I felt her probe my mind, and knew it for a challenge—knew her for Galiess, Rubiy's watchdog. She was a small, fine-boned woman, who looked like she belonged in a salon somewhere, not in a frontier port town. She wore a long, heavy gown—nothing fancy, but still it looked out of place. And it couldn't cover the truth—that she was an old woman, even though she tried to hide it. Her thick silver-tipped hair was a wig, her face had a stretched look to it; her mind was full of musty rooms. The look in her washed-out blue-green eyes said I'd done something to her, without even knowing her. I let her think she was getting a look right into my soul, without giving her anything; using her own concentration against her while I tried to find out what she really wanted. I didn't get much—she was a good telepath. But she didn't catch me, either. That meant I was a better one—and that I had one less thing to worry about. I made myself look away from her and down, knowing that was what she expected.

"My name is Galiess," she said, like she was talking about the weather. I tried to look like it was news to me. "And you are Cat. I suppose you know that we've waited a long time to have you here." Her voice was brittle.

"Not half as long as it seemed to me." I glanced from Jule to Siebeling. His mind was like mirrored glass. I kept my back straight and my voice strong, knowing like I'd always known that when you were in enemy territory you had to hide any weakness. "And I guess I know what you want me for. Rubiy's got bigger eyes than I figured." I rubbed the bond tag on my wrist.

She nodded. "Your time at the mines makes you a risk, but it also makes protecting you worth any risk. He was right about that much. . . ." Her mind shifted. "And I don't expect working for Contract Labor left you with much loyalty to your employers."

I laughed once. "Not much." I couldn't help looking at Siebeling again. He was frowning, and holding his thoughts in a cage woven of perfect half-lies; I knew they were half-lies only because I knew the truth. Galiess already knew there was bad feeling between us; but it barely covered the deeper anger and fear in his mind as he waited for what I said next. "I told Rubiy I wanted in, before. I sure haven't changed my mind. What do you want me to do—just name it." I didn't have to force the hardness in my voice.

"I only want you to obey Siebeling, for now. Nothing more is expected or required of you until Rubiy returns." The way she spoke his name made it sound like the Holy Name of God. "But you'll need your strength back then. I hope your recovery continues to be as rapid." While a hidden part of her mind wished

I'd been dead when the Hydrans had handed me over to her.

She was beginning to realize that I'd been playing with her mind, and she made a sudden, stupid try at getting past my guard. I tied my mind up tight and shut her out completely. She stared at me like she didn't believe it. Finally she said, tripping over the words, "Dr. Siebeling has been told how important you are to us. I'm sure he'll see that you keep improving." She gave Siebeling a warning look. Then she turned to Jule, and the look changed. "Why are you here? Why aren't you at the spaceport? Is working as a clerk too demeaning for you?"

"I brought Cat a meal." Jule waved a hand at the food. "I always do." The words were soft, her voice was even; she almost perfectly blocked the resentment that rose up in her. But I saw her eyes turn cold. "I'll be back at the shipping counter when they expect me to be. If they have any complaints, they'll let you know, I'm sure." It wasn't the first time she'd had to give those answers. Galiess didn't miss a chance to bait her, and I knew from Jule's anger that it wasn't because she deserved it.

"Be sure you remember where you are—and who." Galiess nodded to us all and left the room with her own mind in a snarl.

Jule and Siebeling glanced at each other, their faces grim and tight, with unformed questions passing between them as they waited. When they were sure Galiess was gone for good, Siebeling turned back to me, and I stopped thinking about anything but him.

He caught my wrist, the one with the restamped bond tag. "What the hell are you doing here?" The words dropped on me one by one, like stones. He didn't really expect an answer. He let go of my arm again. I knew for certain then that he hadn't arranged my transfer. Jule stayed where she was at the foot of the bed, her hands clenched in her lap.

I leaned back against the wall, trying not to let him see that I couldn't sit up any longer. "Nothing personal. I just figured I'd rather freeze to death than drown in mud. That's all the choice they gave me. . . . You think I came to Cinder on purpose?"

"I think someone saw that you did." *(Rubiy.)* The name was as plain as if he'd spoken it.

My fingers hugged the plastic tag on my wrist again. "Yeah. It fits . . . it makes sense. He's got the contacts to do that?" I looked up at Siebeling again, but he wasn't listening.

His voice was so quiet when he spoke that I had to strain to hear the words. "The first thing you did when you saw me was try to tell Galiess who I really was. You just had another chance—why didn't you use it?"

I winced, glancing at Jule. She was biting a nail. "I—I didn't know what I was doing, before. I was sick then." My own voice was hardly louder than his.

"You ought to be dead—"

Blood sang in my ears, but all I said was, "Sorry to disappoint you."

His face went white, and I realized that I'd read him wrong. Jule leaned forward, her anger and frustration suddenly back again. "You would have died, if it hadn't been for him, Cat! No one else here understood what was wrong with you, or how to treat it. You owe him your life."

"Maybe he owed something to me." I stuck out my bony wrist with its red band.

Neither of them answered that; and what lay in their minds wasn't an answer, either.

Finally Siebeling said, with an effort, "I only meant that because you're half-Hydran, you have a higher-than-human resistance to the radiation. And you heal more efficiently."

"I know. . . ." I let my arm drop; it felt like lead. "You know what they say about cats—we all got nine lives." I thought about how they would've been safe if he'd let me die. He'd known that, too. "Maybe that is one of 'em I owe to you."

Jule smiled, easing a little, but Siebeling still held himself rigid. I felt his thoughts shift focus.

"And I ain't spending the rest of 'em working for Contract Labor!" I answered him before he could say it. "I ain't going back to the mines. You might as well forget that right now. You heard Galiess—the psions need me, Rubiy wants *me*. There's nothin' you can do about it. You're stuck with me."

"*We're* stuck with you?" Siebeling said, his voice rising a little. "Are you trying to tell me you still want to work with us? After what you tried to do?" I couldn't tell whether he sounded sarcastic or amazed.

"You mean, after what you did to me." I pushed forward, wrapping my arms around my knees to keep myself there. Suddenly I was really hearing his question, and wondering what the hell it meant to me.

Did I still want to work with them? Was I crazy? I thought about the times, down in the mines, when I'd imagined how good it would feel to wring Siebeling's neck.

But then I looked at Jule again: sitting at the foot of the bed like a mediator, aching for an end to the anger and misunderstanding between Siebeling and me. And I saw the ways she'd helped me, trusted me, believed in me. And I thought about Dere Cortelyou tossing me a camph, telling me more than I ever wanted to know about telepathy or half a hundred other things, trying to make me understand why he even cared. . . . About working with the psions at the Sakaffe Institute; about feeling like a part of something for the first time in my life.

And the truth twisted like a knife inside me. I'd let myself get tied to these people, let my life get tangled up in theirs. It was just like it had always been—getting involved was hanging a stone around your neck when you were already drowning. But if fate wanted you to drown, there was nothing you could do. . . . I thought about Galiess and Rubiy, and tried to tell myself that I'd be crazy to trust either of them. But that didn't change how much I could gain by working for them. And it didn't change how much I could lose, working against them, for somebody who hated my guts.

I realized that the silence had gone on way too long while I thought it through. Finally I said, "Yeah, I still want to work with you." *I been a loser all my life. Why change now?* I stopped just short of finishing it out loud.

Jule's belief reached me like a smile. But Siebeling's eyes didn't change, and neither did his mind. He didn't believe me; he'd never trusted me and he never would. "You're a bad liar, for someone with your experience." He moved away from me toward the window.

"You got a lousy bedside manner." I sagged back against the wall again, my hands clenched white-knuckled on the bedding. "Listen, I don't give a damn what you think," putting all the strength I had left into it. "You're stuck in this, and you know it's not gonna solve itself. I can help you, if you let me—you ain't gonna survive with Rubiy if you don't."

Siebeling turned; his disgust caught me behind the eyes. "You're going to protect us from Rubiy?"

"I'm a better telepath now. Better than Galiess. You want to know how I got rid of her so fast? I just let her know that."

A frown pinched his forehead again. He glanced at Jule; she looked at me, surprised but not really surprised. He said, "If that's true, then you were a fool to let her know it."

"Uh-uh." I shook my head, even though I wasn't sure he was wrong. I reached out for the cup of water on the table beside the bed. (And you can believe it. I can make you believe it; I can make you believe anything if I want to.) I looked him straight in the eye as I tore apart his shield and sent the thought into his unguarded mind. He jerked physically; the recoil of his thoughts hit me so hard the cup fell out of my hand.

Jule moved to pick it up from the wet floorboards. She filled it again before she said, very quietly, to

Siebeling, "I tried to tell you." There was no sharpness in it, but there could have been.

He kept frowning, flexing his long-fingered hands, searching for words; still searching his mind for the tendrils of my own probe.

But I'd already let him go again. I was bluffing him, and I couldn't afford to let him find out. I didn't have the strength in me yet to hold out against him for long—even to go on talking much longer. But I had his attention now; I had to use it while I could.

"How?" he asked, finally.

"The aliens, the . . . Hydrans." I lifted a hand to my forehead. "They went into my mind; they changed it. Healed it, somehow . . . all of them together, in a joining. That's how they live—with all their minds bound together. And for a little while they made me a part of it. It was . . . it was . . ."

(Like coming home,) Jule thought.

I glanced at her, with the image moving like a bright bird through my mind. I looked at Siebeling again, at the blank wall of his resentment. "How'd they get involved with Rubiy? And why?"

"By accident. They had nothing to do with any of this, originally." His voice darkened. "But they discovered the presence of human psions here, and Rubiy's sucked them into it as deeply as he can, using them, letting them think he's here to help them by overthrowing the mines."

"Their ancestors promised them. . . ." I said. "What are Hydrans doing here at all? How'd they get this way? Are all Hydrans like this?"

Siebeling broke my gaze. "I don't know," lying. Old memories stirred in his mind, in a mass of tangled feeling.

"Come on, damn it. This's important to me. I know you know—you said you were married to one."

"I don't want to talk about it." His mind warned me away.

"What the hell's wrong? I ain't asking for your lousy life story—"

(Yes, you are,) Jule said silently, only to me. (You can't help it.)

(What—?) I slid into direct contact, so much easier with her than words. I saw Siebeling's face change as he realized what we were doing. (How? Why does he hate me, Jule?)

(He doesn't—)

(He does! He's hated me from the first time he laid eyes on me. Anything I try to do, he takes it wrong. I never did nothing to him!)

(It's not you that he hates. It's—)

I finished it for her. (What I am? A half-breed, a 'cheap gutter thief'?)

She shook her head without moving. (No! Not in the way you think. *Her mind telling me at the same time that I wasn't a cheap gutter thief, that she wouldn't feel me believing that.* But he lost everything, Cat. His wife and son—)

(What's that got to do with me?)

(Everything! It's not you he hates; it's himself.) And in less time than it would have taken to ask again, she showed me her answer: she showed me Siebeling as he'd been when he was young, barely out of med training, so in love with his proud, gentle wife and their green-eyed son that he wanted everybody to know it.

(*He loved them,*) I thought, (*he really loved them—?*)

But his wife had dedicated her life to improving the way Hydrans were treated by the Federation. She'd gone back to her homeworld during a combine's relocation sweep, trying to help save her people from being deported. Siebeling had tried to stop her from going, afraid of what might happen to her. But he'd only made her angrier; in the end she'd gone anyway, taking their young son with her. And she'd died—murdered, he was sure, even though he couldn't prove it. Nobody knew whether the boy had died along with her or been transported with the rest of her people, who'd been scattered over half the worlds of the Federation like dust thrown into the wind. Siebeling saw his wife's body; but he never found out what had happened to their son. No Hydran he found knew what had become of the boy, or else they wouldn't tell him; and the combines involved didn't even care. Siebeling never found his son. (He blames himself, he thinks that he failed them because he wasn't with them, and because he's . . . human. Remember the crystal ball you stole?) I laughed, silently; she glanced away. (It belonged to his wife and their son. It was a Hydran thing, tuned to a Hydran mind. Only someone very much like them could make it change, the way you did. Seeing you reminds him of what happened, you make him overreact without meaning to, because you remind him of—)

"—Of my son?" Siebeling said out loud, shattering the clear wall of silence between us.

Jule froze; her face paled and then turned red as she realized what she'd done.

"God damn it, Jule—" Siebeling began. The rawness in his voice was like a wound; pain, not anger. Whatever he'd been going to say to her, he didn't finish it. But something unspoken moved between them, and this time I was the one who was left out of it. The rigid, clenched way he held himself eased, almost against his will. When he looked back at me again, finally, I sank down into the corner, wishing I could disappear. I didn't want to know, didn't want to hear what he was going to tell me, the excuses, the reasons why I—

He said, "When I finally realized that my son was gone forever, I just wanted to forget . . . what had happened, everything I no longer believed. I stopped living, for a long time." He looked at me like he was really seeing me for once. I felt his own stolen memories stir inside me; the moment when he'd heard about his wife, the long years of hiding inside himself. . . . "Until the FTA offered me a chance to do real psionics research, to actually help psions in a way no one had been able to before. And then I met an Oldcity thief with telepathic amnesia, who always seemed to say the wrong thing and do the wrong thing, until finally I sent him away without really understanding why. . . . Maybe it was because I blamed you, for always making me remember things I wanted to leave alone. Because there is a resemblance. You have the eyes, and your age is about right. . . ."

I remembered the strange conversation we'd had once, back in his office at the Institute. "No. You're wrong. I never had any kin; none that wanted me, anyway."

"But you're not sure. You said you don't remember—"

"I remember. I remember always b-being alone." My eyes were shut against him. I felt him pushing me back toward the cliff edge of darkness at the end of my own memories, where something ugly waited to drag me down. (Don't. Don't.)

"Show me proof." The words rang in my head like heavy bells.

I had to make him leave me alone, and words would never be enough. So I showed him the only proof I could—jagged pieces of my life that would leave his crazy belief torn and bleeding: (I've never been a part of your memories!) I showed them both what it meant to stay alive in Oldcity, enough truth so there wouldn't ever be any more questions; and I showed them the fire and the ashes and the screaming. . . .

My eyes were open and I was staring at Siebeling again. He muttered: "I was wrong. I'm sorry," while his sickened mind shrank away from what it had seen.

But I realized that what I'd shown him hadn't really proved anything. Suddenly I hated myself, for letting him see even that much, and I looked down. I couldn't face Jule at all.

"I'm sorry." Siebeling said it again, too quickly. Relief filled his mind now. He wanted to believe it; he was glad I wasn't his son. It was all he could think about, glad his own son didn't have to live like that; he didn't care whether it had happened to me. . . .

"You bastard, I'd rather be dead than be your son!"

I pushed myself up again. "So you still don't know about the kid, do you? If he didn't have to live like garbage—if he ain't a slave digging ore someplace right now because somebody didn't like his face? Well, maybe I hope you never find out!"

He slapped me. Jule stood frozen, staring at us like we must be out of our minds. Siebeling said, "I was right all along about what you were." And his mind was pushing it all down again. . . . He turned and left the room. Jule stood a second more looking at me; but the pain was too strong inside her, she disappeared without a thought.

(I hope you never find out!) I flung it after Siebeling, before I collapsed again in the tangled bedding. I lay still for a long time with a crushing ache in my chest.

11

I was halfway up the hillside when my knees gave out. I almost managed to make it look like I'd meant to sit down. The view wasn't bad, except that you could still see the town, and I didn't want to think about it now—not the blank-walled room where I'd memorized every crack in the plaster from flat on my back; not the miners in the happy house down below it just waiting to spot my bond tag, or the psions waiting to spot a lie, or the spaceport, or anything else human. . . . I was free from all that, even if it was only for an hour, and all I really wanted was to reach the top of the hill. But in one and a half gravities I still felt like crawling, and I'd never have gotten this far without a stick in my hand and Dere Cortelyou walking beside me. He came up here whenever he could, "to get away from my mind," he'd said.

"Next time," Dere said, following my eyes and reading my thought.

"Yeah, sure." I answered him out loud, because like most human psions he wasn't used to not talking, or to having his questions answered before they were asked. There was a reason why humans didn't make more joinings. I wiped my forehead on the sleeve of my parka, feeling the cold spring air chill my flushed skin. *If there is a next time.* I didn't let him hear that; hadn't let him know what I already knew—that Rubiy had come back during the night. I was trying not to think about it myself, right now. It was too good just to be with somebody who felt sane and calm and didn't want anything from me.

Dere sat down beside me. I leaned back on my elbows; the soft thick moss grass was like velvet under my hands. The air smelled heavy with new life; rustling tendrils of bark spilled down the trunks of the trees. Beyond the golden green of young leaves the sky went on forever. Just thinking about how deep it was, how endless, made me giddy. All my senses felt more alive in this one moment than they'd ever been in my whole life—because in my whole life I'd never had a moment like this, in a place like this; and because with Rubiy back I knew more clearly than I ever had that I had to take it while I could. I wished that Jule could be with us, or that she could be sharing what was in my mind right now; that I could feel a poem take root in it, to crystallize the feeling and make it last forever.

But Jule's mind didn't lie open to my feelings or to my need the way it had before: *before I was well*, she told herself; *before I'd said what I had to Siebeling*. And knowing that, I kept away from her thoughts and shielded my own. "Where did all this come from?" I said, to keep myself from thinking, and Dere from wondering. I lifted a hand across the view of green. "Did it just happen?"

He laughed, folding a piece of bark between his fingers. "No. Life is rarely that simple." His mind shrank tight around the irony; for a second his mind screamed tension, out here where he could, before he got it back under control. Even he wasn't really sane and calm, playing spy in a nest of mind readers—especially not him. He'd been right before, back on Ardattee, when he'd told me that he wasn't much of a telepath. I knew it a lot better than he did now, with my new clearer mindsight; knew how hard he struggled to keep his thoughts to himself, and how afraid he was that he wouldn't be able to. But he was still the same Dere, and he couldn't leave a question unanswered. "Every species of living thing you see here was transported to Cinder from somewhere else, originally." He spat out the end of a camph and fished another one out of his jacket.

"By humans?" I said, starting to get interested. I watched his hands. "Gimme one of those," reaching out.

He shook his head. "Doctor's orders. You're still sick."

"I could be dead, tomorrow. All of us could." I wagged my fingers. "C'mon."

His cold-reddened face went a little gray; but he reached into his pocket and brought out another camph.

I stuck it into my mouth, and laughed once. "Funny."

"What?"

"How worried Siebeling is about my health now. He didn't give a damn what happened to me with Contract Labor."

He glanced at my bond tag. "Maybe he thought you'd be better off with them than you were in Oldcity." Always ready to excuse and forgive. "Contract Labor builds worlds. And it can give someone with no skills a chance to learn one. I've seen it work on Hadder's World— I've seen combine contract laborers who went on to good solid company jobs. The FTA colonized Sephtat with government contract labor, and now it's independent, one of the biggest exporters—"

I swore, and drove it into his brain with the rush of ugly memories that filled me up. "'Builds worlds,' hell! It mangles them, and it uses warm bodies because they're cheaper than machines!"

He put his hands up to his head; brought them down again, slowly. When I saw his face, I was sorry, but I didn't let it show. I let him tell me he was sorry, instead; that he hadn't known what I'd been through, that I was right and he was wrong. Because I needed to hear it from somebody, even if it was only him. He said, "I know. . . . Ardan's a bitter man, hard on everyone—especially himself." The same thing Jule always said. "Not an easy man to understand, or love."

"Jule don't seem to have no trouble." I looked away, drowning my thoughts in the endless sighing green of the mountains.

"Jule has a gift most of us don't have." He didn't mean just her psi. "And she has the problems to go with it."

I chewed on the camph, watching the sky, the ribbons and veils of color against the deepening blue; until suddenly I heard what lay between the words. I looked back at him. "You're the one, ain't you? The one who—who stopped her from drowning; who told her about Siebeling and the Institute and the research?"

He nodded, glancing down, his smooth brows twitching. "It was dark. She doesn't remember, or recognize, me." He meant that he thought it was better that way.

"You done a good thing, anyway."

He sighed, plucking at wisps of moss grass. "To answer your question: no, the humans didn't bring life to Cinder. It was all here waiting for us when we arrived . . . along with the ones who brought it all here before us."

"You mean the Hydrans?" I sat up again, locking my hands across the ankles of my boots. "What the hell were they doing here?"

He shrugged. "I'm not sure. I'm not that familiar with Colonial history. Siebeling could probably tell you—" He broke off, seeing my expression. "Well, you can always . . ." He stopped again. "I can look it up for you." His job here was taking care of the tape library.

"Yeah, I know. . . ." I grinned a little. "If I ever get out of this, I guess I oughta take up reading." He laughed. "You know anything about the Hydrans? The ones here, they—they live inside that thing you told me about, a joining, all the time. Are they all like that?"

"Not that I've ever heard." He shook his head. "But they probably all have the potential, in a way humans don't—because they have every other psi talent anyone's ever discovered. They got the name *Hydran* because we encountered them first in the Beta Hydrae system—but it took on a double edge when we learned what they could do with their minds. Beta Hydrae is

a star in the constellation they call Hydra on Earth;
in human mythology the Hydra was a many-headed
monster."

I made a face.

"But no one can really deny that they're more like
we are than we want to admit. There have been xeno-
biologists who've claimed that Earth is a world of defective Hydrans—psionic deaf-mutes, mental cripples."

Something turned inside me; suddenly I was listening to him talk about humans like they were strangers,
almost aliens. . . . "What happened, then? If the Hydrans could kill a human just by thinking about it,
how come the Federation took over all their worlds?"
Because I knew that was true; knew the Hydrans lived
among humans like something less, the ones who were
still alive.

His round face got soft with guilt. "They can't de-
fend themselves." He opened his mind and showed
me: just because they *could* kill with a thought, Hydran
minds had developed in a way that kept them from
ever doing it. If a Hydran killed another being, the act
destroyed built-in mental guards; the telepathic shock
of the death would recoil and kill the killer. They
couldn't commit any violent act without sharing in the
consequences. I realized then why the Hydrans here
had never been able to drive out the human miners.
And that it was why they'd been easy prey whenever
the Human Federation decided it wanted something
they had.

He showed me how once they'd had an interstellar
civilization more highly developed than even our own—
one that had been so different it almost seemed like

magic to humans, because it was built on psi. It had
passed its peak by the time we found them, and we
hurried it on into collapse—taking what we could use
and calling the rest worthless, like the frightened bar-
barians we were. . . . (I saw it all happening in Dere's
mind, wrapped in his words.) We'd pulled down their
cultures, ruined their worlds, destroyed millions of lives,
and all they'd been able to bring against it was pleas
and protests. That hadn't been enough to save them.
I thought about Siebeling's wife. And now the last of
their people were living like strangers on their own
worlds, or relocated on worlds the humans used as
dumping grounds, among the people who'd destroyed
them and who despised them, because they couldn't
kill the way humans could. . . .

And I thought about my mother, or my father;
whichever one had been Hydran. And I thought about
the one who must have been human. . . . I sat, chin
on my knees, looking down the green slope at the far,
glittering snowfields, and I didn't say anything for a
while, because of the lump in my throat.

Finally Cortelyou said, "You don't know what happened to them?"

My parents. I tangled my thoughts, angry at letting
myself slip that far. "I *know*; it's in here someplace."
I touched my head. "I just can't *remember*."

"Siebeling—"

"I don't want to talk about Siebeling." I cut him off
before he could even finish the thought. I thought
about the Hydrans instead—who shared everything,
and knew everything about each other, even about
me.

"Cat, what happened to you when you were with the aliens? Something did, I don't need Siebeling's pointing it out to know you're a hundred times the telepath you were."

I shrugged. "They did it. I dunno how. They made me join with them, and something just . . . came loose."

"You made a real joining? What was it like?" His voice was hushed, almost embarrassed. His mind filled with sudden, hopeless longing, with envy for what I'd shared . . . with a need and a bitter loneliness I'd never thought I'd see inside anybody else, especially him. But maybe it was there all along, inside every human being, that voice crying and never being answered. And maybe for a telepath, living like a one-eyed man in the land of the blind, the loneliness was worst of all.

"I . . . uh, well . . ." I looked at the ground, wishing I could show him somehow. Because I wasn't good at words; because words were too solid, too clumsy and heavy, never really meant to show what I felt anyway. . . . "It was—like all the highs I ever had, and all the burnouts. Confused and bright. A thousand voices singing all at once. . . . Like an ocean, like a whirlpool. . . . Like drowning. . . ." I moved my hands. (I don't know how to tell you.)

He half smiled. "I know." His own stubby hands clung together. "How did it make you feel?"

"Scared" was all that came out of my mouth. But I couldn't tell him that what made me feel that way was knowing it could fill my every need.

He was disappointed. I felt him force his mind away from it. "How good is your telepathy now?"

I looked up at him again. "Better than anybody I seen here."

He raised his eyebrows. "Better than Rubiy? That's what Siebeling claims you told him."

I pressed my mouth together. "Did he tell you to find out?"

"No."

"Then I'll tell you the truth. I dunno how good I am, compared to him. I never felt a mind like his. It's like a wall."

"Your mind is a wall to me now, when you want to keep me out. And it's as clear as the sky when you want to communicate."

"Yeah?" I stretched my arms, letting the stiffness out. But he was watching me too close, and I felt the stray thread of a thought tickle my own . . . *relief*, that I still didn't know his secret. . . . *His secret?* I eased further into his mind, following the strand back, not bothering to hide what I was doing. He tried to tangle his thoughts, to turn me away with confusions and distractions and half-truths leading nowhere. But I followed the true thought on and on, seeing the paths he tried to make me ignore and choosing them each time, feeling his panic grow. . . .

Until finally the truth burst into my mind: "Dere—you're a Corpse?"

He slumped forward. The tension that had been rising for months drained out of him at last, and only a dull weariness was left in his mind. "So it does show."

"You wanted me to do it—" It was half an apology and half a challenge.

He nodded, still hunched forward.

"Why? I mean—you, a Corpse? You said you were just a corporate telepath."

"And every one of you believed me. Jule and Ardan still believe it—for their own good. What I told you wasn't a lie; it just was not the whole truth. I do work for the Seleusid combine. But I'm part of their security force, their private army." Pride glittered in the words, but pride was cutting him up inside; and everything I knew about what it had cost him to get where he was and stay there was still true. He was still a paid snitch, used by deadheads who would never understand.

"How'd you get involved in this? Somebody order you to do it?"

"It was my idea. The FTA needed to know how to deal with psions, so they asked one. And I told them it would take psions to stop psions. I thought it would give us a chance to show them that we can be loyal, useful, productive citizens—"

"How many Hydrans have you helped Seleusid kick off their own worlds, Dere?"

He looked up at me then, his hazel eyes green with anger; but he looked away again. I didn't try to find out what he had to be ashamed of.

"Nothing," he said. "I have nothing to be ashamed of."

(But you got plenty to be afraid of.) If the rest of us thought we had a lot to hide from Rubiy, it was nothing compared to what was in Dere's mind. And he wasn't much more of a telepath than I used to be. "What did you think you were gonna do once you'd got in with Rubiy? What are we gonna do? You got any plans?"

I didn't think his face could get any grimmer, but it did. "Rubiy is a professional. He made sure we were completely isolated before we got to Cinder. There's been no way to get a message out, because there's always someone *listening*. Even when you can't see them, you can feel them. . . ." His fists clenched. "But the mines or the FTA have to be warned, somehow—and it has to be soon, before Rubiy comes back."

"You know what he's planning to do?"

The hazel eyes sharpened, for a minute he wasn't sure about me. . . . But then his mind loosened again, and he shook his head.

"Why should you trust me?" I said, realizing that he did. "Nobody else does."

He shrugged. "Because I don't have any choice, now. And because Jule trusts you. Like her, I think that if you were going to betray us, it would already have happened. . . . All I know is that you're supposed to be the long-awaited key to help them get into the mines."

"How?" I pulled my legs up under me.

"I was hoping you could tell me."

"They didn't show me no secret passages while I was in there, if that's what you mean." The muscles in my back were pulling tight again. "Galiess won't talk till Rubiy gets back, and she ain't given me a real chance to read her, if she even knows."

"Whatever it is, they seem to be sure it'll work this time. God knows what demands they'll make on the Federation."

(And God knows what'll happen to us. That's the worst part, ain't it? You know that if I can read your secret, so can Rubiy. Once he comes back your life isn't worth a damn, if you can't stop his plans first; maybe all our lives—)

"Stop it, for God's sake!" For a minute I thought he was going to hit me. "I'm sorry"—he took a deep breath—"but don't answer questions for me before you even ask them!"

I almost laughed. "Bet you never figured you'd be saying that to me." And I realized how much I'd begun to depend on my Gift; as if I'd grown another eye to see with, another ear.

Half a grin grew on his face. He fumbled for another camph and put it in his mouth. "That's for damn sure. My star pupil. . . ." His voice trailed. He handed me another camph.

I took the camph, balancing it between my fingers. Then I said, as gently as I knew how, "Dere, Rubiy's already back."

He froze. "When? How long?"

"Since last night."

"God . . ." he said. Suddenly his eyes unfocused; I felt circuits opening and closing in his brain, but what happened then was nothing my own mind could understand. He let out a cry, like something had torn him apart inside.

I jerked back, not knowing what was happening to him. *Rubiy?* But we were alone, even inside our minds; I was sure of it. "Dere?" I put out my hand, brushing his arm. "What's wrong?"

He shuddered; I pulled my hand away. He wiped his mouth. "I . . . I had a sending."

A sending . . . precognition. I'd almost forgotten that he was anything besides a telepath. "About what?" His mind was jumbled with shock, I couldn't read him.

"About death. My death. Rubiy . . ." His voice was weak and stumbling. "It's too late."

"No, it ain't. You're just scared it will be; it ain't sure. That's the wild card talent, you said it yourself."

But he shook his head, glaring his anger at me. "Not this time. It's in every image. Every one. And so is Rubiy. And so are you. . . ."

"Me?" I pushed up on my knees. "I ain't done nothin' to you. I ain't going to, I swear." (I swear it!)

He climbed to his feet, every movement belonging to a dead man. "I know. I'm sorry," he said thickly. "I need some time alone now." He stumbled on up the hill, not looking back. His flickering shadow trailed him like the darkness in his mind.

I sat where I was, alone inside my own darkness, until the sky started to darken to match it. I got up then, stiff and numb, and started back down the hill alone.

12

(Hello, Cat.)

The sudden voice inside my head turned me around on the slope. I lost my balance and someone's hands caught me from behind, steadying me. Rubiy's.

"You shouldn't be out here alone. You're hardly steady on your feet." Rubiy smiled, but only with his mouth. I hadn't forgotten that smile, or anything about his face. I looked into his ice-green eyes, and saw the bottomless green of a crevasse: shining, shadowy, deadly. His hands were still on my shoulders, holding me like the talons of a hunting bird would hold some poor squirming thing it had trapped in the night. I knew the feel of hands like that. . . . I jerked loose with all my strength, staggering back.

"Did I frighten you?" He held out his empty hands to me, amused. He wasn't dressed for a walk outside, but he didn't seem to feel the cold.

I swallowed. "Takes—more'n a 'hello' to do that." The shock had knocked everything I'd been thinking a minute ago out of my head; I was glad. "I wasn't alone. I was with Cortelyou."

"I know," he said.

I didn't flinch. I kept my mind woven tight, with just enough ends dangling loose to make it seem like I wasn't trying to hide something. "He's still up there."

I pointed with my chin. "I got tired," answering him before he asked.

He liked that; his face almost looked human. "You're old friends, I take it." There was something lying between the words that I didn't like.

"Yeah. I guess so." I rubbed my neck.

"I was pleased to learn that you were strong enough to go walking. Your recovery strengthens my trust in Siebeling and his skills."

"Yeah, he's all heart."

He raised an eyebrow. "You don't seem surprised to see me."

I shrugged. "Should I be?" I showed him that I knew how he'd tried the doors of my mind last night— and set off alarms.

He played with a smile again. "The telepath you were when I last saw you wouldn't have known. But I'm told the Hydrans did what those fools on Ardattee couldn't do for you. You're good; Galiess was right. You're even better than Galiess, in fact. . . . How good are you, now?" He threw it at me like a challenge, sparking with excitement, eagerness, hope—a dark glint of envy—dying to take my measure. That was why he was out here, why we were here alone.

I shied back from the first real contact I'd had with his emotions, the first proof that he even had any. "I— dunno. Good enough, I guess." It sounded dumb and sullen. I pushed my hands into my pockets and shifted my weight from foot to foot. My mind left his challenge lying in the air between us.

(Didn't I tell you so?) his mind said. He smoothed a strand of dark hair the wind had loosened. "False modesty doesn't appeal to me. But loyalty does. After the ordeal you went through, I would imagine you're ready to do anything you have to to help us take control of Federation Mining."

I nodded. "You made sure of that," taking a chance.

He shrugged, an easy twitch of his shoulders. "Siebeling made sure of that—in his clumsy, backhanded way. I merely made use of an opportunity." His thoughts were as cold as his eyes.

And a warm body. My hands flexed inside my gloves. "So now I got something you can use. Why am I so important, what's the deal?" I had to ask it, not really expecting him to answer.

But he said, "Until now we've been missing the key to get us into the mines compound. We'd been able to come this far, to reach the world and establish ourselves in the very town. But the identity screens at the mines are too rigid, and the security checks on their actual personnel are too complete. We couldn't get any further. We can't walk in, and we can't teleport in— you can't teleport to a place you've never been." The muscles in his cheek tightened with his jaw; for a second I felt his long months of frustration. "But *you* have been inside, now; thanks to Contract Labor. So we are able to manipulate them from a direction they never anticipated."

(Up through the sewers,) I thought. I realized he still hadn't answered my question.

(Exactly.) Cool laughter slipped into my mind.

"But I can't teleport—I can't get back into the mines. So what good's that gonna do you?" I felt a kind of relief as I said it, because I didn't see how—

My hand jerked out of my pocket with a sudden twist; but I hadn't done it, and he hadn't touched me. . . . *Telekinesis*. He had: my wrist hung in front of my eyes, showing me the bond tag. "You can go back any time you want to."

I was still a bondie. All I had to do was let someone know it. "But . . ." fighting to keep control of my voice, "but, I mean, so I'm back inside. I can't get out again. You're still outside. What good's that gonna do!"

(Cat.) His hand reached out and stroked my arm. His mind made soothing waves, but that didn't ease anything. And then I felt another whisper of real emotion, an echo of the images he'd shown me back in Quarro, telling me, *(he understood, I could trust him, he'd been where I'd been, he knew what I'd been through; we were the same. . . .)* "It isn't forever. Only a day or so. That's all I'll need, all I want from you. And then you'll be free again, and the Federation will be in our hands—" The energy of his vision crackled between us. "You can make a joining; you've made one before." It wasn't really a question; he knew about the Hydrans. He felt me acknowledge it, and then at last he began to show me his plan:

I was going to turn myself in, and they'd take me back to the mines. Once I was there Rubiy would make a joining with me, and use me as a fix to teleport himself into the mines. He knew the layout and he'd sabotage the ventilating system with gas, leaving them all unconscious, and the mines wide open for the rest of his psions to come in and take it over. Once they were in charge of the mines compound, they'd also

be in control of the energy shield that protected Cinder
from any direct attack as well as from radiation—an invisible wall of electromagnetic force out in space around
us. And then we'd be in the control seat, holding the
Federation's most important resource for ransom. The
combines who'd hired him to do this, to attack the
FTA at its heart, thought he was doing it for them;
but they were wrong. . . .

His mind shut me out again, as if suddenly he felt
like he'd shown me enough, or maybe too much.

I shook my head. "It—all sounds so easy." So easy
it scared me.

"It is; now that we have you."

"I thought . . . I heard it ain't that easy to make a
joining—not for humans."

"Not for the average human psion. We are not average, you and I. You had no trouble joining with the
Hydrans."

"I didn't even have a choice, with them. But I
thought there had to be a—a *need.*"

"I have a need—the need to see this plan work!
And when the time comes, you'll find you have enough
need to see the mines under our thumb. . . ." The
promise in his voice made me feel worse than I already
did.

"Why do we have to make a joining at all? Why
can't I do what you want, there?"

"You haven't the skills, and you won't have the
equipment. Besides, it may be—difficult for you to move
freely." And besides, he wanted the triumph to be *his.*
His eyes were alive now, searching my face, measuring
my reaction. "Do your own part willingly and well,

and I'll reward you. Believe me, this is only the beginning. You've had nothing all your life; now you'll have everything—"

Power sang through me—his power, my power, shared power, *(All this could be mine.)* It blazed up like wildfire, made me drunk, gave me a rush . . . and left me empty, as suddenly as it had come. (If you are loyal.) Rubiy left the words branded on my mind.

I shook my head, dazed, when I should have been nodding. And I couldn't stop myself from thinking about Cortelyou—not sure if Rubiy had put him back into my mind, or my own guilt had. "When—uh, when am I supposed to—go back?" I only said it to cover what I was thinking, but it was still hard to say.

"Soon. When I'm sure you're ready." He wasn't talking about my health. But in the back of his mind he was already sure that *we were the same*. He reached out, tracing the line of my jaw with his fingers, letting his arm slip across my shoulders. "You're a handsome boy, as well as Gifted."

I laughed nervously, wondering why the first person who'd ever said that to me had to be him.

"Galiess is envious of more than your telepathy, you know. . . ." His mind brushed against mine.

"I'm cold," I said, and it was the truth—suddenly I was cold to my bones. "I better go back down." I edged away.

"Of course." His hand closed gently around my arm.

"I can make it by myself."

"Of course." He let his hand drop again, brushing my hip. "You need a little more time . . . to think over the things I've told you."

I nodded. He disappeared. I made sure he was even gone from my mind before I went on down the hill, feeling afraid of something I couldn't even name.

By the time I reached town it was getting dark, even though it was only the middle of the day. Bright banks of lights were coming on in the streets, but they weren't enough to clear the settling of night. Cortelyou was still somewhere out in the hills; I could feel his mind dimly, distant and closed. The starport lay on my right, silhouetted by the glow of the landing grid eaten out of the hillside beyond it. A couple of cargo shuttles were sitting on the field; I recognized the insignia on the side of them both: Centauri Transport. I turned toward the port entrance, drawn by the sight of the ships.

The lobby was nearly empty. The floor was a tiled picture of the Crab Nebula, with a colored fountain spewing up from its center like the heart of an exploding star, all golds and reds. The walls were midnight blue, glowing with hidden light. I was surprised; the outside of the building looked like the warehouse it was. I stood blinking in the brightness until my mind caught a familiar murmur of thought, and I finally understood what had made me come: *Jule*. I found her with my mind before my eyes found her, standing behind a counter in a half-hidden corner of the room. Somebody in a Centauri Transport uniform was talking to her. At first I thought he was just another horny spacer trying to pick her up. Her irritation stung like hot needles.

But then he handed her something that looked like

a message. She read it, and her mind flashed anger/
disbelief/suspicion/anger. She wadded the message up
and put it in her pocket. I couldn't tell what she said
to the officer, but I read the cold refusal in her mind.
He actually took her by the arm then, trying to pull
her away from behind the counter. She opened up her
mind and let him see what she thought of him. He
dropped her arm and backed away like she'd slugged
him. He almost ran toward the exit that led to the
landing field.

I crossed the room to the shipping area; she was the
only one there by the time I reached it. She started as
she finally noticed me. She looked like I felt, shaken
and exhausted. I moved to lean on the counter, needing the support.

(Don't do that!) Her voice inside my head made
me pull back. (Your bond tag will set off alarms. Keep
it away from things.)

I froze, tingling with panic, but nothing happened.
Slowly I put out my left hand, watching her face. I
leaned on it, pretending to relax, keeping my other
arm clear. (Jule—)

Her gray eyes sent me a look that was almost angry.
She was thinking about what it meant for both of us
if anybody noticed. "You shouldn't be here, Cat.
Galiess—"

(Can go to hell!) I made her wince. "Look, I . . . I
need some information."

I felt her wondering why I couldn't have waited, or
even asked her about it long-distance, mind-to-mind,
with less risk. . . . And then I felt her suddenly *know*
why, the way she always did.

Her face softened; she was realizing it had been too long—"Cat, I'm sorry about what happened before . . . for what Ardan said, and for what I didn't say. There was a lot of blindness. Even when you're a telepath—or an empath—it's still so easy to be wrong. Isn't it? . . ." She put a hand up to her eyes, and for half a second she wasn't seeing me. "Because we're still human beings first, always trapped behind a one-way glass of self-centeredness. And somehow that makes it so easy to say the wrong thing."

"I wasn't wrong." I hadn't expected this now. I felt my anger starting fresh, too easily. "I know what Siebeling was thinking. He'd rather have his son be dead than be me."

She shook her head. (No! Listen to what I'm trying to tell you.) "Ardan never meant he was glad you weren't his son. He was only glad that his son hadn't had to suffer what you did. You let yourself misread."

I didn't say anything; I only let myself remember. . . .

"He didn't know what the mines would be like for you. Cat, he didn't know." And she hadn't known, either; she was ashamed that she hadn't understood, that even with empathy she could never really go where I'd been.

Her eyes were hurting me. I looked away. I had what I'd wanted, her understanding; but there was still no sharing between us, only walls. What she said was true. A human could never trust or share completely, the way the Hydrans did. They'd always be too afraid . . . of seeing themselves.

I knew she was watching my face and thinking about things I wished she'd leave alone, angry at herself over me when she didn't need to be. I wanted to tell her that, but I didn't know how. So I said, "Jule, Rubiy is back," and I made myself look at her, just to stop her thoughts.

It worked better than I'd meant it to. Her mind tangled into a wild wall of defense, almost choking me out. She let it loosen again, relaxing but still on guard. "How do you know?"

"I've talked to him." I looked down at my hand, watched it tighten on the counter edge.

"And it made you afraid." She half frowned, because it wasn't for the reasons she'd expected. I felt her trying to read what was too out of focus even for me to understand.

"It ain't just that he's good, or even that he told me how he's gonna take the mines. . . ." Her eyes widened, but she didn't interrupt. "It's . . . there's something else, something more, that I almost caught: more than just what I can do for him, something he—wants. I mean, he wants *me*."

Her frown sharpened, questioning.

"Yeah, like that. It's all right; I can handle that. But it's more than just that. Deeper. Stronger, like he wants—" *My soul.* I broke off. "I don't understand it; I don't think I want to understand it. Because that's what really scared me, Jule. Because . . . we were the same, once, him and me. . . ."

"And you might still be?" She shook her head, telling me, (Don't be afraid of that. There's no need.) "You were never alike, really."

And I told myself that as long as she believed that, it would be true . . . not really believing it, anyway.

"You said Rubiy told you how he plans to take the mines?" Her voice was barely louder than a thought.

I nodded, and showed her what he'd said.

"So it's true. He really has what he needs. . . ."

"Me." I made a face.

For a minute she couldn't even answer; her feeling of helplessness was so strong I could taste it. "When— when are you—is this going to happen?"

"I dunno. Soon." I couldn't refuse to go, or Rubiy would be on to us all. But if I did go. . . . I covered the bond tag with my hand.

She took a deep breath, silent again for a long minute. She was thinking that (we'd find an answer, we would, we'd find a way. . . .)

"What did that Centauri spacer want?"

"Nothing. He was just. . . . He tried to get me to leave Cinder. He had a 'cast from my father, saying I was in danger." Her mouth thinned. She wondered how they'd found her, how they could know unless they knew. . . . Her mind broke the chain of thought, sick with suspicion. "You said you wanted some information?" She forced the change of subject herself, this time. She spread her fingers over the terminal touchboard in front of her, trying to look calm.

I'd gotten enough that I didn't bother to ask why she hadn't tried to give the spacer a warning to take away. But if her family still wanted her safe . . . "Uh— information." I'd only said I did because I needed something to say; but now I realized that maybe I'd had a reason after all. "How often do ships come here?"

"Not often. Every few weeks Centauri sends a

freighter—usually to bring supplies from the Colonies and pick up telhassium shipments. The FTA controls the traffic in this sector, and they keep Cinder as isolated as possible." Centauri again. I realized she probably knew more about shipping than anybody on this planet.

"But there's a ship in orbit here now. The one Rubiy came in on."

She nodded. "For another couple of days. Why?"

"Dere—Derezady needs to know."

"Why?" There was frustration in her voice.

"He didn't say." I couldn't tell her any more; what she didn't know couldn't hurt her. "How do people get on board? Does anybody watch, or check?"

"Of course." Another small frown formed, like a ripple on the face of water, and was gone.

"I'm not thinking of myself," I said.

She glanced down, and nodded once. "The security guards check every passenger; and all the guards are Rubiy's, so they double-check, to be sure Galiess intended the passengers to leave. But he knows that."

"What do you need to convince them?"

"I don't know. . . . Why don't you ask Galiess?" Jule's voice dropped to a whisper; her eyes looked past me in sudden warning.

I turned, almost forgetting to keep my hand clear, and saw Galiess coming toward us. She was wearing the same kind of heavy jacket I had on, and an expression that would've killed me if it could.

"What are you doing here?" Her hand closed on my sleeve, jerking me away from the counter. But she still didn't try to get into my mind. "Are you insane?"

"Jeezu. I was just looking around." I tried to look stupid.

"Don't lie to me." But all she meant was that she thought I was hot for Jule. (You're not invisible. While you wear a bond tag, you keep your face out of sight!)

"Okay. Don't get so tight about it." I pushed my hands into my pockets. "Look," I said, trying to get back on safe ground, "Rubiy told me everything—"

"When?"

"Half an hour ago."

(Already?) Her face reddened as she swallowed her anger. "Don't talk about that here."

I shrugged. "Don't worry. But he told me what he wants me to do. I'm an important part of all this. I want to know more about it, I'm sick of bein' shut up in a room. I ain't your prisoner," not so sure I wasn't.

But she nodded, stiffly, like someone forced her to do it. "All right, if that will keep you happy." She sounded like she was talking to a moron. I didn't care, as long as it got me what I wanted. I glanced past her at Jule, saw the confusion and surprise on Jule's face. I shrugged again.

As she led me away, she glanced back at Jule. "Isn't one man enough for you?" The envy in her voice was as sharp as a spear. I would've laughed, except that somehow it wasn't funny.

And that was how I got the back-alley tour of town, what there was of it. Galiess introduced me to a few of the psions who were working as shopkeepers and workers. She didn't tell them about what I was going to do, because she said it could endanger the plan. But still I felt a kind of excitement running through them, as if they knew their long wait was finally coming to an end. Most of them didn't pay much attention to me; I was just another hired brain. One or two of them looked at my face a little too long.

Galiess showed me what lay underneath the town, too: a network of tunnels and metal-walled rooms had been dug out beneath the buildings. They were used for storing the supplies the townies and miners needed to live—and now they were used for storing things that could make them die: weapons and equipment Rubiy had had smuggled in for his takeover. I asked all the questions I could, and all the while I was trying to figure answers to the ones I couldn't ask. By the time we'd seen it all, I was so tired I could hardly see straight. I let it show, stumbling and weaving on my feet. I could tell that Galiess was satisfied that she'd put me back in my place.

When she left me at my room, I collapsed across the bed and lay there for an hour before I even wanted to move again. But it had all been worth it. Because I'd already learned everything I needed to know, and made all the trouble I was going to; and she never even knew it. It was so easy. I got up and sat by the window with half a bottle of strange-tasting leftover brew; listening to the music drift up from below and flipping the torus coin I'd taken from her into the air—the coin that was Dere's ticket out of here. I had the key, and I was going to be the answer to everything; but not for Rubiy. And when they learned what I'd done, they'd all be so grateful—Dere and Jule and even Siebeling. He'd have to see I wasn't just the cheap gutter thief he thought I was. And Jule. . . .

The next day I found Dere picking at his food in the back room of the tape library. He looked totally burned out. After his wide-awake nightmare yesterday, I had a little trouble getting him to go for another walk; but I couldn't tell him what I'd done with all the psions and deadheads picking through the loops out front. Most of them were bored out of their minds, right then, but I didn't want to be the one to give them something to think about. Not yet. I finished most of Dere's food for him, and said finally, mind-to-mind, (Come on, you told me you needed to get away from it all. . . .)

His hands twitched on the scarred wood of the shelf where his food had been; his thoughts were jumbled. He got up then, and we went out the back way. I made sure all the way up into the hills that nobody followed us, even with their mind.

"It's safe," I said finally, sitting down on an outcrop of blue stone.

"For what?" When he got out a camph, his fingers weren't real steady.

"You want a way to stop what's happening, Dere?"

He didn't answer; he didn't need to. Finally he said, "So you think you have one?" He almost didn't want to ask, too afraid of being disappointed.

"I know I do." I grinned. "There's a ship in orbit right now. I know how you can get onto a shuttle at the starport. And I've got the thing you need to do it."

"How did you learn—"

"I was with Galiess. I picked her brains." I held my hand out, showing him the small brass coin with a square hole through the middle of it. It was from Galiess's homeworld; she was the only one here who carried them. "She uses these as her marker. Give this to the guards at the port, and tell them you have to go up to the ship. Say, 'Special check,' and *believe* she sent you. That's all you gotta do. They'll let you by."

"My God . . ." His own gloved hand closed over the coin. He put it in his pocket like a jewel. "How— where the hell did you get it?"

"I picked her pocket, too."

He stared at me like he didn't believe it.

I shrugged. "It was easy. I'm pretty good. I had a lot of, uh, on-the-job training."

He laughed, for the first time since I'd seen him here, and clapped me on the shoulder. Suddenly he looked ten years younger, and felt like it, too. "If I can get to that ship, I can radio a warning from orbit. . . . What about Galiess? Will she miss this?" He patted his pocket.

I shook my head. "She's got dozens. She'll never miss one. But check out the ship's crew before you trust them. Some of them may be playin' both sides. . . . Just keep your mind together, that's all you got to do."

His expression turned to something I couldn't read; for a minute he was looking at me like he'd never really seen me before. But then he took a deep breath and said, "Does anyone else know about this? Ardan, or Jule? Did you tell them about me?"

I shook my head again.

"Good. Let it stay that way. What they don't know can't hurt them. You can handle it." He smiled. "Sometimes I think you're the only one of us who can."

"Yeah, sure." I thought about Rubiy yesterday, wondering if I should tell him about my "interview." But the memory of his death-sending was too close to the surface inside him, eating at his control. I was afraid to push it, afraid to say anything that would make him doubt himself now. "Just make sure the FTA remembers what side I'm on when they come to get us out of this, will you?" I held up my wrist, letting the bond tag show. "They ain't been too grateful so far."

He laughed again. "Don't worry."

"I always worry." I let my arm drop.

(Because of you, I think our worries are finally over.) He grinned at me. (Thank you. Thank you.)

I smiled then too, felt the smile get wider and stronger as we started back down the hill; thinking that maybe I'd finally done something right.

13

I pulled on my sweater in a back room at the port hospital as Siebeling finished telling me, with all the enthusiasm of an undertaker, that I was just about healthy. Jule had told him everything about Rubiy's plans for me and the mines.

But I couldn't even tell him there was nothing to worry about. I took out a camph and stuck it into my mouth, just to watch him frown. I offered him the pack and he shook his head, frowning deeper. And then it happened. The box dropped out of my fingers as the wave of cold terror flooded my mind—not my terror *(fusion, confusion)*; somebody else's, somebody I knew too well. . . . *Cortelyou.*

"What is it?" Siebeling's face was full of surprise now.

"I . . . I . . . something's gone wrong." The words slipped out before I could stop them.

"I can see that. Are you in pain? What—" The words blurred into meaningless noise.

I covered my ears with my hands. "Shut up! I'm trying to hear something." But the terror had choked off. There was nothing left for me to trace through the maze of too much mind noise that was the hospital and the starport beyond it. . . . *The starport.* He'd been close by, and a slip like that could only mean one thing. He'd tried to get to the ship, and something had gone wrong.

"Cat? Cat—" Siebeling was shouting at me. I focused on his face again, saw his eyes, felt his tension turn into fear. I couldn't deal with it. I left the room, left him shouting after me.

I almost ran through the hallways that led to the starport; reaching ahead with my mind but not finding Cortelyou or any answers. I came out into the hall with the mosaic floor; but no one there felt anything strange now, no one looked angry or betrayed. Then I felt the touch of Jule's thoughts; saw her in the distance, doing what she was supposed to, but letting me know by a whisper of feeling that she'd caught Cortelyou's fear and knew something was wrong.

But before I could even answer her, someone was beside me. Rubiy. For a minute I thought he'd actually teleported into the middle of the starport. But then I realized that he'd walked in, just like anyone else—I just hadn't sensed him coming. Somehow I managed not to jerk or shudder; somehow I choked off the panic that splintered my mind at the sight of him.

"You shouldn't be here," he said. "Galiess warned you that it was dangerous."

I tried to shrug. "I just . . . wanted to see Jule." *What did he want—what?*

"See her in less obvious places. Come with me, instead. There's someone else I want you to see. Something I've been waiting to show you." He took hold of my arm. I turned away with him, knowing I didn't have a choice. Could it be he didn't know about Dere? Everything about him was as empty as a clear sky. He could've been inviting me to look at the sunset. But somehow I knew it wasn't going to be that simple. "You're on edge," he said. His grip tightened a little on my arm.

"It's an old habit."

We left the starport and walked down the street a way. The wind was even colder than usual, and the sky was a lid of heavy, mud-colored clouds. The street-lamps were shivering to life even though it was barely midmorning. It made me think about Oldcity. And then I was back to wondering about Dere, and trying not to. We reached the general store that Galiess had shown me a couple of days ago. It looked closed to me, but Rubiy unlatched the door and we went inside. The store was closed; no one was there. We went down into the storage tunnels.

Galiess was waiting for us, with a stungun and a couple of psions I didn't know—men, heavy and tough-looking, dressed in the uniforms of port guards. And Dere, standing like a rumpled bird between them, under the gun. I stopped dead at the foot of the steps as his eyes found me. "What—?" saying it to cover the sick lurch of my thoughts; knowing exactly what.

Dere swayed as he saw me—as his death-sending turned to reality. The guards took hold of him, holding him up. My hands tightened on the rough wood of the railing.

Rubiy turned to look back at me, measuring my re-action; I felt the minds of Galiess and the two guards beating against my control. "What's goin' on?" I said it again, keeping my voice steady. "Dere?" *Dere, don't give out, don't lose it all now, for God's sake.* I didn't even dare to reach out and share strength with him; I just tried to make myself believe I didn't know what it was all about, hanging onto the confusion to save my life. Believing that they couldn't know the whole truth yet or we'd all be dead. *Wouldn't we? Don't even think about it!* The muscles in my face were frozen; I felt like I'd come down with lockjaw.

Dere didn't answer, either. The knowledge that his own death was looking back at him with my eyes turned his mind into jangling noise. . . . I realized that he was letting it feed, using his fear to block out the other knowledge that he couldn't afford to let slip. He hadn't been a telepath all his life for nothing.

"I'm afraid Cortelyou has more to answer for than he's willing to admit to you," Rubiy said. The confidence in his voice made my breath catch.

"I don't get it." I shook my head. "What've you got a gun on him for?"

"Because he tried to reach the crew of the ship that's in port just now, and warn them about what we're planning to do here. Fortunately he spoke to someone who works for me."

I felt the bottom drop out of my thoughts, even though I'd been expecting it. . . . *My idea, it was my idea.* I turned it into disbelief, betrayal. "Dere, you did that? Why? We could—we could get rich. . . ." I mouthed all the words I should have been saying, while my eyes tried to read his face for blame. *I didn't set you up, I swear*—choking off even the thought.

And the answer was there: that he knew, he didn't blame me, I was only a tool of a fate no one could control. . . . "For the greater good, Cat." His voice was steady now, but his face was the color of chalk.

"You're leaving out whose greater good," Rubiy said mildly. "Derezady Cortelyou is a Corporate Security agent. I've known his real identity ever since Ardattee. I brought him here in order to be sure he remained harmless to us . . . and to see whether he betrayed anyone else from the Sakaffe Institute."

"And since we haven't learned anything yet, I think it's time we stopped waiting and probed." Galiess bared her glance at me, letting me know she was sure I'd been in this with Cortelyou, and that Rubiy would see for himself when he took Dere's mind apart.

I felt my eyes go wide. I turned the shock of his knowing the truth about Dere into the shock I ought to feel at hearing about it. "Dere, you're a Corpse?" The words grated against the memory of my saying them for real. "How could you work for them—you're a psion!"

He pulled loose from the guards' hold and stood straighter between them. "Yes, I am a Corporate Security agent. And I'm proud of it." He met Rubiy's stare for the first time. "I'm doing all I can to prove that a psion can live a normal life among other human beings."

"You call it a normal life, serving as a lackey to the law that oppresses us?" Rubiy's face came alive. "You're a coward, a parasite, a traitor! We're not human beings, and we never will be; not to the deadheads. We have to strike back. If we want justice, we have to take it!"

"Then you make yourself less than a human being—

you can't blame that on your victims." Cortelyou lifted
his chin, and I felt his mind fill with a kind of hopeless courage, the way Rubiy's was filled with hate. Dere
was challenging Rubiy, feeding his fury and making it
hotter. "Two wrongs only make a greater wrong. We
can only make the deadheads see us as no threat if we
are no threat. They'll let us live a normal life among
them only if they aren't afraid of us. We have to work
within the law—it's the only way. It's the renegades who
make them afraid, and bring down punishment on us
all." Dere caught my eyes and pointed at Rubiy, his
hand trembling with anger—or fear. But none of what
he said was meant for me.

"But it doesn't work that way!" Rubiy's own hand
jerked like he was throwing something away. "I know
it doesn't—and he knows it doesn't!" He glanced at me.
"They'll do to us what they did to the Hydrans if we
don't fight them. Cat knows what it feels like to crawl,
to carry the hatred of the world on his back. He never
had a chance at anything better because he was born
a psion—even though he was born to be better than any
human who ever lived." And he wasn't seeing me when
he looked at me—he was seeing himself. "This is why
I brought you here, Cat. You call this man your friend.
But now I want you to see him for what he really is—
a puppet, a traitor to his own kind, who wants us to
lose everything we've worked for, everything we deserve. I let him have the freedom to do what he did
because I wanted you to understand his crimes, and
the kind of punishment he deserves. Do you understand?" The whipcrack of his voice stung me.

I glanced from him to Dere, back at him again, feeling a band of pain tightening in my chest. I nodded, all I could do. Knowing with a kind of despair that I did understand: that he was right; but so was Cortelyou. And that both of them were just as wrong. My hands twisted the stiff leather of my belt.

"Name his punishment," Rubiy said softly, letting me know what he wanted to hear.

I didn't answer.

"Go on, Cityboy!" Dere said. "You always were a leech, looking for a quick credit and an easy way out. You're two of a kind. He'll kill me anyway—tell him what he wants to hear. Tell him I have to die!" And his eyes under the birdwing brows begged me, (Say it, say it—)

"Kill him." The words were acid in my mouth. "He deserves it, kill him!"

Rubiy smiled.

"Wait—" Galiess said suddenly.

But it was already happening. I felt the power surge, and Rubiy uncoiled a lash of psi energy. Dere's face twisted; his hands flew up to his chest. His mind filled with fear and outrage and all the things you scraped up from the bottoms of nightmares, went white-black with agony. . . . And then it was empty, and he was falling.

The railing of the stairs bit into my spine as I sagged against it, holding myself up with my hands, blind, deaf, and numb. All my senses stopped as my mind closed down to save itself from his death. They came back little by little, until I could watch Rubiy move to Dere's body, stand looking down at his face; still smiling the same inhuman smile. He'd reached out with his psi and stopped Dere's heart in his chest. He'd just killed a man in the most personal way anybody could think of, but there was no sign of it on his own face. He blocked so perfectly that he didn't feel a thing. . . . *No*. He'd felt something: he'd enjoyed it.

He turned back to me, but I kept my eyes on Dere. My mind kept searching for Dere, feeling the nothingness inside me where he'd been. I could see him, I could almost touch him; but I couldn't feel him at all. *Dead*. He was dead. He was gone and he'd never come back. And it was all my fault. . . .

"Have no regrets," Rubiy said. "He was our enemy."

"He was my friend." I looked up at him at last.

"Look at him!" Galiess moved suddenly, the stungun still in her fist; she pointed it at me like a finger. The two guards stirred beside her, the expression coming back into their blank, stunned faces. "He's involved, I tell you. You're a fool if you can't feel it. And you let Cortelyou die without probing him, when you could have learned everything, the truth!"

Rubiy turned back to her—angry, but not making a move to stop her. "You're right," he said, and lifted his hands. "Of course. As ever, my teacher and my guide. But we can still learn the truth . . . we still have Cat. We'll let him prove whether you're wrong about him. You have nothing to hide, do you, Cat?" Back to me.

"No," I whispered.

"Then open your mind to me." He'd been waiting for this; I saw the hunger for it come into his eyes.

I shut my own eyes, focusing inward. For a minute I thought I wouldn't be able to unweave the bruised and battered wall of my guard, because I hated what was going to happen so much. But if I refused him, I'd die just like Dere, and all for nothing. . . . I forced myself to let go, felt the fabric of my mind begin to loosen and separate; making filaments of thought into gateways, dropping my guard strand by strand and welcoming him in.

Cold maggot-fingers of thought crawled into my mind, heavy and clumsy; he didn't bother to be gentle about it. Probing further and deeper into every twist and secret place, he pulled out all the things it wasn't his right to see, helping himself like he owned me, like I was nobody, not even human—using me the way they'd done at the Institute, the way even the Hydrans had done. And I had to let him . . . had to hate him, like I'd hated all the others; had to hate myself, my stinking half-breed blood, the reason why they all did it to me.

And somehow I still had to make myself believe the lies snarled up in the strands of my own thoughts, lose him somewhere in the tangle of half-truths woven to cover the real truth. I turned him away again and again, until he was dizzy and dazzled, until I felt him begin to withdraw. . . .

But he still wondered. And so he tried once more, with a sudden hard blow that hit me like a fist. Old fears rose to help him, and for a piece out of forever I couldn't hold onto my control. The lies slid and smeared into everything else, and I didn't know if I even. . . . And then he came up against the locked door of the secret room in the deepest pit of my soul, and heard something behind it, screaming. He tried to force the block, but he couldn't. I wouldn't let him, not even to save my life. And finally, after a time that seemed like forever, he backed off. I knew then that he'd finished with me at last. He let me go, he thought he knew my limit, he'd taken everything there was to get, he was satisfied . . . he was still the best.

I stood at the bottom of the stairs, my hands locked over the railing; realizing that my mind was really my own again, and it was over. *It was over* . . . I'd beaten Rubiy. And he was the best.

"He's innocent. He knew nothing about Cortelyou's real identity; none of them did." Rubiy's voice reached me from another world; his hand smoothed my hair back from my sweating face. "They are exactly what they seem to be. Are you satisfied?"

And Galiess: "If you are, Rubiy." The stungun trembled in her hand.

I turned and climbed the steps without waiting for a dismissal. I made it all the way through the silent, empty store and out to the street before I got sick to my stomach.

14

It was pouring rain outside. The noise it made on the roof of the covered walkway was like the end of the world. I could barely even hear the bunch of mine workers laugh at me as they staggered past. "Wha'sh the matter, sonny, can't hold your—"

"Have a little hair of the—"

"Didn't I see you somepla—?"

I pushed away from the building and the drunken questions and stumbled out into the street. The sleeting rain drenched me and froze me as I walked, until my body was as numb as my mind. I didn't know where I was going to until the door slid open and I was looking at Jule.

"Cat?" She blinked at me like her mind was light-years away. "Where were you? What . . ." I didn't say anything. She stood aside to let me in.

Siebeling was there, sitting on the couch in the one large room that was her apartment. He stood up when he saw me. I didn't mind seeing him for once—it was right that he should be here, we all shared this together. "Dere is dead."

(*Dead, dead? dead? . . .*) It echoed from my mind into theirs and back again.

(I knew, I knew something—) Jule's face twisted. "Oh, God!"

Siebeling sat down again, as if his legs wouldn't hold him up. "How do you know?" Even his voice was weak.

"I was there." My own voice shook; I hardly knew it for mine. Jule's eyes came back to my face. "Rubiy . . . he just . . . stopped it, Dere's heart. Just like that." I snapped my fingers. "Just like . . . that."

Jule took my arm and led me to a chair at her table. I stood staring at it until she made me sit down. She brought shawls and sweaters and wrapped me in them, before she sat down across from me. "*Why*, Cat? What happened at the spaceport? You felt it too, I saw you come in, and you knew. But then Rubiy took you away."

I nodded, pressing my hands together on the table-top to stop them from trembling. The old fight scars on my knuckles stood out white and silver against my skin. "He made me watch. Dere—Dere tried to warn the ship that was in port . . . only, they turned him over to Rubiy! Rubiy knew—he knew all along what Dere was. . . ."

"He knew?" (*He knew?*) Words and thoughts jumbled. (Us, he knows about us—?)

(No!) I projected it without trying. "Dere was a Corpse! That's what he knew—and that's all he knows!" I didn't have enough control left to keep their half-shaped questions out, so I took hold of their minds and made them understand: how Rubiy had used Cortelyou, always knowing that in the end he'd have to kill him. How he'd trapped Cortelyou in a be-trayal to test my loyalty. How Dere had made Rubiy angry enough to kill him without probing him, because he knew that if Rubiy did he'd learn the truth about us all. . . .

Their relief and understanding filled me; but then the feelings changed again, to horror and guilt, as the real understanding hit. Words came out of their mouths, sounds of grief that didn't even register when the real grief was drowning my mind.

". . . and he just let you walk away from it?" Siebeling's voice broke through as his mind started to focus again. "He didn't even question your story, or ours?"

"Yeah, he questioned me." I looked up again at him, glaring, and touched my head. "He probed *me*, to get the truth." I pressed my hands together again; my bond tag rattled on the wet tabletop.

"After he made you watch a man die?" Jule's hand crossed the table between us and closed over mine.

I nodded, not trusting my voice for a minute. "But—but—I tricked him, Jule, I still kept him away from us. I couldn't let him win, after . . . after Dere . . ." My mind was still searching, still finding nothing. "But I had to be open to him, I had to let him have anything he wanted, so he wouldn't suspect. And I hate it, when they do that, I *hate* it. God! It's like . . . like being . . ." I bit my lip, shaking my head. And the human part of me wondered how the Hydrans could show their entire lives to everyone, to a bunch of strangers.

"They don't share their lives with everyone," she murmured. "They never join with humans, with strangers—only with each other, with someone they know as their own. And the important thing is that their privacy is given, not taken. That's the difference between a joining and a—a violation." Her head filled with pasts; she broke away from my mind, let go of my hands. One of her hands rose to her mouth, she started to bite a nail.

I caught her hand and pulled it down. I touched her mind; the shared feeling grew, warm, bright, and strong between us again. I knew that it wasn't the Gift I hated, any more than I could blame fire because someone had used it to burn me. And I knew that if I was given a choice right now, I wouldn't change what I was. "I guess it is. And I beat him. That's the important thing." *I beat Rubiy.*

"You expect us to believe that?" Siebeling said suddenly. His mind drove between us. "Rubiy probed you and he didn't learn anything? He set Dere up and used his murder just to test you? Why you? Why not all of us?"

"Because—because I'm his key. Because Dere was my friend. Because—" *Because he wants me.* "How the hell do I know!" My fist came down on the table.

"It's a lot easier for me to believe that maybe you set Cortelyou up. Jule told me you were asking about ships—for Cortelyou you said. That you went out of the spaceport with Galiess afterward." His thoughts were turning on me, to keep from turning on themselves.

"Dere was scared Rubiy would learn what he really was, and find out about us all. He needed a way to get a message out fast. I found one for him."

"And got him killed."

"Yes!" I pushed up out of my seat. "But not because

I was tryin' to!" Still knowing it was my fault, *my fault....* Touching the hole in my mind that someone had filled who'd been more of a friend to me than a whole city had back on Ardattee. I sat down again and put my head in my hands.

"You can't even hide your guilt. Why just Cortelyou? Because he was Corporate Security? Why didn't you betray us all? Or maybe you have already, and we just don't know it. You're vicious, lying gutter filth, and that's all you'll ever be!"

"You bastard—" I moved in my chair, my hands turning into fists.

But Jule was beside me suddenly, her hands on my shoulders. (No, Cat, no, no. . . .) "Stop it, Ardan!" Her mind was a shield protecting me, absorbing Siebeling's anger and turning it aside. "Not again, not this time. He's telling the truth."

He's telling the truth. Rubiy's words echoed hers in my mind, making my stomach twist.

"He claims he could convince Rubiy that black is white. He could be doing the same to us."

For just a second I felt her mind waver and search. "No. The wound is too deep. I know him. He couldn't lie that deeply to me. You're wrong, Ardan." Her voice faltered. She lifted her head as if she was afraid of a blow; but it passed. "He came here for help, he's been through something terrible. If you can't believe him, then believe me, at least. You have to believe someone."

Siebeling stood up. A wave of blind hatred washed over him, and I couldn't tell who he hated more, me or himself. . . . "I don't need anyone to tell me the truth! That we're caught in a trap because I got us into this. . . . That because of him we have no hope of getting out of it again! He betrayed Cortelyou. He'll help Rubiy take over the mines and blackmail the Federation—his only loyalty is to himself. He's an irresponsible kid, he's never done an unselfish thing in his life. If you expect anything better .of him, if you keep protecting him, then you're committing suicide. But that doesn't matter anyway, because when he's ready he'll betray me—and you, too." He started toward the door. Jule's fingers dug into my shoulders until I winced, but she didn't answer him.

He stopped at the door, his hand on the open-plate, and turned back. He glanced from her to me and back at her again; something happened between them for a long minute that they closed me out of. But his face didn't change. "I don't need that. I don't need anyone." He went out the door and he didn't come back.

Jule's hands let me go, I heard her move away from me. I slumped in my chair, fumbling in my pockets for the pack of camphs. I found it, stared at it for a minute, thinking about Dere. And then I crumpled the whole pack and threw it at the door. "Shit!" I stood up. "I didn't mean for it to happen! Dere was my *friend*, I only wanted to help him. Why don't he believe that! Why can't he—" I stopped, as I saw her face. She was standing very still, and I thought no one should have to feel what I saw then in her eyes. She was trying to keep control, *(but her emotions were too strong for her, they'd always been too strong, and now. . . .)* A rush of agony poured out of her mind.

I took a deep breath, clenching my hands:

> what's wrong?
> Jule . . .   you want me out of here?
> are you all right?

She looked at me with panic in her eyes, and a tear slipped out and down. "Damn it, Cat!" Then all the tears broke free and she was sobbing, (Don't do that!)

I hung onto my chair. "I'm sorry."

"It's—not your fault. It doesn't matter. He doesn't matter. . . ." Her hand rose to cover her mouth. "How could I be so blind!"

Siebeling. Siebeling had made this happen. "Jule, he didn't mean it."

"You know . . . what he said. And you know it was the truth. He doesn't need me. He doesn't even want me, he doesn't care."

"He couldn't have meant it like that. He knows you . . ." I fell over the words, feeling helpless, feeling like a fool. "Better than anybody." *Except me.*

"It is true! He's felt that way . . . ever since he lost his wife and son. I thought this was different, that I was. But I was wrong again!" She bit her lips, wiping at her eyes.

I went to her and put my arms around her. She held onto me, sagging against my shoulder, sobbing again. Her grief filled my mind and became my own; until just for a second I wanted to break away. But I knew that everything had already gone far beyond that, and at least I had to give her something to hold onto.

And she said, so softly I barely heard it, "I hate everything." I held her closer, feeling her warmth, and kissed the shining midnight of her hair. "No, Jule, no. . . . Everything's gonna be all right." My throat was so tight that I could barely get the words out. My mind accepted her need, the way her mind had always accepted mine; asking no questions, only trying to show her that she wasn't alone, she'd never have to be alone. . . .

And after a while the sobbing died away. I swallowed hard and said, "Jule . . . I never learned a poem in Oldcity that you'd want to hear. How about a joke?"

Jule pulled back to look at me as if I'd lost my mind, and I grinned.

"What would a five-hundred-kilo talking rat say?"

She shook her head. "I—I don't know."

Dropping my voice about an octave, I said, " 'Here, kitty, kitty . . .' "

She said, "Oh . . ." She started to giggle, and then she started to laugh. For a minute we stood there like a couple of idiots, laughing, and the tears were still running down her cheeks. And then I wasn't sure I had the right to, but I said, "Do you want to talk about it?" She stiffened against me, against answering; but then she nodded. We sat down again at the table. I watched her with her face in her hands and her dark hair slipping down. For the first time I noticed the wildflowers she'd brought in to make the room her own, wilting now between us in a bowl. They smelled like spring.

She didn't say anything for a while. She almost seemed afraid to look at me. "It's stupid . . . how hard it is to talk about yourself . . . it's such a stupid story."

But she opened her mind at last, and began to show it to me.

I entered the memories as she let them rise: memories of a little girl whose mind always made her feel too much when she looked at everyone; who had to share every emotion, and couldn't even keep her own to herself. . . . Memories of growing up in a shining, empty world where objects had more meaning than human lives, with people you *knew* didn't care about you, or even each other, anymore. . . . Knowing that your very existence was a humiliation to them, another blow driving them further apart. Memories of finally leaving them and your whole life behind, because you couldn't live with your own emotions and their lack of them any more. Moving on and on, trying to escape what there was no escape from—living everyone else's hurts and hatreds and lacks, because you couldn't help it. Caring about their pain, because you couldn't help it; being used and hurt, again and again, because you cared too much. And all she wanted was peace, and someone she didn't have to be wrong about.

But then she was remembering Siebeling, she'd really believed he was the one— A sob caught in her throat. (*Because it was all true. . . .*)

"Jule, what are you ashamed of?"

"I drive everyone away! I'm weak. I'm neurotic, I don't know how to have a real relationship. I tried to drown myself—I couldn't even live with myself."

"It ain't true." I shook her gently. "There's nothing weak about you. Humans . . . shouldn't have to live inside everyone else, too; they have to have protection. But when you're born a freak, you don't have it, and nobody else knows how to give it to you. . . . I mean, it was never your fault. You can't blame yourself for the way you were born."

She frowned.

"I know what I'm saying, Jule," knowing I wasn't saying it right. "Listen to me. You're no fool for trying to love him, or wanting his love. And anybody who'd ever let you go is the real fool."

She sighed, a long, shaky sigh.

"Siebeling don't blame you for suffering, for hurting. He helped you learn to stop having to feel everything and be hurt by it. He knows how hard it was." If he was even half of what she thought of him, he did; but right then I had a hard time pretending to believe he was even human.

She almost smiled, but then her face twisted like she still didn't know what to feel.

"He didn't mean it, Jule. I ought to know, if anybody does. He's half out of his mind over what's happening here; he ain't thinking straight, he's too full of guilt and too confused. Ain't that what you kept trying to show me? He didn't even know what he was saying." And I didn't think about what I was saying, didn't choke on the words, only wanting to say whatever I had to to make her stop feeling that way. "He's scared and angry, because he's in love with you, and he's afraid to admit it because he's afraid of losing you like he lost his wife."

She stood up. "Is it true—?" She shivered.

"It's all true." I just let it come, not sure where it

was coming from, not even sure who I was talking about anymore, because— "Because he ain't the only one who feels that way." I only knew what I'd said after the words were out—and it was only after I heard them that I knew they were true. (I love you. I love you.)

She reached out across the table and took my hands. She kissed me once—my mind filled up with her emotions, with all the tenderness I'd ever known. She whispered. "Thank you, Cat . . . you're the best, the only real friend I've ever had." She looked up at me again, with her storm-cloud eyes.

But her lover would always be Siebeling. And as I understood that, something snapped inside me, like a broken-off piece of her pain. Suddenly I was five years old, hurting so bad I wanted to cry. Why him? Why did it have to be him, why couldn't it be me? I'd never had anything!

But love was blind, they said, love was crazy—love didn't have any heart, and so it ripped out your own. Jule had taught me how to care; I knew I'd never be able to stop caring about her now. I moved around the table and held her again, just for a minute, pretending she was mine. And then finally I said, "It's gonna be all right. Everything's gonna be all right. I promise you."

I left her apartment, and went out into the night.

15

I turned on the light.

"How the hell did you get in here?" Siebeling leaped up out of his chair; he'd been sitting like a stone in the darkness of his room. The look on his face was worth the effort.

"Slip's secret." I twitched my mouth. "And what the hell do I want—since you're gonna ask that next. I'm here because you got only two people you can count on in this snakepit, and you left both of them bleeding. I came to make you listen to some true things, you piece of—"

"Get out."

"Uh-uh." I shook my head, moving toward him, feeling the grief and rage caught inside me build again at the sight of him. "I ain't getting out of here until I make you understand." I reached out and caught him by the front of his thick sweater, and shoved him up hard against the wall. He started to struggle, but he hadn't learned to fight on the streets. I pinched a nerve; he yelped and stopped struggling. "Yeah, that's right, Doc. I can be everything you think I am, if you make me. Don't make me do it—because it ain't what I want." I let go of him and backed off. "I just want you to *listen*."

He straightened away from the wall, his eyes dark

had told me about him, that I'd told back to her, was true: some part of me had always seen it, there inside him. The one he really hated was himself. He'd never understood why his family had been destroyed while he went on living—and so he'd stopped living too, even though his body still went through the motions. He was suffering as much as the psions he treated, but there was no one he could turn to for help, no one who understood what he'd lost. He'd tried to do something good with the Sakaffe psionics research, something to help him feel like he had a right to be alive. But all that had done was cause a good man's death, and trap him in a hopeless situation; and Jule. . . . His face collapsed.

He cared about her, all right. If I'd been blind and deaf, I'd still have been sure of it—the feeling was that strong. He'd hurt her because he was afraid—afraid of losing her, afraid to face her death, and his own. And I saw how much he wanted her, and wanted to make it all right; how much he wanted to stop hurting himself and everyone else, he'd been so wrong about everything. But it had been such an old—habit, to break free of, being so wrong. And now he'd thought there was no hope left. . . .

He didn't say anything, either; as if there was nothing he could say, to her.

And I still wanted to hate him, but somehow I couldn't. Because I'd seen into his mind—but more than that, because I understood what I saw. I wasn't the same burned-out shadow walker who'd been dumped in his office the day I met Jule, any more than I was still the psionic deaf-mute I'd been when I met the Hydrans. I'd changed. More than just my Gift had come back to life inside me; and like it or not, I couldn't twist the knife in his wounds, any more than I could stop loving Jule. . . . I let all my angry words out in a sigh between my teeth. "She'll know, Doc. She always knows. But go and tell her anyhow." I started for the door.

"Cat, wait—" he called after me.

"Go to hell." I opened the door and went out.

I went back out into the nameless street again, moving like a shadow walker, not wanting anybody's mind or even their eyes to touch me. Moving because I couldn't rest—not alone with my memory in my dead, empty room. The rain had ended and the sky was clearing; quicksilver puddles shimmered everywhere. The street stopped beyond the spaceport but I went on up into the hills, the only place I'd ever felt free for even an afternoon; the last place that I'd seen Dere smile.

I went farther than I ever had. The light of the sky was enough to let my eyes find a way. I only stopped when even the memories had to let my body rest; dropping down on the hillside in the spongy grass. The sighing of the trees and the hiss of venting steam was all around me, with the faint rustling music of tiny wild things in the darkness. No human sound, no human eyes, no human mind to ruin the perfect peace.

A cool wind moved through my hair. I looked up for the first time, and I thought that if the days were beautiful, there wasn't even a word for this. The Crab

Nebula lay across the clearing sky like golden fishnet, in a black sea rippling with aurora. I lay looking up at it for a long time, opening all my senses, letting my mind escape into the universal darkness. Wanting to stay there forever and let the beauty of it fill me. . . .

A tendril of alien thought curled into the pattern of my own. My mind tumbled in blind panic, trying to protect itself—until I heard the voice that wasn't a single voice but a choir of thought calling me. Not human . . . *Hydran*. I stood up, searching the darkness, and suddenly they were all around me, maybe a dozen of them, as silently as ghosts.

(What . . . what are you doing here?) I looked from face to face, knowing that their eyes saw me just as clearly in the darkness, and that their minds could see clear through me. A couple of them were albino-white, but I wasn't really sure if any of them were the ones I'd seen before. It was hard to focus on their faces when my mind's eye couldn't even separate them.

They asked me, (Why I was surprised to find them here, when this was their place, created by their ancestors? Their ancestors were not born to live in the dark heart of this world. They longed for the sky and the world of living things as much as the outsiders who had stolen those things away from them.)

I looked down.

They showed me that they came here often, in secret, (to gather what they needed to feed and clothe their bodies . . . and to feed their spirit.)

I nodded, and let my mind loosen again, reaching out to become a part of their whole. But I kept control this time, I didn't lose myself as I sank into the image.

I joined with them, needing to share in the filling of their spirit, needing it more than I could know.

But as I joined, I couldn't stop the memories of tonight that welled up like blood from a wound. The memories bled into the sea of their shared mind, and yet they didn't break away. Deep waters swallowed my grief, purified it, held it suspended as they shared their strength with me.

But I felt their stunned surprise, the deeper fear beneath it, as they absorbed the truth about the human psions who had promised them deliverance. . . . (Murder—the human psions had murdered one of their own and forced the Chosen)—me, they meant me—(to be a witness. They were psions, how could they do such a terrible thing and survive?)

(They're human,) I thought. (They're good at surviving.)

And they were asking themselves, (How could they not have seen—?) But sharing their question, I saw that there was no way they could have known—because even though they were the best telepaths I'd ever met, their own minds were so open, so freely shared, that they had no defenses; they didn't even know what a lie was. Without the lie itself, they had no way of telling a lie from the truth. Rubiy must have known that and used it against them, used them like he used everyone else.

But then they were asking me for an answer, (Because there was a strangeness that was more than alien in some of the human minds. . . . There was an unrightness, perhaps a)—the image blurred until it was almost lost—(deceit.) They could learn. They weren't the fools Rubiy figured they were, after all, and I was glad.

But now I had to try to make them understand the truth behind the lies, the way they'd been betrayed, the hope they'd lost— (This is hard . . . but you're right. They weren't telling you the truth, they're—deceiving you. We call it 'lying.' Humans do it all the time, because most of them can't read minds. . . .) And I told them, not hiding what I felt about Rubiy, or how good it felt to show them the truth. (. . . So they lied to you, to keep you out of their way while they took over the mines. They tangled up their thoughts with a false image because you couldn't understand the difference—they thought you couldn't, anyway. Does that make any kind of sense to you?) I let them sink deeper into my mind, as they tried to get hold of something that kept slipping away, and then the word/feeling came back.

(They understood, now. . . . But it was not clear why these new outsiders wanted the unholy place, if it was not because they came to fulfill the promise.)

(Well, they want power, I suppose.) I tried to show them what the blue crystals meant to humans. (So controlling the mines means they'd have the FTA— the ones who control the Human Federation—by the throat.)

It was like dropping a stone into water and getting no ripples: (Not clear . . . there was no need . . . no purpose. . . .) As if they didn't have any idea why anyone would even want power. I tried to remember what I knew about power to let them see why. And I guess they did, because I felt something sharp and sudden form then that hurt my head. I didn't know exactly what I'd been thinking of, myself, until the thought came, (It was the suffering of those weaker than themselves that they wanted.) I caught images they must have picked up from my own mind, about the mines, and the Labor Crows . . . and Oldcity.

(Yeah, I guess that's about right. But power can be used for good—) Except that right then I couldn't think of an example.

A feeling that was almost disbelief patterned in my head; they were whispering, (What ugly, twisted mind-paths these aliens had chosen.) And I remembered what Dere had said, about humans being defective Hydrans.

I felt their hope curdling. (They understood at last that these human psions had used their gift falsely, only meaning to do further harm. But if they suc-ceeded, what would become of the outsiders who held the unholy place?)

The question surprised me. (I don't know.) I figured Rubiy would have to keep the ones who ran the mines alive to get what he wanted. But then I thought about the bondies—nobody would help them, whoever won.

(They saw that there was no good that would come out of this, for anyone.)

I looked up at the ring of dim faces again, seeing that there was nothing left for them now; the thing that gave them life and meaning was being destroyed because of something they didn't even understand. There was no way they could stop it, now. Their last hope of someone to save them, of a new beginning, was gone. And I was sorry I had to be the one who'd told them; I was sorry for everything.

(But they knew it was better to know the truth, good to know that in some ways at least they had been wise. . . .) The circle of their thoughts drew closer around me. Even if I wasn't the answer they'd been promised by their ancestors, I was still the one who had shown them the truth.

I looked down at my hands, wondering like an idiot whether they wondered why I wasn't blue anymore. And then, because there wasn't anything to lose by trying, I tried to show them how Siebeling and Jule were working against Rubiy, trying to stop him.

They listened. And then they asked me, (Why would I help the ones who tried to save the place where I was a slave?)

My mind tried to shut them out—

(Because there was someone who mattered.) They answered their own question, and I saw then that they already knew about Jule and the others, and everything that had happened between us.

(Yeah, someone who matters.) For a minute I felt the old, human resentment rise against their understanding too much. But only for a minute. (So you see, we could use any help. . . .)

There was a silence inside my head. Finally they answered; but it was only to tell me, (They had to consider these things further.)

I nodded. (I don't blame you. You don't owe us nothing.) Except revenge—but I knew they couldn't take that. I felt hopeless and empty. My legs were

getting shaky; I wondered how long we'd been standing there. I realized that they were telling me there
was nothing left to say or share except loss, (And that
was not appropriate to this place.) Their solid reality
flickered. I felt them begin to loosen the ties that bound
their minds to mine, knew that they were about to disappear again, and go back into their hidden world.

(Wait! I—I need to ask one more thing.) Their
presence grew strong again. (You must have seen
most of what's in my memory, that time you . . . I
mean, I heard the mind is never supposed to forget
anything, just that sometimes you forget how to find
something you want. I need to know something that
happened a long time ago. . . . *And under it, wanting
to know about my parents, and why—?*)

They knew my secret. But they wouldn't give me an
answer. (Because they also knew that among the outsiders there was a purpose to forgetting; it protected
a mind that was solitary, easily broken, and slow to
heal. The ways of the outsiders were mine, I had been
raised into them and I would have to live with them.
I had learned to forget; I would have to learn that
there was a reason for forgetting. It was better to leave
some things alone.)

(They would not interfere against us. Whatever we
did, they would not oppose it, for my sake. But I had
seen the truth, there was no choice either way for
them. They must think longer on this.)

I nodded again, and my hands made fists. The circle
of their mind began to close me out, gently. But my
own mind didn't want to let go, suddenly afraid of

losing the contact that eased all pain: my lifeline, the only bond with my people. *My people*—

But I lost it anyway. They didn't belong to me; they never had. I knew it as they disappeared with a sound of the wind sighing. I'd lost my true people forever; I was stuck with being human. And that was the same as being an orphan, and right then I hated it.

I went back down alone again, feeling as cold as if I'd died along with Dere. After a while I began to see the lights of town, and the mines compound out on the snowy plain. I thought about what a cheap, cruddy place the port town was, like an old scar on the green hills. Humans destroyed everything they touched. But I didn't have anywhere else left to go, or any other choice than to play out this loser's game of Last Chance with Rubiy. Even if nobody else helped me or even believed me, even if Siebeling still thought I was nothing but a croach and a lousy half-breed kid . . . even if Jule still loved him. I'd never had a real choice in my life; any more than I'd ever really been young.

16

Somebody was shaking me awake, their fingers digging into my shoulder and their irritation digging into my brain. I crawled up out of black dreamlessness, through the Oldcity memories I always woke into, through layers of time. I reached out with my mind, expecting to find Jule, or maybe Siebeling . . . finding Galiess instead. And then the memory of where I was and what had happened yesterday caught me like a prod, shocking me awake.

I raised my head. Sunlight silhouetted her, throwing her face into shadow. I lifted a hand to my eyes, but I didn't need to see her expression. I pushed my memories into a cell and held them there, clearing my thoughts. I couldn't think about it now, *not now*. . . .

"Get up," she said, letting me go like having to touch me disgusted her. "You've spent long enough being useless."

I frowned. "Get off it. What do you care if I sleep? I got nothin' better to do."

"You do now. Sit up and listen."

I sat up, slowly, yawning until my jaw cracked. (I'm all ears.)

She stiffened. "Rubiy showed you what was expected of you. You've proved you're strong enough—

and you've proved your trust, to him." Not to her. "It's time for you to do your part."

It took me a minute to remember that what she meant was me going back to the mines. "It's time? Right now?" My fingers traced the ragged trail of an old scar along my ribs. "Ain't this kind of sudden?"

"What did you expect, a parade?" She wasn't going to give me a chance to ruin anything—or even to get any satisfaction out of it.

I frowned. "Maybe just a chance to ask some questions."

"You're to turn yourself in at the spaceport, and let yourself be taken back to the mines. At an appropriate time you'll begin a joining with Rubiy, who will be open for your contact. That's your entire role and responsibility—and all you need to know."

"If you say so." I shrugged. "One question—do I get time to put on my pants?"

She left the room.

We walked along the street toward the starport side by side, but it wasn't like we were walking together: I was going there alone, and she was making sure I did. The clear afternoon air was bright and still; it gave me chills, but not because I felt cold. I stopped across from the ramp in front of the shining glass starport entrance and looked on past it into the wilderness. Green hills burned my eyes; I kept looking up until I saw the cobwebbed sky. I wondered how much of it I'd be seeing after today.

"You know what to do," she said. "You're being

watched, always. And always remember . . . we're your
only protection. If you don't do what you've been told,
our plan will fail—and you'll be a slave there until you
die."

I looked down again. "You don't really want me to
go, do you?" Saying that instead of what was filling
my mind. "What's the matter, you jealous? If you want
to take my place . . ." I waved at the entrance, trying
to force a laugh.

But sparks leaped from live wires in her mind. She
did want to go in my place—wanted to hold the place
of honor that belonged to her, do the final deed that
would put the Federation Mines into Rubiy's hands
and secure the future. It was her right, *hers*, not mine:
She'd spent the best part of her life working toward
this triumph, working for Rubiy, with Rubiy; molding
him, teaching him, serving him, worshiping him. He
was her creation, and her god. She'd taken him out of
the gutter when he was nothing but a hoodlum—
angry, helpless, but burning with potential. She'd never
known how to take control of her own life; he'd solved
that problem for her. Soon he'd had her begging him to
use her, any way he wanted. She'd devoted her life to
helping him learn, helping him succeed . . . made herself his willing slave.

And this was how he repaid her: by deciding that
she had outlived her usefulness, her ability, his need for
her . . . his love for her. Letting himself be seduced,
pushing her aside for this dirty half-breed with the
morals of an animal. . . . Her control fell apart completely. For half a second I saw the raw heart of her

betrayal, and I thought she was going to use her psi against me right there in the street.

But she got her control back almost before it was gone. She had put her life in Rubiy's hands; it was his to use or throw away. She would accept his decision in this, gracefully, as she had always done. . . . No matter how much she detested it, and me. Her hands flexed inside her gloves, and her mouth trembled.

I let go of my own defenses, taking a deep breath. For a minute I almost felt sorry for her.

A couple of town psions pushed past us with sidelong glances. I turned and followed them up the ramp without saying anything.

I stopped once I got inside, letting her hate drain out of me. I had my own problems to worry about. I stood staring down at the mosaic of a star gone nova under my feet; thinking it fit the position I was in right now about as well as anything could. Now all I had to do was find somebody who was waiting to turn me back into a piece of property. I looked around, wondering how to start: I didn't see any guards who looked like I was on their minds. I began to think it would be a laugh if I couldn't find anybody who wanted me.

Then I saw Jule, through the light-fountain, leaning against a counter and talking to some woman. I started toward her, wanting to see her once more before I had to go; to carry her smile with me, to give me courage.

She was facing away from me, listening, as I came up to the night-blue counter. I put out a hand to rest on, not even thinking about it. And then suddenly my wrist jerked down and slammed flat against the counter edge. It startled me; my hand was trapped somehow and I couldn't move it. The counter turned blood-red for a meter on either side of me.

The woman at the counter turned, and then she was backing away from me. I was jerking at my trapped hand; my eyes caught Jule's staring back at me. I could see her fist pressing her chest, she was shaking her head. (*Too late, it's too late.* . . .) I looked down at my own wrist and the world snapped back together: the bond tag. Suddenly it was all real, what I was doing here, and the thought hit me: *What if this doesn't work?*

I quit struggling as a handful of port guards circled me with their stunguns out. I kept my eyes on Jule, and I said, "Help—" She gave me a sad, helpless smile, while one of the guards put a lock on my hands. Then they told her to push a button. She did, and my hand came loose from the counter. They led me away. I could feel her thoughts following me; her mind filled with gratitude. *She knew.* Siebeling had told her everything. I looked back and smiled.

A couple of the guards led me to an empty office, and shut the door against the people still staring at us out in the lobby. They pushed me down into a chair and looked at me; one of them wiped the back of his hand across my face. "No dust. He hasn't been at the mines long; or else he's been out long enough to throw off the effects. You watch him; I'll call in a report."

He left the room. The other one sat behind the desk with his gun pointing across it at me. I shifted in the molded plastic seat and tried to get comfortable; but it was the wrong shape, and I didn't feel much like relaxing. I thought about Jule, about trying to reach her with my mind. But the guard was a telepath, and a good one. I didn't want him eavesdropping; he was too close for comfort. I made myself stop thinking about her. But then I started to think about the mines; and I didn't want to think about that, either. I looked back at the guard. He sighed and shifted his gun. I said, "Nice weather," because I had to do something.

"I suppose so, to you." He looked at me kind of funny. "How'd you get loose, anyway? I thought that was impossible." But he was a psion, and I couldn't help feeling he should have known why I was here.

I said, "I teleported," and he frowned. I kept my mind loose and empty, and watched him wonder. Galiess hadn't even told her own people the truth about me, or what I was supposed to be doing. Making sure I didn't get any special treatment—or any credit. At least I wouldn't have to worry about her anymore. Only about me, about how I was going to make them listen to me at the mines. Joraleman would be there; he was all right, he knew what had happened. And when it was all over, they'd let me go, because they'd have proof that I'd been an agent. Sure, they had to. . . .

The door opened. The guard was back already, and Kielhosa was with him. I shut my eyes and wished I really could teleport.

The trip out from town and down to the snow was the same as before, except that this time my hands weren't free, and this time Kielhosa had a stungun. He didn't say a word; but I knew what he was thinking, so maybe it was just as well. He'd been in town on his time off, *(Just his goddamn lousy luck)*. . . . And mine.

I hoped Joraleman would be there when we reached the snowtrack, but he wasn't. There were only a couple of bondies, loading supplies, and a guard sitting on an empty box watching them. Kielhosa came up alongside him and made me stop. "Got room for two more?"

"You're going back early?" The guard looked surprised.

"Not by choice." Kielhosa glared at me. "I've got a special delivery to make. How much longer is this going to take?"

"Nearly done." The guard stood up and stretched. I looked at the prod shimmering in his hand. "I had to wear out my arm, though. Your prize specimens don't break their backs getting the job done. Where'd that one come from—a new recruit?" He laughed.

"To them it's a holiday. And no. This rat thought he could resign." His hand on my shoulder shook me. "They picked him up at the spaceport."

Out of the corner of my eye I saw the bondies look up. Kielhosa was making sure they heard. Their blue faces startled me; I'd forgotten what they looked like.

"Oh, yeah? How'd he get away from you?"

"Long story, and I don't even know all of it. He's been out for a while. But they all turn up eventually, if they don't starve or freeze."

"And twenty lashes'll convince anybody not to try it again." The guard glanced back at me, snapping the prod with a jerk of his hand. He enjoyed thinking about it.

And I wondered how I could ever have been so stupid. The guard moved away, herding the bondies toward the back of the snowtrack with the last of the supplies. I heard a door slam. Kielhosa pushed me toward the 'track. I climbed up into the cab and sat in the backseat. It was too cramped for my legs. Kielhosa shoved me over against the far window, cursing, and sat beside me. The guard sat up front. The bondie who was driving now turned to stare past the seat at me. Then he started the 'track and I looked out at the snow, feeling like I'd swallowed a stone. *What did you expect them to do, shake your hand? Twenty lashes . . .* my God, how much was that? All my fingers, and all my toes. . . . But I hadn't been trying to get away. I was going back to tell them about the plot. I was on their side—I had to remember that. They wouldn't give me a beating when they understood. I twisted in the seat. "Hey, Kielhosa—"

17

They didn't believe me. Kielhosa took me to the Mines Directorate; I stood on the perfect white carpet and told them all I knew. They listened to every word. And then they started to laugh. Joraleman wasn't even there to back me up; when it was too late, I'd found out from Kielhosa that he was still back in town. The directors called me a liar; all they saw was a scared kid, a trapped rat trying to save his own skin, and nothing I could do with words or even with my mind could make them see me any other way. The head director told Kielhosa to have me punished.

But instead Kielhosa said, "Sir, I think you should know this is the bondie who saved Chief Purchaser Joraleman's life. If we could at least wait until Joraleman gets back . . ." He hesitated.

The director's face darkened. "Him? This is him? The psion, the mind reader?" His own mind filled up with fear. "What the hell do you mean, exposing us to—Get him out of here! And add another dozen to his sentence, for wasting our time."

And so I walked between two guards across the compound yard, where a hundred others stood waiting and watching. The white glare of light on the endless snow was blinding me, and I didn't think I was going to make it to where the other bondies were stand-

ing. They'd brought out all the poor shivering blue-
faces who weren't digging ore to watch what happened
to me. So that they'd never try what I'd tried. *(But I
hadn't!)* One of the guards shook his head. I tripped
over nothing; it seemed to take forever to cross the
yard. I could see the faces of the others, like blue
beads strung out across the glare, and all of a sudden
I remembered Mikah. And I knew that if he was
standing there, he'd think I'd lied to him about escaping. I didn't want that; I felt bad about it, as if it
really mattered. I couldn't make my mind search him
out, couldn't even look along the line of faces. . . . It
was too bright to see anything; I couldn't think,
couldn't even feel.

But I could see the gray-silver metal post in front
of my face. I tried to pull away but they fastened my
hands up above my head, the metal pressed smooth
and cold against my skin. The bitter taste of fright was
in my mouth. Somebody's hands tore my shirt down
the back. I started to shiver. Someone else was speaking; the words fell on my ears without making any
sense, words about me. I could see the guard waiting
with the glowing arch of the prod out of the corner
of my eyes. I remembered how being hit a full blow
just once, for wising off down in the mines, had felt.
I tried to believe that this wasn't going to be twenty
times worse; and a dozen more, for passing as human.
. . . I tried to remember to count, so it wouldn't be as
bad, so I'd know there was going to be an end. . . . I
wished to God they'd get it over with! I—

"Begin."

The prod made a high song coming through the air,

and when it struck my back, it went *snap*. A blistering pain like the burn of hot grease spread across my back, and I forgot the cold burn of the metal post against my cheek. I tried to count *one*, but it was just a gasp, my teeth gritted together. And *two* came, while I was trying to disappear into the metal, and laid another line of sticky fire across my back. I made a sound and choked it off. I heard the prod sing again, bracing myself; my stomach knotted, and then it was *three*. I bit my lip until it bled. Again, and that was *five*; no, wrong, *four seven*? And I couldn't count on my fingers now because they were balled into fists. Again, and I knew I wasn't going to be brave . . . again, and it didn't matter anymore. I buried my face against the cold post and let the cry come, letting the pain out the only way I could. There was nothing I could do but let it hit me again, and again, until I thought I couldn't hurt any more than I did; and then it would hit me again. I sagged against the post and my wrists bled as the cuffs cut into them. I barely knew it. I thought I was learning what it was like to be burned alive. I thought I was going to vomit. I thought I was going to pass out, but I couldn't let go of the pain no matter how I tried. . . . My whole life was caught up in an endless loop; there was no beginning or end, it was going to go on forever, and I was going to see and hear and taste and feel it all. . . .

And then it was over. They freed my hands and pulled me away. I heard a voice I didn't recognize still begging them to stop, a voice that couldn't belong to me. . . . My legs wouldn't hold me up.

They took me away. I felt dull sickness and fear

follow me along the line of blank blue faces. But everything was far away, now, like a star in a mirror. Then something struck my face, flat and gray—I was on my stomach on a cot. Someone chained my foot to the bed. And then I was alone in the small empty room, while the part of me that was still conscious made dry sobbing noises in the back of my throat.

I lay there for a long time, hurting, and the only sound I heard was my own voice. Finally that stopped, too. I knew at the edge of my mind where I was, in the infirmary, in the ward set aside for the bondies. No one else was in the room. I was glad, because right then I hated everybody in the goddamn universe.

It was a long time before someone came back again. Hollow footsteps crossed the ward, and stopped. A voice muttered, "God!"; a hand touched my shoulder. I swore and it moved away. I started to hope that I was alone again.

But the voice said, "I'm sorry, kid. I'm sorry this happened."

It was Joraleman. I wanted to say, "Me, too," but I couldn't do it.

He waited a minute, before he said, "Kielhosa called me. Your timing stinks, you know that? Why'd you have to get yourself picked up when I wasn't here to get you a break? They could have waited for me to get back—! But why the hell did you have to antagonize the directors with that lunatic story? You weren't telling them the truth." It wasn't even a question.

I tried to turn my head, tried to get out just one word: "Yes!"

"Wait." He kneeled down. "I've got some pain-killer." He pulled back my ruined shirt as carefully as he could, but it still felt like half of my back went with it. I whimpered and swore. Through the red agony in my mind I felt his own mind jerk with disgust at what he saw. "God, I'd never make it as a medic." He sounded sick. I shut out the image of what he was seeing. A hiss of spray struck my back, in an instant of fierce freezing cold. But the cold spread and faded, the fire died . . . the world started to stretch out beyond the edges of pain. I looked up at him then, and said, "Thanks." It sounded rusted-up.

"Forget it." He glanced away. "Look, the story I got from Kielhosa sounds pretty paranoid even to me; I've got to admit that. What in the Holy Name made you try to tell a thing like that to the Directorate?"

I rubbed my eyes. ". . . Seemed like . . . a good idea at the time. Kielhosa—he asked them to wait for you; he tried to keep them from punishing me."

I couldn't keep watching his face, but I felt him half smile. "He's a friend of mine; he owes me a couple. And he knows what I owe to you. Besides, not everyone around here thinks a beating is the answer to all questions. What's the matter, did you expect him to hate you forever, for pulling a fast one on him over the snowtrack? He's even starting to think it's funny, in a way. But with what he heard today, I'd say it's convinced him that you're a pathological liar."

I groaned.

"Maybe it lost in translation. Try telling it again, to me."

I heard him sit down on the next cot. My eyes kept

falling shut. "That's all I ever wanted. . . . You got to believe me, Joraleman; you know what happened to the snowtrack! You said it wasn't an accident. Didn't you tell nobody? They acted like they didn't know—"

"Yes, I told them; I told them what I could remember. . . ." He stopped. "After it happened, it was like trying to remember a dream—parts were clear, and parts were hazy. I still don't remember everything. Sometimes a piece comes back." Like he hardly believed now that it had ever been real. "But trouble with the Spooks isn't the same thing as a plot to take over the mines."

"Don't you remember what happened to the snow-track?"

"Yes! Yes, I couldn't forget that. I put that in the report, at least." He sighed. "They said it was simple equipment malfunction—we haven't had a decent mechanic here for months." He was thinking that no one even questioned it; that nobody believed anyone would threaten the supply of telhassium, or that they could get close if they tried.

"If they don't even believe you . . . ?" My voice started to fall apart. "What's the use of tellin' it and tellin' it, if nobody ever believes it? Why should I even try? The hell with you, you lousy bastards. You deserve anything you get, and I'm damned if I care. Jule's crazy . . . Why'd she have to love Siebeling. . . ? Why did I . . . ?" slipping off into the clouds on the edge of sleep.

Joraleman reached out and shook me. "Come on, I'll listen, at least. Try to tell me the rest of it."

I swore at him again. "Awright, all right, ask Kielhosa, he heard it! There's a group of psions in the port town, planning to take over the mines. . . ." Somehow I pulled my thoughts back again long enough to tell him the rest. ". . . And I was supposed to come back here like this, so Rubiy'd have a focus for teleportation. He's planning to gas everybody so his people can walk in and take over. If I don't make a joining, they can't do nothing—but then the ones I'm with will die. I figured if I could warn you, you'd help . . . go to the town, clear 'em out. I told Kielhosa everything, but he didn't really believe it, none of 'em did."

"You can't exactly blame them—that story would be hard to take even if you were wearing a uniform, and not a bond tag. But he said he remembered some funny things happening around you when he bought your contract. That's why he got you a hearing with the directors. That, and because you saved my life."

"Yeah. When they learned who I was, they were so grateful they gave me an extra beating." *Psion, mind reader, freak . . .*

Joraleman muttered a curse, and shook his head. "Ignorance breeds fear."

"You think you ain't afraid of me? You think you got nothin' to hide—?"

His mind spasmed with guilt. For a second he glared at me. And then he sighed. "That's the problem, you see. For most people, the only one who sees into their soul is God. And most of us wish even God was a little nearsighted."

(The land of the blind,) I thought.

"What did you say?" He blinked and shook his head again.

"Forget it."

"If you were—are—working with those FTA agents, what are you doing wearing a bond tag at all? You didn't plan that—?" He frowned.

"No. I . . . got thrown out of the group, back on Ardattee."

"And they turned you over to Contract Labor?"

"Yeah. It's a long story."

"It must be. But you're still helping them—and us?"

I didn't say anything.

"Why?"

I turned my face away. "It's personal."

Joraleman didn't say anything more for a while. Then, finally, he said, "I'll talk to them."

I couldn't remember who he meant. He left then, but I hardly knew it. Nobody was going to help me; nobody'd listen to a bondslave freak. I'd done everything I could—but I'd failed, I'd ruined our last chance. Jule and Siebeling would be trapped, maybe they'd die, and I'd be a slave forever. . . . And it wasn't *fair*. My hands made fists, the bond tag cut into my swollen wrist. My back felt like raw meat. I was only a lousy kid! Half a year ago I was nothing but a Cityboy slip who couldn't spell his own name. How was I supposed to be able to change anything?

Ever since the day I first laid eyes on Quarro, and saw what it could mean to live a free life, everyone I'd met had been putting their chains on me—chains of need, chains of greed, chains of blame. I moved my foot, hearing the chain around my ankle rattle, loud in the empty silence. Half a year ago I could hardly carry the weight of my own life—how the hell was I supposed to save the galaxy all alone? All alone . . . I'd always been all alone. . . .

I slept, finally. And somewhere in the darkness of my dreams I met the one I only knew from dream to dream, who disappeared even from my memory each time I opened my eyes to the light. The one who had been as alone as I was, who knew all the bitterness of the lost; who wandered now, lost in my dreams, forever. The one whose mind had touched my own with love once, somewhere in another life; whose arms had held me safe; whose voice could whisper hope when there was none left even in her mind; who sang me to sleep with a vision of going home. . . . Whose ghost moved through abandoned hallways of my mind, and showed me where to find strength when I thought I didn't have any left; who made me go on living when I wished I was dead. The one whose name I could never say, because her true name was hidden in the heart of her mind. The one whose face was always hidden, too; who would never let me remember it, no matter how I cried to see her again, no matter how much I needed her, no matter how hard I tried, how far I reached, to be held in the warm circle of her arms. . . .

I came awake into blackness. I blinked; grays drifted up and steadied, but I didn't really focus. My mind was wrapped around something that the rest of me still didn't know; it was pulling me out of sleep like it always had back on the streets when there was a need: I was tense and listening. I tried to lie still until I could figure out why.

The lights were out for the night, but I knew somehow that it was close to a new day. I knew where I was, and I knew there was someone else asleep in the ward now, a couple of cots away. He coughed and moved as I lay listening. I felt my hand, numb with sleep, clenched in a fist. I felt something more, fire licking the edge of my nerves—my back, the pain-killer wearing off. . . . And then I remembered what I'd dreamed: inside walls of nightmare the gentle thought of *her*; needing to reach her, across impossible distances of time and space, impassible barriers of loss. Reaching out with all my strength that still could never be enough—

Until suddenly, somehow it was enough, and more: My mind blazed up, caught in a tapestry of nameless colors growing brighter and brighter, filling the emptiness inside me like nothing I'd ever known. A rightness filled me, a belonging, all the answers I'd ever need, all the comfort and understanding and love.

But I couldn't hold onto it: I felt the strands begin to separate, saw the colors fading. I didn't have the strength; I was losing control. *No*— I threw all the strength I had left into it, feeding the bright fabric everything I could; because if it fell apart and left me empty now, I wouldn't be able to stand it.

But then the fabric tore, and I was lying dazed in the dark, not knowing whether it was a dream, not wanting to know; with my body and my mind still drawn as tight as wire. Waiting and listening . . . *for what*?

"Cat?"

I froze. And then I lifted my head, trying to look

over my shoulder; the pain made me dizzy. Jule was
standing there beside the cot in a long pale gown.
Jule. I could see her face, soft against the darkness,
and her black hair falling around her. I stared at her,
trying not to blink back the pain-tears, because I knew
when I did she'd disappear. (*Don't let me wake up.
Stay. You're beautiful, you're beautiful. . . .*)

She moved, came toward me—touched me. I caught
hold of her wrist; solid flesh. She was real. I blinked,
and felt two tears slip out and down.

(*How did I get here?*) She was staring down at me,
but she didn't believe what she saw. She looked past
me into the darkness. (*I've never been here!*) Her eyes
came back to me, I saw the panic in them. She didn't
bother with her voice. (It is real. But how, Cat? I've
never seen this place! I shouldn't have come out . . .
anywhere.)

My head dropped back onto the hard mattress. I let
go of her, lay just watching her. The answer came
without me even having to think about it. (A joining.)

She reached out and pushed my hair back from my
eyes. (You're that strong?)

It almost wasn't a question. I didn't try to answer it.

She smiled a little then, kneeling down beside me.
(It was like nothing I've ever known. So intense—
enough to pull me here, to you. I thought it never
happened. I felt you calling me in a dream tonight,
so far away; but it wasn't a dream and . . . Cat, what
happened to you? *Pain, and such fear. . . .*) She shuddered, remembering. Her memory ran through me,
and my hand closed hard on her wrist again.

(I tried to tell them! I tried, I told them what was happening, but they didn't believe me. They laughed at me! They beat me, for escaping. And for being a psion. . . .) I swallowed hard against sickness rising. (Everything went wrong. Joraleman was gone, and they laughed . . . they wouldn't listen, they wouldn't even wait. I tried everything to make them—!) Jule put her fingers up, touching my face, and stopped the thoughts with her own. I felt the aching sorrow in her mind.

She leaned forward, trying to look at my back; one hand touched it, as lightly as a birdwing, and jerked away at my gasp. Then suddenly tears were running down her own face. Her eyes met mine, her pupils were wide and black, open clear down to her soul. My wounds were her wounds and hers were mine; our thoughts were bound together in a second of perfect understanding. My lips found hers; we tasted the salt of blood and tears.

And in the same instant, we felt the mind that gathered like smoke in the shared space of our own: *Rubiy*. The fragile bond shattered like its strands were made of glass, and suddenly we were two separate people staring at each other across the dark again. Our minds were clear; Rubiy's contact had broken with the joining-spell. But we both knew that what really mattered was his reaching our minds at all. He knew what had happened.

"We did it—what he wanted you to do," Jule whispered, looking down. "But you found my mind, not his."

"It wasn't a mistake."

"But now he knows he can do it, too."

"Not if I don't let him. Not if you don't go back. Stay here, Jule—you can make them believe the truth!"

"I can't . . . I can't leave Ardan there. If I don't go back, Rubiy will kill him; he'll know we're betraying him."

"But if you do . . ."

"I have to! I'll find another way!" Her voice rose. "We've been making plans, Ardan thinks he's found a way to get the—"

The bondie who'd been asleep a few beds away began to cough again. He sat up, wheezing, and looked over at us. "Hey, what the hell—"

Jule stiffened and turned like a wild thing, and then she was . . . gone.

My hand that had been holding hers closed over nothing. The other bondie was staring back across the empty room at me. I shut my eyes, with my fingers digging into the edge of the mattress, and tried to look like I was sleeping.

He said, "Hey?" a couple more times in the darkness, and then he lay down again. I heard him swear and gasp for breath. I touched his mind; it was knotted with misery and despair: (*God, don't let me go crazy, please, please, not crazy too. . . .*) And because I'd caused it, I tried to use my mind to ease his fear, to help him forget, for a while. . . . I felt him drift down into sleep again.

I kept my eyes shut a while longer against the emptiness in my own mind—until I found Jule calling me, from far away, and heard her promise. . . .

18

With the new day, the medic on duty came into the ward again. I opened my eyes to watch him check out the other bondie. The bondie coughed and mumbled, halfway into delirium. The medic gave him a shot of something. I felt him thinking there wasn't much point to it as he moved away again. I'd always heard it wasn't easy to get into the infirmary—as long as you could move, you could work. And by the time you couldn't, it was probably too late. This was a small room.

"How's the back?" The medic was standing beside me now. He didn't bother to look at my back, and I didn't try to look at him.

"It hurts." I hadn't moved for hours, afraid even to breathe too deeply.

"That's the point." He left me food and water; on the floor where I couldn't reach them. As he was walking away, I went into his mind and let him feel exactly how much I hurt. I heard him yelp, and the crash as he dropped something. I smiled, just a little.

The rest of that day was the longest day of my life. I tried to concentrate on Jule, on what had happened the night before and what Rubiy would want to do about it. But a red haze of pain filled up my mind until I couldn't focus my thoughts enough even to worry much about it.

After what seemed like forever someone came into the ward again. I heard two voices this time, arguing; one of them was Joraleman's.

". . . against the rules!" the medic shouted.

"I don't give a damn," Joraleman said. He sounded like he was right beside the bed. I opened my eyes and saw his legs in rust-colored uniform pants. "I'll do it myself."

"You can't treat a patient!" The medic came after him.

"Then you do it. Do your duty as a healer, for God's sake. I'll take the responsibility." Joraleman's voice was heavy with disgust. He pushed something at the medic, and sat down on the next bed, waiting.

The medic's hands came at me with a blade, but before I could jerk back, he began to cut away the rags of my shirt with it. I lay still, biting my lip. He sprayed pain-killer on my back, and then something else that covered the burns like a soft skin.

I took a deep breath, and another, without feeling the pain nail me to the cot. Then I moved one numb arm, slowly, stretching it out, and the other one.

"Give it a chance to set," the medic said. "And don't make a lot of sudden moves. Not that you're going anywhere." He gave the chain around my leg a tug. "That's all I can do for him," to Joraleman. He left the room.

"How are you feeling?" Joraleman asked me.

"Better'n I was five minutes ago." I tried to grin.

He smiled, but it was weak. "I can do this much for you, Cat." His big hands twisted together in the space between his knees. "But that's all I can do. I tried to get a hearing today, but . . ." His hands spread in a shrug. "Nothing."

I nodded, not even surprised. "What did they say?"

"That I've gone soft." He laughed once, his eyes shut against seeing my back.

"What're you doin' out here, anyway, Joraleman?"

He opened his eyes. "My job. I'm just another bureaucrat, putting in my time until transfer. The hardship pay is excellent, if I finish my tour. And my time's almost up." He sighed. "It's not like this everywhere."

"Yeah, sure." I looked at my wrist, at the bond tag. "How much do I owe on my contract now?"

He read a number off my tag, and did something with the computer remote on his belt. "Still close to five thousand credits."

"Five thousand . . . still?" I whispered. "Jeezu. I never been worth more'n fifty in my whole life."

He didn't say anything. The bondie in the other bed started to cough.

I pulled myself to the edge of the cot and reached down for the water and food. My hands were swollen and clumsy; he helped me feed myself. Then he got up again. "I've got to get back to work. But I'll try again tomorrow. If I can get in to see Tanake, he might be more willing to listen. . . ."

"I hope you got that much time left."

He looked back at me, startled into a frown. But he only shook his head and went out of the room.

The other bondie was coughing again. When he

stopped, he tried to push himself up. He said, "When I was—" and then he collapsed, unconscious, and I never found out what he was trying to say to me.

I lay then and waited until night came again in the civilized levels of the complex. Then I let my mind loose into the nameless sea, searching for Jule. And she answered me at last, like she'd promised me she would. Everything was still all right. I caught the bright ribbon of her thought and fused it to my own.

Her mind wove into mine and I felt the joining begin. But this time she wasn't alone. The cord of someone else's thought wrapped itself around the strands of hers, and as her mind joined with mine, the joining was tripled. Before I could shape the hundred questions crowded into my brain, or even stop what was happening, the bright warmth that had begun inside me turned white-hot. Reality wrenched itself apart inside my head, the space behind my eyes filled with starbursts. And then the contact tore again, the way it had the first time.

Only this time it wasn't just Jule standing by me when my eyes cleared. Rubiy was with her, and I knew then that time had finally run out for us. Jule's face was full of quiet desperation; Rubiy's burned with triumph. It throbbed inside me like the blood in my veins, and all I could think about suddenly was Cortelyou's heart stopping. . . .

Jule kneeled down beside me. Her mind touched me softly; she forced everything out of her own thoughts but her concern for me.

Rubiy's mind came down out of the stars as he looked at us. (Cat!) In the darkness his grinning face looked like a death's-head. He focused his triumph, force-feeding me the giddy electric shock of his exultation until I had to put up a wall to protect myself. I lost Jule's contact in static. He showed me my share in it all, my power, his approval, his pride: (Didn't I tell you, when the time came, you would find the need, and make the joining? *Even if it hadn't worked out exactly the way he'd planned.*)

Find the need. Suddenly I remembered what had made me find the need, just the way he'd promised. Pain gnawed my blistered back as I pushed up onto an elbow. He'd known—he'd known what would happen to me. (Thanks for bein' so sure.) I couldn't hide the anger, didn't even want to.

His mind flashed surprise and confusion, before it shut off like a switch. He didn't know why I felt angry, why I resented it. (You suffered: You paid a small price for a great reward. We've all made sacrifices to reach this goal; only a fool would whine about them. Pain is nothing—learn to ignore it.) Like he'd learned to ignore pain, and every other shred of human feeling he'd been born with.

I didn't try to answer. I glanced at Jule, standing with her fists clenched and her mouth pressed tight. She was looking at the chain that held me on the cot.

(Then you begin to understand.) I felt his annoyance; I was spoiling the pure pleasure of his moment of victory. (You'll understand everything, when we're through. You'll know then that I'm right.) He turned back to Jule. (But first we have to complete our business with the Federation. The maintenance systems control center is on this level of the complex. We should be able to reach it directly from here.) He began to move away. Jule started after him, moving like she was stepping onto a tightrope.

(Wait!) I threw it into his mind. He stopped. (I want to come with you. Don't leave me here. I don't want to be like this, helpless, when it happens.) I wore my best victim face, hoping he could see it. (They hate psions.)

He frowned. (You'll be safe where you are. You'd only get in our way. I'll come back for you—)

(I'm fine!) Somehow I sat up, holding my breath. I was glad I didn't have to lie out loud. (Like you said, I can learn to ignore pain. I want to be there when— when you take this place over for good.) I reached out to him, letting my swollen hand tremble a little.

His frown faded.

I put one foot on the floor; the chain on the other leg rattled. I kept my eyes on him, pleading, waiting, praying. . . .

He reached over and put his hand on my leg, let it slide down to cover the metal cuff. I felt the power focus in his mind. . . . The cuff fell open, and I was free. I sat gaping at it for a minute before I finally got up off the cot. The thought hit me that my whole life would've been a hell of a lot easier if I'd only been born a teek instead of a 'path. I laughed at the irony, without really meaning to.

Jule and Rubiy were both wearing miners' uniforms, because the halls outside would be monitored. They were both armed. Jule's hair was hidden under a security guard's helmet; she was tall and thin enough to pass for a man. Rubiy took off his jacket and helped me into it. Even with the bandageskin the medic had put on my back, I thought the pain when it settled on my shoulders was going to be more than I could take. But I didn't have any choice, and so I took it anyway. I sealed the jacket up the front, my hands and face wet with sweat. Jule watched my fingers, her eyes full of apology and relief. Neither of us alone could stop him, but together we still had half a chance.

I glanced at the other bondie as we left the ward. He didn't even stir; his mind was down somewhere deeper than sleep. I wasn't sure whether he was lucky or not.

Moving through the halls was no problem—because nobody here expected any problems, the security before you got this far was too good. We reached the systems center without anyone questioning us. When we got there, the entrance was sealed by an identity lock. Rubiy set his hand against the plate like he really expected it to open. He focused his psi against it, like he had with my cuff, and in a few seconds it hummed open. I glanced at Jule; a kind of dazed awe filled her mind. I wondered if Siebeling had ever even thought about using his Gift that way.

We went inside. The lights came up as we entered a room filled with more monitors and terminals and screens than I'd ever imagined seeing at one time. If living in Oldcity had been living like a parasite in the guts of some alien being, this was like being a virus inside a brain. No one was watching over it—it kept its own nightwatch, monitored its own systems, like a sleeping body. And Rubiy had come here to infect it. . . . And we'd come here to stop him. I was hardly even thinking about my back now.

Rubiy moved along the walls, forgetting us as he looked up and down the instrument banks. Jule touched her stungun, looked a question at me, not letting it form in her conscious mind. I glanced at the gun Rubiy was wearing, and back at hers. Jule and I had to make any move we tried at the same time. Our only chance to take him by surprise and survive would be if we could split his attention, hoping one of us could put him out before he could tear open our defenses and kill us. I raised a hand, (Wait), and let myself drift across the room. Rubiy was calling up information on a terminal. He finished as I stopped beside him, and looked up at me, pulling a headset off.

I managed a smile. "How's it goin'?"

"Perfectly." He reached into his jacket, and pulled out something sealed in shiny packets. "Now for the final step." I followed him, as he moved to another section of instruments and began to feel his way over a touchboard.

"What're those?" I pointed at the packets.

"Those are what we'll be feeding into the air conditioning system." He didn't look up.

I laughed. "It looks like candy!"

"I don't recommend them. The chemical is a form of a sodium compound that was once widely used as an anesthetic—and a 'truth serum.' "

I froze. My hand fell back to my side.

"They probably don't taste very good." He smiled, enjoying his own wit.

I laughed a little too loud. "How's it work, anyway? How long will this keep everybody asleep? It's not gonna last forever—don't it leak out? What happens then?"

"The gas is harmless. We can keep them unconscious for as long as we need to, until everything is under control. This system is self-contained, the gas can't 'leak out.' It purifies and recirculates the same air."

"Won't it clear out the gas, then?"

"Ordinarily it would. But most of these systems have a regulator built into them—"

"So you can use them to gas people?"

He looked up at me just for a second, with his irritation starting to show. "I hardly think that was the purpose intended by the manufacturer." He looked down at what he was doing again. "It's used for air hydration control, mass immunization, disinfectants—similar functions."

"Oh." I let my hand drift out in a slip's move that was so automatic it was almost instinctive. "Well, ain't it gonna gas us, then?" My fingers closed over cool metal.

"I can bypass—"

I jerked his stungun loose—(Now, Jule, now!)—trying to leap clear—

But my legs didn't do what I expected. I stumbled, and in the same split second Rubiy's arm lashed out and knocked me into the panel; I heard Jule cry out as her own stungun tore itself loose from her hands. I had one glimpse of the total rage on Rubiy's face before the pain of my wrenched back blurred it out, before the same rage smashed into our minds. I felt

my body shudder with the blow, felt my heart constrict
and miss a beat as my mind barely blocked his attack.
The stungun had fallen out of my hands. Rubiy's
hands reached out—

I felt psi energy overload the circuits of my mind
suddenly, sweeping all the barriers of my control
aside, forcing me to join—*not Rubiy, not Jule, not even
human. . . .*

Hydran. The combined strength of their mind
poured into me, building inside me like the static
charge of a lightning bolt. Rubiy fell away from me,
his face changing, mirroring my own as I was transformed; no fury left on it, but only confusion and disbelief. I saw his power, *saw* it, shining around him
like an aura—but it couldn't reach me now. I saw
Jule too, her face slack with shock, her own psi aura
haloing her. The whole room shimmered with lifeless
light and whispered with silent noise. I didn't feel pain
now. I didn't even feel human; my consciousness was
like foam on a cresting surge of energy. Static crackled
between my fingers, my hair lifted on an invisible
breeze. . . .

I watched Rubiy lurch across the room to where Jule
clung to the wall, too dazed by what was happening
to get out of his way. He caught her in his arms, holding her between us like a shield—not knowing there
was nothing I could have done to stop him.

And then suddenly something sucked me down into
my own mind, made me forget them both; and all I
could think about was where I stood now—in the Federation Mines, in this hell of misery and torture and
slow death. All I could see was spending the rest of

my life as a slave; all I could feel was the pain in my back, the betrayal, the suffering, the humiliation. . . . And suddenly I knew that I had the power in me now to make it end forever.

(Yes.) I spoke the word where only they would hear me. (Yes. I will. . . .) I felt them answer me; and knew that what they showed me then would stay with me forever, too.

And then the lightning struck—through me, around me, below me . . . everywhere. I think I remember seeing Rubiy and Jule disappear together, before my vision turned inside out. I think I remember screaming.

The thunder followed, deep in the levels of the compound below me.

19

Liquid fire trickled into my mouth, dripped down my throat, filled my nose with fumes that made me gag. Reaction caught me with a heavy hand and dragged me into the real world like a newborn. I was blinking and blinking, starting to wonder if I'd gone blind when suddenly my mind opened to the light. "What . . . what . . . where am I?"

Joraleman stood looking down at me like he thought my next question was going to be "Who am I?" and he wasn't sure what the answer was. "In my office."

I was lying on my stomach on a couch, staring at a holo of some other world projected on the wall behind him. At first I didn't know it from the real thing. My eyesight strobed again, turning the view into a negative, and back. I put a hand up to my eyes. My head felt like it was really to split in half.

"Here." He pressed a cup into my hands, winced as a spark of static leaped between us. "On my homeworld we call this Holy Water. They claim it can put life back in the dead."

I fumbled it up to my mouth and took another swallow. It was a lot like drinking molten lead. "If"— I gasped—"if it don't kill you first." I drank some more, a sip at a time. "How'd I get here? What . . . . happened?"

He sat down on the corner of his desk and took a drink from the cloth-covered decanter, grimacing. My eyes still weren't working right—he wore a halo of pale rainbows. "I found you wandering in the hall like a burnout a few hours ago. A lot of other people were doing the same thing, at the time. . . ." He shook his head. "You were really telling the truth." I began to see how dazed he looked—like someone who'd seen the end of the world. "Needless to say, it was a shock, if not exactly a complete surprise, around here. But how the hell did it *happen*—I thought you said the plan was just for a takeover. . . ." He rubbed his head, rumpling his yellow hair.

I didn't answer him, because I couldn't. I shut my eyes, trying to focus on the aching chaos inside. The last thing I remembered: *I remembered being chained to a cot . . . Jule . . . Rubiy . . . the chain dropping away. The control room; Rubiy by the computer board, turning on us just as we were about to . . . And then something alien filling my head; my whole body like a jar full of lightning. . . .* I opened my eyes again. "It didn't happen. The takeover Rubiy planned, it didn't happen. We stopped him before he could use the gas. . . ." And then Rubiy had disappeared, and Jule with him. And I hadn't been transformed by wildfire so much as I'd been a kind of transformer for it: knowing that if I thought the word, it would be set free. . . .

"But you didn't stop them—they've destroyed everything!" He took another drink from the cloth-covered bottle.

"What're you talking about?"

"The underground vaults have collapsed. Some are

full of molten rock. Everything's in ruins. Why would they do that? And what kind of weapon—" His voice broke off.

I took a gulp of my own drink. "Did . . . how many people were . . . killed?"

"Nobody! That's the damnedest part of it—nobody was seriously hurt." He wiped his mouth; rainbows splintered and danced.

I sighed as the tension flowed out of me. Joraleman was staring at me. I said, "It wasn't part of the plan. . . . It was the Hydrans."

"The Spooks?" He straightened. "Why?"

"Why do you think?" I sat up finally, swearing at what it did to my back. Joraleman watched me, not saying anything, until I got my face under control. "Why do you think?" I said it again, meeting his eyes. "They knew what Rubiy was planning, because I told them. They told me they had to think about it . . . and they did. They decided to stop him; and they got what they wanted all along, too. God, did they get it. . . ."

He shook his head. "Why now? Why not a long time ago, if they were going to do it at all?"

Because they'd been waiting for a focus, a key . . . just like Rubiy had. And they'd finally found one.

(What happened to you?) But he didn't say it out loud. Because suddenly he knew the answer. He looked down. "A higher justice," he mumbled, and took another drink.

I thought about what would happen to me if he ever told anybody the truth. And then I thought about how he hadn't even. . . . "You're protecting me. Why'd you bring me here, instead of turning me in?"

He looked up again and his mouth twisted. "Because you were right. And because when I found you, you weren't in any shape to answer a lot of angry questions."

"How long was I like that?"

He glanced at something on his desk. "Close to five hours now."

Jule. Jule disappearing, along with Rubiy. . . . I pulled myself to my feet. "We got to talk to somebody. The psions in the town, somebody's got to stop them. Rubiy's back there, and he knows—"

"It's already been taken care of." He held up a hand.

"It has?" I swayed.

He nodded; the haze of distortion shimmered around him. "We got a radio call from somebody named Siebeling—"

"Siebeling!" I sat down again. "Is he all right?"

"As far as I know. All I know is we got his call right after the disaster, and he claims he turned the psions' own show back on them somehow. We sent out a security force. They ought to be back any time, if—" Something buzzed on his desk. He turned away, "Joraleman," he said, speaking into the intercom.

I closed my eyes and stopped listening, concentrating on what I'd just heard. Siebeling was all right. Then somehow he must have gotten the best of Rubiy, and Jule must be with him. I wanted to find them, but my mind was too full of noise: too full of the suffocating fog of shock trapped here inside the dome, hundreds of human beings numb with it, filling all the levels of the compound; too full of the jangling static of my own pain. I quit trying and made myself relax.

Joraleman left his desk and went to the door, saying something I didn't really hear. He left me there alone, and after a while I dozed off.

I don't know how long I slept. I woke up again just as the door opened; knowing whose face I was about to see. . . . I got up from the couch.

"Cat!" Siebeling said. An aura shone around him, twice as bright as Joraleman's. His happiness and his relief were blinding. I rubbed my eyes, realizing then that the light I saw around him wasn't really light at all.

And then Siebeling was hugging me like a long-lost friend. I yelped and pushed free as the burns on my back came alive. Siebeling's hands dropped; surprise and sudden guilt flashed around him.

"Hey—" trying to keep my voice even, fumbling for a grin, "hey, Doc. You look like you're really glad to see me for once." I laughed.

But his guilt only doubled, flashing crimson. And I'd be lying if I didn't admit I enjoyed it. He said, "Jule told me everything. . . . Will you let me look at it?"

I unsealed the jacket and shrugged it off my shoulders, gritting my teeth. I heard him suck in his breath.

"Second and third degree burns, and they left them like that—?"

"That's the point." I pulled the jacket on again before I could think about how much it would hurt.

He looked away at Joraleman, his face hardening. "This is barbaric. How can you—"

"It ain't his fault," I said. "He would've stopped it, if he could."

Siebeling nodded, grim-faced. "Then will you help me see that he gets decent medical treatment?"

Joraleman was looking at patterns in the rug. "That might be . . . difficult, under the circumstances." He glanced up, with his face red.

Siebeling opened his mouth, shut it again without saying anything.

"Where's Jule? Didn't she come with you?" I changed the subject to the only thing I wanted to hear.

"No." Siebeling looked back at me. "Isn't she here?" His mind took a sick lurch. "Where's Rubiy? What happened?"

"He ain't here. He got away. I thought you'd . . . ?" But he hadn't.

"My God, where the hell are they?" Panic leaped into his voice. "What's he done to her?"

"I think maybe I've got an idea," Joraleman said slowly. "I heard outside that we've lost control of the planetary shield. It doesn't answer commands from the equipment here—and while it doesn't, there's no way in or out of Cinder. We're trapped, like flies in a bottle. Somebody broke into the computer and tampered with the programming."

"Rubiy." I nodded. "He did somethin' in the systems room. But how's that tell us where he is now?"

"He could be at the transmitting station. He could be controlling it directly from there, if he's that good. He could still be holding this world hostage, single-handed." He reached for the intercom on his desk again. "Maybe it's about time we had another talk with somebody on top. . . . Joraleman here." He'd called Kielhosa—the voice that answered him was one I was never going to forget.

". . . if they know so damned much about it! Why didn't they stop it before, if that's what they were here for?"

"But remember what the kid told me, Keel: they were cut off, they couldn't get a message. . . . Never mind, we can fill you in later. Listen, is Tanake back at the systems center? We'll meet you there, five minutes. Uh, one more thing, a favor: give me your word that whoever shows up you'll keep your mouth shut?"

Kielhosa grunted. "So it's the kid. You know damn well that he's mines property. Is it him?"

"All I have here are a couple of Corporate Security agents. Well, what about it—have I got your word?"

There was a long silence. Then Kielhosa's voice said, "You've got it." He started to say something else, but changed it. "Make it fifteen minutes; Tanake's not back yet."

"Right." Joraleman switched off, looking at me. "I owe you this much, Cat. . . . We can join the others at the systems center, that'll give you all a chance to fill each other in." Siebeling nodded, a motion full of angry tension. Joraleman shrugged apologetically. "I'm afraid it's the best we can do. Meanwhile, maybe you'll join me in a drink?" He passed Siebeling a cup; the top of the decanter was full of them. I sat down and he filled mine again. I took a long swallow, trying to get numb from the inside out. Joraleman poured for Siebeling and poured some more for himself. "I'm

Meade Joraleman, by the way. I'm Chief Purchaser here. I don't remember our ever being formally introduced out there."

"Ardan Siebeling." Siebeling shook hands, trying to force himself to keep calm. I felt him groping for something to say, anything that would fill up his mind. "Frankly, you don't seem to be very disturbed by all this . . . ?"

"You mean, the fact that in spite of everything you tried to do, you are now sitting on top of the most expensive pile of rubble in this part of the galaxy?" He shrugged again, and sat down in his desk chair. His voice was slurring a little. "I'm beyond surprise, Dr. Siebeling. . . . And I have to admit this isn't my first toast of the day. I've been drinking to my resignation. The nice thing about this stuff is that it doesn't give you a hangover." He leaned back in his seat, looking up at the holo on the wall. "Before you accuse me of leaving the leaky ship, let me assure you the idea isn't a whim as of this afternoon. It's been a while coming." He glanced at me.

I said, "I'll drink to that," and I did.

Siebeling nodded.

Joraleman set down his cup. "We ought to be drinking to you. How the hell did you manage to subdue an army of psion traitors single-handed, anyway?"

Siebeling looked at the cup on the desk. It rose a few inches into the air and hung there, before it settled gently back again.

Joraleman shook his head. "Of course."

Siebeling didn't even smile. He took a deep breath, forcing himself to concentrate, and told Joraleman

302 Joan D. Vinge

about the underground storage tunnels. He'd put gas into the ventilating system, just like they'd planned for the mines, after everyone had gathered there for their final orders. He'd set free the handful of miners who'd been locked up in town by the psions, and they'd helped him clean up the ones who'd gotten clear of the gas. . . . He told the whole story like he wasn't even thinking about it. He was thinking about Jule. So was I.

Joraleman grinned and shook his head again.

"So what's gonna happen here, now? Are the mines gonna be shut down?" I asked it to stop thinking about her.

Joraleman nodded. "They'll have to be, at least for the present. But don't get your hopes up; the Federation runs on telhassium. We'll be reconstructing, the faster the better. Time is money."

"Oh."

He held another drink out to me and I took it. "To the Spooks." I lifted my cup.

They looked at me.

"Just kidding." I took another long swallow, looking at my bond tag.

Joraleman half smiled. "Sure. To a higher justice. . . ."

I put my cup down, starting to feel a little gorked, remembering that I was drinking on an empty stomach. The colors around Siebeling and Joraleman hurt my head. I leaned over and looked at my own reflection in the tabletop beside me. It was only a reflection, no halos, and it looked like death warmed over. There were dark smudges of bruise around my eyes, like something had hit me in the face, and dried blood on my upper lip from a nosebleed I didn't remember having. I looked away again.

Joraleman glanced at the clock in his desk. "We can go on down, if you're ready." Siebeling nodded, more than ready. Joraleman looked back at me. "How about you, kid?"

"Sure." I shrugged, and wished I hadn't. "Let's go." We went to the lift and down a couple of levels. I wished it could have been up, instead; but I didn't let it show.

There was a handful of officials waiting for us in the hall outside the systems center. One of them was Kielhosa. He gave Joraleman a dirty look and muttered something. I stopped behind Siebeling and didn't look at anyone. They were all wearing halos to my mind's eye, flickering like the night sky. Siebeling's stood out like the sun.

Joraleman was making introductions. One of the guards said to me, "I've seen you somewhere, kid."

"That's 'Corpse,' to you." I frowned. So did he. He didn't take his eyes off me. I looked away as Joraleman introduced the man named Tanake; the one he'd told me might listen to my story, once. Tanake looked at me like he really believed I was a Corpse. If he wondered why I was wearing a miner's jacket, he didn't ask. I nodded. His hair had gone white, his face was aging; something about the lines of it made me think of the Hydrans. I glanced back at Kielhosa; but he was gone. I stared at the place where he'd been standing, trying to rest against the cold wall of the hallway. My back hurt like hell under the weight of my jacket, and my head hurt worse. Everyone was asking questions, but they were all a blur to me. I let Siebeling give all the answers.

Finally Kielhosa showed up again, followed by a mob of security guards. My legs almost gave out on me before I saw that they were guarding a group of prisoners and not coming to get me. One of the prisoners was Galiess, crowned with splintering light. She looked at Siebeling and then right at me, as if nobody else existed. Kielhosa was asking permission to question them about Rubiy and the planetary shield. Tanake agreed. I thought about what he could do to get answers, and my knees got weak again. Kielhosa gave a signal and the guards started Galiess moving again. Her eyes stayed on me as she passed. I'd never seen a look like that; I never wanted to see it again. Her mind wove into mine: (I told him what you were, I told him to get rid of you; but he wouldn't listen. He thought he knew everything; but he didn't understand anything. And now you've ruined him. He should have listened to me. . . .) The contact was gone, and so was she.

I looked down. Siebeling and the rest of them had gone into the systems center. I followed them inside. The monitor screens looked out across piles of rubble like blind eyes, like the brain of a ruined body. The whole room shimmered with a dim blue radiance, as if I could even see the life-force of machines.

Siebeling was standing with the others where the engineers were trying to make the shield respond. The energy fog around him crackled, and I heard his voice rising, angry and impatient. I moved toward the viewscreens instead, too tense and restless to stand and listen. I tried to lean on the metal panel, jerked back as it gave me a shock. I kept my hands away from it as I looked from scene to scene: dust and broken stone and twisted metal all deep down below the room I stood in. Tiny figures moved through all the scenes, already starting to put the chaos back in order. I wondered how many bondies had stood in this room even once. And then I found a screen that looked out over the snow outside the complex. The crumpled, shining plain lay cold and peaceful between the scenes of ruin. The compound's lights turned the snow to stars, and beyond them the night's rippling sky turned it blue. I thought about Jule out there somewhere with Rubiy, and suddenly all that mattered was making contact; finding her, finding out what he wanted. I let my mind out into the dark.

And he must have been there, waiting. His mind caught in mine like a hook and I couldn't pull loose, while he made me understand what he wanted. And locked inside his sending was another mind: Jule's. . . .

And then Siebeling was beside me, whispering, "Cat!" His voice jarred me back into the room. "What's the matter with you? You're projecting, stop it—" The words were low and urgent; his mind was forcing me to remember where we were, and what these people thought of psions.

I waved my hands. (Will you listen?) Controlling my thoughts, I said, "It's Jule—Rubiy, I mean! Rubiy's got Jule with him. He just showed me where he is."

Siebeling took a step back.

"He knows everything. He knows what happened

here, and what you did. He's waiting for us now at the shield transmitter. I could feel him thinking that he knew we'd try to come after her. It's what he wants. If we don't show . . . he'll kill her."

"You're sure?"

"I'm sure." My hands tightened.

Joraleman said, "One of the psions has the woman you were looking for?"

"Yeah. Rubiy, the one I told you about, who got away—" Turning, I backed into the guard who'd been watching me the whole time. I couldn't stop the sound it squeezed out of me.

Everything clicked together in his mind, I could almost hear it; he had hold of my arm before I could get away. "Sir!" He pushed up my sleeve. The bond tag stood out as red as fire.

"Shit." I pulled away from him.

"We'll straighten all that out later. Go on with what you were saying." Siebeling said it quietly, as if nothing had happened at all.

I flexed my hands. "Rubiy. . . ." But I couldn't remember my own name by then. Joraleman looked embarrassed, and Tanake . . . Tanake said, "Go on, bondsman." And I realized then that he'd seen through it all along; he'd known what they were hiding and tried to pretend he didn't. But now . . . "I'm sorry." He looked at me. The guard had his stungun out; Tanake waved it away.

I nodded, and sighed. "Rubiy got away, the head psion—he's the one who's got control of the shield. He's got Jule and he wants us—Siebeling and me.

If we don't do what he wants, he'll shut off the entire shield."

You could have heard a feather drop in the room. Without the planetary shield the radiation pouring in from outside would kill everyone on the planet's surface. "He'll just kill you, too," Joraleman said finally. "What good is that going to do anybody?"

Siebeling shook his head. "We're not helpless. Remember we're psions, too. Give us this last chance to try to trap him. Help us, and we'll help you."

Tanake put his hands behind his back. "So if you answer his challenge, he may possibly let you get close enough to stop him. . . . If you fail, what will this madman ask for next?"

Siebeling shook his head. "I don't know."

"We have the weaponry to destroy the force barrier that seals off the control station—and the station itself, and anyone in it—if we have to."

Siebeling's face froze.

"You do that and you got no way to be sure you'll get control of the shield back." I read the worry that lay in the minds of his engineers and said it out loud. "You want to risk that?"

Tanake looked back at me, startled, and then at the engineers. "No. And I don't particularly want to cause needless deaths, either. All right, Siebeling—if you want to take the risk instead, you can try it your way. We'll give you any equipment you need."

I took a deep breath.

"Bondsman, I think I anticipate your questions. You've been poorly paid for your part in this. I wish there was something we could do; but now . . . At any rate, for the present I can leave you in the custody of Dr. Siebeling."

I thought he must be a mind reader. I nodded again, my mouth tight.

"You're free to go with him, then. I think you are needed." He figured they wouldn't have any trouble getting me back. But I knew he was doing the best he could for me, and maybe that was more than I could have expected. "I only wish things could have turned out more happily for all concerned. Good hunting."

20

We were in a snowtrack together, just Siebeling and me under the light-curtains of night, following a course that would take us to Jule and Rubiy. Tanake had given us everything we'd asked for, including the 'track. Siebeling even knew how to drive one; but he didn't know why I thought that was funny. I finished a cup of coffee from the thermal bottle, and glanced over at him again. "You want some?"

He started. He shook his head, looking out at the night. The halo of his thoughts still shimmered around him. He hadn't said anything for nearly an hour.

So I said, "Hey, Doc." He looked at me. "I see— light around you."

He glanced down at himself, back at me. "What do you mean?"

"I ain't sure," not knowing how to explain it. "Even machinery glows, ever since the Hydrans . . . did what they did, at the mines."

"It's true, then, everything Joraleman told me? I thought he must have been—exaggerating." (*Crazy*). "The Hydrans focused telekinetic energy through you, to cause so much destruction?" He sounded like he'd never really be able to believe it.

"Oh, yeah. . . ." I put a hand up to my head. "Believe it. I was there when it happened, and I got the headache to prove it." Somehow it didn't come out sounding like a joke.

"Why didn't you tell me? I could have given you something." They'd let him treat my back, but I hadn't said anything about my head.

"I didn't want anything. I don't want no drugs; it could get in the way of my Gift if—when I have to use it. I can handle the pain." I was handling it; Rubiy was right. Somewhere I was finding the control, because I had to. I wondered if Rubiy was going to be right about this meeting, too. "Don't worry about me."

Siebeling looked at me for a minute, and then he shook his head. "And you're seeing some sort of energy?"

"I don't see it, exactly. I *feel* it, like colored noise. Humans more than anything else. Psions are like suns." I wondered if the Hydrans saw the world like that, and I wished suddenly that I could see myself from the outside. "It's . . . I dunno—"

"It's incredible." A part of him wished he could get me into a lab and study me. "I've never heard of anything like this. I think you're probably very lucky you've got a mind left."

"The Hydrans wouldn't hurt me. They know me, they trust me, they think—" I broke off, remembering the message they'd left in my mind. "The first time they saw me they knew I was alien, like they were; even though I was from the mines." It wasn't hard to say that, anymore. "It didn't surprise them that one of their own people could come from outside. They remembered it from—way back. But the oldest memories are tangled up now. They don't seem to know anymore what a lot of it really means."

"They gave a lot to you."

I touched my head. "Yeah. More than I knew. . . . They tried to make a joining with me, the first time they saw me. But with them a joining really is total, it's every part of them, and I couldn't do it. . . . I still can't, really. There's always things I want to hold back; even though they made me a real psion. They said it's because I was raised like a human. Humans can't let go of themselves and give everything that way, they ain't strong enough."

"You weren't just raised like a human; you are human. As much as you are Hydran." Like he thought I could forget that.

"My bad luck." I frowned. "Anyway, I couldn't take the joining, it almost. . . . But when it happened, it changed me, my psi . . . all the barriers came down. . . . And when it happened, I saw a lot of what they remembered. Are all Hydrans like that? Do they share everything? And what are they doing here?"

"I don't know much about these people, really. I don't think anyone does. Even to another Hydran the amount of telepathic communion they share would seem extreme—isolation and hardship have forced them so close together just for survival. Most other Hydrans lost any group mind practice long ago. If my wife and I had been that far apart psychologically, we'd never have . . . been what we were. But I do remember a few things. For instance, their belief in a god-being. . . ." He leaned back in the seat.

So we kept talking, to keep from thinking—talking about the Hydrans of Cinder and what they'd been once. About what it must have meant to be part of a whole civilization that was united in a way the Human Federation could never be. About Cinder becoming life for the Hydran colonists and giving them shelter when their empire failed, until it had become a holy thing, a religion, to them. And about why they'd come all the way to the Crab:

"The Hydrans were miners? They mined telhassium, too. . . . Why?"

"Probably for the same reasons we do."

"My people . . ." I felt my face twist.

Siebeling said, gently, "There's nothing to indicate that they used slave labor. Respect for every part of life is as much a part of them as psionic ability; it has to be, to protect them from themselves. But don't see them as simplistic saints and martyrs, either. They have their imperfections, they share the whole spectrum of emotion with human beings; they have their resentments and anger and selfish impulses, even if they can't act on them as easily. And the ones you met here have had a long time and good reasons to grow inbred and xenophobic. They used you—even if you let them—to get what they wanted; just the way Rubiy tried to do. Accept your heritage, but accept it honestly. Don't deny your humanity for a dream."

I didn't say anything, but I guess he understood what showed on my face. Because suddenly he looked down, and he was thinking about me being half and half . . . like his son had been half and half. The son who would never hear those words from him. Thinking about how

I'd made him remember his loss, and see what had happened to his own life—made him look at it until he finally knew he had to live with it. And that all the thanks he'd given me was to make things worse than ever for me; that he'd hurt me just like he'd hurt . . . Jule, and everyone else. He said, "Cat, I don't know how—"

"Look, just forget about it. It don't matter now." I realized that it really didn't, anymore . . . any more than it mattered now if I never learned whether he was my father.

He didn't say anything else for a while. But then he started to talk again, as if he was trying to explain something; I wasn't sure whether it was all meant for me or not. "When you feel that if you looked around you, everything you'd see would be sick, with no way to cure it, you close your eyes—and your mind—until you don't see anything anymore. Even a private hell is more appealing than a public one . . . sometimes." He wanted me to understand why he hadn't known what he was doing to me when he sent me back to Contract Labor.

"Yeah, I guess." I felt him look at me. "Jule knew."

"Yes . . ." And it was back in his mind again, losing her, grief and fear for the only other one he'd shared as much with—the only other woman he'd ever loved as much as his wife. His wife: golden, her skin, her hair . . . she was beautiful . . . and he'd lost her, too. And remembering all that again now was almost more than he could bear.

I didn't know what to say, so for a while I didn't say anything. Then I said, "Starfall," which was what they said in Oldcity, when your house burned, when the surplus food allotment was contaminated . . . when somebody lost everything. And I wanted him to know that in a way I did understand, but it seemed like it wasn't enough. I thought about the time he'd said he was sorry to me, maybe he had meant it. I wondered what I'd really expected him to feel. "What did your kid look like?"

"My kid . . ." He stopped, and took a deep breath. "He probably would have looked a lot like you, actually."

"I wish I could have met him."

He glanced at me, and smiled just a little.

The sun came up, fading the colored night into sea-blue. And I finally knew, without being told. . . . "Now. Stop, we're there." I looked out over the control panel. There was nothing to see except snow and sky glaring; but my inner sight showed me an energy source so bright it was almost black. I frowned. "Is it underground? There's nothing out there, but I can feel—"

"Something's out there; the instruments are going crazy. A shield generator would have to have at least part of its plant above ground; probably Rubiy's left the scatter screen up around it. I think we'll be seeing it any time now." His hands tightened on the wheel.

I nodded. "Look, I've been thinking—let me go in first, alone, all right?"

"You?"

"Yeah. Stay out here and back me up. I mean, we don't know what he's planning—but he's out for re-

venge, and it could be anything. And I just figure . . .
that I could handle it better, being the telepath. There's
no way we can take him by surprise now. This way, if
something happens, at least he won't get us both at
once, like he did with Jule and me." I pulled on my
mittens.

"I see. . . . Are you sure you can do this?"

I shrugged. "I don't know. I won't know till I try.
But he's got to know now that I beat him once, at
least: when he tried to probe me after he murdered
Dere. He ain't perfect. That ought to be good for
something."

"You tricked Rubiy." He'd known it for days, but
now he finally believed it.

I grinned. "See, Doc, I ain't such a deadhead, after
all. If I did it once, I can trick him again. Dere always
said that's how psions play the game to win. Like playing Last Chance." I twitched my hand, catching ima-
ginary game pieces; trying to make myself believe it.

Siebeling didn't say anything. He was thinking about
what I'd said, and about Jule out there. And he wanted
to be a telepath more than— "All right."

I pushed the faceplate on my parka hood down and
opened the door.

"Wait."

I looked back at him.

"Do you want to try a joining?" He was almost embarrassed, as if he felt like he didn't really have the
right to ask.

"Yeah. . . . No." I thought this was something I had
to do myself; something I owed to Rubiy. And some
part of me still wasn't sure I could count on being

joined to Siebeling, if Jule wasn't there between us. "It's better if we're not tied. But if I need help"—I jumped down into the snow—"you'll know it!"

"Be careful. Don't . . . take any chances."

"Not with Jule's life." Ahead of me was only white noise. I started walking toward it.

21

There wasn't anything—and then there was, right in front of me, as if it had been there all along. The shield control. Even though I knew what was happening, it startled me more than it should have. I stopped where I was, holding the cold, bright air in my lungs.

The building was a huge metal bowl flipped upside down, with a ring of towers and filament wires wrapping it like a web. The bowl was coated with ice, in layers that had rippled and run, flowed and refrozen along lines of force until it looked like a spun sugar castle. The silver-coated towers dripped icicles like frozen tears. And all around it a forest of the crystal trees made their glittering music. The sight took my breath away, for a long minute I stood there forgetting everything but my eyes. But then I remembered what this place was, and how it had cut off a whole world from the rest of the galaxy. I made my eyes search out the entrance, and started toward it.

And as I walked, I thought about what I was doing here. And how half a year ago, back in Oldcity, there wasn't anything that could have gotten me to do this . . . nobody I would have done it for. Then I thought about how I'd never wished I was back in Oldcity instead, no matter what was happening to me here.

No matter what. I focused my thoughts and wove my mind into a wall, blocking the bright noise of the shield's energy and my own battered body. None of that was important now; it was only static, and once I stopped listening, it didn't exist. There was no trace in my mind of anyone else's trying to reach me—not Jule, not Rubiy. I took out my stungun, and then I went into the building.

The hallway was dark after the brightness of the snow, but not too dark for my cat eyes. I pushed back my hood and unfastened my parka so I could move easily. There was humming in the air, and something more—the crackling overflow of trapped energies, that made my skin tingle. I couldn't help wondering if it was something more than the shield. But still there was no touch against my mind. I could almost be here alone. I didn't let my mind explore; letting Rubiy make the first move instead. I could see light up ahead now, real light, coming from one of the control rooms.

I reached the doorway and stepped into the light. The first thing I saw was Jule, just sitting there, waiting. But not because she wanted to. Her dark hair floated on the charged air as she turned her head to look at me; her mouth was open as if she was trying to warn me, but couldn't. Her gray eyes were the eyes of something caught in a trap.

"Well, Cat. It seems I'm a good judge of human nature after all."

I raised my head. Rubiy was waiting for me across the room. He was sitting in front of a control panel, with circuitry creeping up the walls, surrounding us all. Making me think about webs: spiderwebs, mindwebs.

I raised the stungun, and like some fool in a threedy show I said, "You're under arrest, Rubiy. If you move I'll—"

The stungun jerked itself out of my hand and flew across the room. I watched it drop down on the panel behind him. I'd been so caught up in protecting my body from a mind attack that I'd forgotten to watch the gun. I kept trying to swallow, but all of a sudden my throat was as dry as dirt.

"You won't be needing that." His face was as calm and unreadable as ever, as if nothing ever touched him.

I shrugged, trying to match his expression. "I've come. What do you want?"

"So, you really came to risk your life for Jule taMing? For the daughter of Centauri Transport?"

I nodded, holding my mind closed as tight as a fist. But still he didn't try anything against it.

"And even you were working for Corporate Security all along. My compliments to them. Your cover was ingenious."

"Good enough to fool you." I touched my bond tag.

"So it seems. . . . And you're still wearing that. It must be satisfying to know you've been so well-rewarded for your loyalty to the Federation Mines." He lifted an eyebrow.

I tried to laugh, but the truth made it stick in my throat. "Look, what do you want with us?"

"What do you want, Cat? To take me prisoner, and go back to the mines as your reward? Is that why you came? Is it worth that—are they worth that to you?"

"Shut up." I went to stand beside Jule and touched her shoulder. I couldn't reach into her mind.

"Cat. I'll tell you what I want. . . ."

I looked back at him. And suddenly I was seeing a real face, tight with strain and fear, his eyes that saw his own humiliation and death ahead. And his mind was open—he'd dropped his guard to me.

His mind clawed at me: (I want to get out of this! Help me, Cat, you're the only one who can. Turn me in and they'll destroy me, they'll destroy you, too. Help me—and I'll teach you every trick I know. I'll make you a better telepath than I am. Work with me and you can still have everything I promised, everything you ever wanted—!)

I felt my hands cover my ears as if they could shut him out. *Lies, why should he . . . ?* But I took a step toward him. Jule gasped, as if she felt my control slipping. . . .

But his mind was open to me, it was all true. And I'd known all along that this was what he'd wanted me for, what he'd planned for me all along. He couldn't believe that I hadn't understood—that Galiess was too old, that he needed someone new and smart, someone young. Galiess knew he'd chosen me—she resented it, and that was why she'd resented me. But she was loyal; together they would have helped me, they would have taught me . . . I was only a raw beginner. I'd created sophisticated results out of blind ignorance, I didn't even know the things I could really do.

Or what I had done. No one had ever tricked him before. But I'd tricked him. I pulled him down, me, the half-breed kid—but he didn't hate me for it. He admired me. If I helped him now, we could still escape this trap together. He'd take me with him, there wasn't anything I couldn't be, or have. . . . And my mind was full of what it would be like, again: the worlds and the wonder, the satisfaction, knowing they all had to ask *me*. . . .

And this was why I'd been afraid to face him. Because now I wanted it all. I wanted to know what I could really do with my mind. I wanted to be everything I could be, proud of my Gift and in control. . . . I wanted to know how it would feel to have everything money could buy, power, respect. . . . (Everything I want—everything?) I looked at Jule; my hand slid down her back in a caress.

Her face froze as she understood; but then her eyes said that she understood everything, before they dropped away. And that she knew there was no hope. (Jule, I—) I pulled my hand back.

(Take her, if you want her!) Ruby caught my mind. (Use her, stop being a fool! Don't you know who she is; what the taMings stand for? They're one of the most powerful and corrupt shipping families in the Federation! They're part of the cartel that hired me to take over the Federation Mines! You've let her seduce you all along: for what? Have you forgotten Oldcity, the slums of Quarro? She never cared about you, none of them do. They're all alike, parasites feeding off the combines that feed off the gutter scum—you and me, Cityboy! Always the ones who suffer and bleed . . . because they keep it that way. Because they need it! We make the systems work, our suffering, our despair. They're using you, they've always used you. Hate them. . . .)

The way he hated them. I touched his hatred, and

black bitterness, rage like cold diamonds, ripped me
inside. There was no light in the world, only a craving
hunger, the need to survive. There was nothing I
wouldn't do, nothing I couldn't do to them; they deserved it all and it was my right. . . .

But it wasn't my right. I was only half human . . .
and half Hydran. And now at last I saw what that
really meant—that a part of every other Hydran lived
in that half of me: a presence born into me like instinct, the presence of the people who rejected the
ultimate use of power. To take a life was the unforgivable wrong; to destroy another was to destroy yourself.

"No . . . I can't." I stood beside Jule again, my mind
torn in two, my hands tightening into fists. Jule, who
was only Jule, who'd never done anything to me but
show me she believed in me. But at the same time I
knew that everything he said was true, and that another
part of me hated half the universe for the things they'd
done to me, to him, to so many others like us for so
long, so long. . . . That he had the right to hate them.
That we were the same . . . once.

But not now. Now I saw how hate and power had
twisted him into the thing he hated. He didn't give a
damn for anybody, including me. He'd destroy the
only thing that had ever mattered to me—the thing I
shared with Jule, and Siebeling—and use me to do it.
He'd use me worse than anyone had; he'd destroy me
with his mind sickness. . . . He was crazy, and I couldn't
let him do it. I had to stop him—

I had to look at him. His face was a lie; his eyes
didn't show me anything. I knew then that it was too

late to stop anything. I'd let him through my guard, and into my mind—

He took control of it.

Then I learned about triumph, and thought maybe I was going to die of it: he held my mind cupped in his hands, he could smack them together and smash it like a bug; every time I breathed it was only because he let me. He waited, letting me feel it, letting me see how strong he was; that no one could stop him, we were all crazy even to have tried.

He nodded, and his mind's hand loosened around me. "I've misjudged you twice, now, it seems. The first time I underestimated you, and I paid for it. At least this time I didn't make that mistake. This time the mistake was yours, half-breed: you've lost sight of reality. I am—disappointed. I'd hoped. . . . But your choice is plain enough."

So I knew what would happen next. We were all going to die. And it wouldn't even be because we'd ruined his plans; it would be because we'd hurt his damn pride. Now he was going to prove that he was still the strongest, and the best. He didn't have anything else left, no way to escape, no future; but he could still have that much. He'd get his final satisfaction from the three of us, and especially from one half-breed bondie who'd ruined everything. . . . *(Siebeling!)* I called him without even meaning to. *No, don't think about him, he'll—*

Rubiy smiled. (Think about him all you like; I already know. He's coming to join us now. We'll wait for him; I think it won't be long.)

He picked something up from the control panel,

came and put it into my hands, cold metal. Static
sparked in my palms as it touched them, and made me
flinch. I tried to feel surprised, looking down at it, but
I couldn't. It was a six/ten energy hand weapon. In my
whole life I'd only seen one a couple of times, on Citi-
corpses in riot squads.

I looked up into his smile, and didn't need to ask
what he wanted me to do with it. But the pictures
came into my mind, where I couldn't close my eyes to
keep them out; and I saw my hand press the button—
to kill Siebeling, and then Jule, and finally myself. I
wouldn't be able to stop it, and neither would they,
because he'd have control of us all. He could make us
do anything to each other. *Anything.* My mind started
to form images of . . . *No!* I jerked the gun up, trying
to aim it at him.

And then suddenly my throat closed and I couldn't
get any air; I couldn't even make a sound. Seconds
passed and more seconds and more; the paralysis didn't
come undone. The room floated around me. I got too
dizzy to stand; I went down on my hands and knees
with my chest on fire, clawing at my throat. . . . And
then he let me go, and I crouched panting with my
head down, my eyes shut.

(Get up.)

I got up, somehow.

(Pick up the gun.)

I did.

Rubiy came over to me and caught my jaw with his
hand, looking into my eyes. (Yes, I could kill you all
myself—it would be simpler. But this way I'll enjoy
it so much more.) He let go of me again. (Consider

the irony of the situation, Cat, while you have the time left. I find the arrangement fitting.)

(You bastard, I'm not gonna kill for you, I won't, I . . . can't.)

And he knew I couldn't kill, because I was Hydran—he knew what it would do to me. But he knew I would kill, because I wasn't Hydran enough—or strong enough to stop him. Because he was the best, he was stronger than any of us. *But not stronger than all of us.* (Jule—!) This time slipping free, finding her in the darkness of our mind prison; linking, feeling her mind flow into mine.

Her hand rose and clutched at mine. But we were barely touching fingertips through the cage bars. It was only because Rubiy chose to let it happen, because he enjoyed pulling our strings. . . .

(Cat!) Her voice filled my mind; she knew everything Rubiy had shown me. (Why did you come? I wasn't worth it. . . .) And her guilt was a weakness that Rubiy used against her, like he used my own guilt, and my half-alienness. He was playing us all against ourselves, we were flies in his web, and every time we struggled we only pulled it tighter around us. (Jule, he can't make me use this thing.) I looked at the gun, trying to make myself believe that; but knowing, too, that he knew every secret fear, and how to turn them all against me.

And then he reached out and broke our contact. Jule's fingers slid down mine, my hand dropped . . . I was alone.

And Siebeling was coming. I felt Rubiy focus his mind like a part of my own, to take Siebeling over; I felt like it was my own mind being lost all over again. Now he had us all. Not wanting to, I turned to watch the door, and I waited.

I saw Siebeling come into the light. His face was stiff, like Jule's face; the face of something trapped and helpless. His eyes went from Jule to me to Rubiy, and back to me. I had the gun pointed at him. His eyes asked the question—

(No, I don't want to do it!) But I couldn't reach into his mind and make him sure, any more than I could find Jule again. My hand held a gun on him, and all he knew was that he was going to die.

"Dr. Siebeling." Rubiy nodded. "Now the circle is complete, and we can finish this." He said it out loud; I wondered why he bothered. I felt his mind begin to push me, gently at first and then a little harder; because he had plenty of time, and he wanted to enjoy this. And it wasn't like pain; it wasn't anything I could fight back against, or even get hold of. It was just the understanding that if I didn't do the thing he wanted me to do, in the end my mind would shatter into a million pieces like glass. *I couldn't do it . . . I couldn't . . . but I couldn't stop it.* My hand began to shake, I watched while my other hand rose to steady it . . . he was trying to make my fingers close over the button . . . now both hands were on the gun. But Jule and Siebeling were all I could see. And they were all I had—

And I held him. My fingers froze like a part of the metal, he couldn't make me fire.

It shook him. His control of me slipped a little: he'd taken on too much, he didn't have any reserves left, he couldn't control us all for long. He wasn't a god— he was pulling a bluff too! And I tore his web, found

Siebeling first, (Join with me!) But Siebeling's mind turned me back; he wouldn't join. He thought I wanted to kill him. The words formed in my mind, his words: (You lying gutter thief. I should have known better than to trust you.)

(Stop it—) My hands were slipping.

(I should have know what—*no, I*—what you were.) And then everything he'd always thought of me, despising me, denying me: (I should have known.)

"God damn you. . . ." My voice broke.

(No, Cat! I don't!) Horror filled his face.

Rubiy pushed me and I pressed the button.

I knew what he'd done then, I jerked my hand aside, but it was too late. The energy beam caught Siebeling and dumped him against the wall. Jule screamed with his pain, and my mind echoed with it.

And then he disappeared from my mind. Rubiy's gloating pride filled the emptiness. *It was a trick, another trick;* and Siebeling was dead. I whimpered and swayed on my feet, but Rubiy controlled my whole body, holding me there. I felt my head pull around to look at Jule. She sat with everything and nothing in her eyes and on her face.

"I'm sorry, Jule. I'm sorry, I'm sorry. . . ." I felt my hands swing around with the gun. She just kept on staring.

Now there were only the two of us left; Rubiy knew he could make us do anything. Now it was Jule's turn to die. He'd made me kill once, and after I killed Jule too, he wouldn't even have to force me to use the gun on myself. Because I wouldn't want to live.

I saw Jule behind my eyes, and what I was going to

do to her—to Jule, for him. And I knew that there had to be something stronger than Rubiy, and stronger than hate, in what she meant to me. Finding that thing was all that mattered, she was all that mattered. . . . *Find her, find her, nothing else is real.* . . .

And I did find her, caught her, cried, (Jule! join with me—) I felt the blackness close in on me again, but I wove her mind into a band of light, I *made* her join. The power wavered and grew in me, until it felt as strong as it ever had, and suddenly even stronger, as if someone else— The gun swung back and away and back like it was caught in a magnetic field.

Rubiy's mind struggled to tear us apart, but our minds were one, fused by the fire of need. He tried to stop our hearts, but he couldn't reach us. He probed the pain center in my mind and ripped away the block I'd set there; my body cried out with the shock. But that didn't matter, I didn't really feel it; the pain was diluted, absorbed, shared.

And then his attack shifted again; he caught me from behind and his mind forced me down into hell. And hell was my own face mirrored in his eyes, my own stinking face: Cat the gutter thief, Cat the drug dreamer, the slip, the boytoy, Anything-for-a-credit-Cat, seeing my whole rotten, wasted life stripped of its lies. I struggled in his web, trapping myself, until there was nowhere to hide. . . . I relived all the ugliness that had made me what I was, every memory as sharp as hunger. . . . I remembered everything. Until finally he drove me back against the locked door in the deepest part of my mind—the barrier I'd built myself at the beginning of my life. Until I had nowhere else to go, nothing left but to surrender or to break—

I broke through, into the time I couldn't remember, and memory poured into the darkness: *Sleep, my little one . . . dream of the stars and sun . . .* her voice, singing away my fear. I could see her face, the face that smiled only for me, at last; I could reach the mind that touched me with love. And nothing mattered but the joy I felt holding the hand that held everything. . . . *Dream a world of your own. . . .* How could I ever have forgotten that face? . . . *Dream of a life, dream of a time. . . .*

And then, answering me, Rubiy—tearing me loose from that hand . . . *dream of my love . . .* making me remember why, making me follow the strand to its end, the end of the song and the memory and the only *happiness security peace love* I'd ever known. I watched my dreams die again in an Oldcity alley splattered red with death: hearing her screams, the screams that nobody answered, the screams inside my head that only I could hear—the agony, the nightmare. . . . Crying and crying to get free, (But there's no escape, Cat, only death her death your death . . . *death. . . .*) And Rubiy showing me how it had to end.

But I wasn't alone anymore! The past was dead, but I was bound to a new life. I was joined more than just mind to mind—soul to soul—and I knew that I never had to be lost and alone again. Strength that was more than just my own strength shrouded me in light, warm pure light, shielding me, shaping me, forcing, forcing— and I was a mirror, I shone with light. (No escape!

Rubiy, there's no escape. We've already won!) I felt the terror that had trapped me turn back on him, and the truth drove it home. And I broke him, heard him cry, (No, *stop, I don't want to die—!)*

But he'd shown me the truth and I wanted my revenge; my mind flashed free like a coiled spring. I couldn't stop . . . I pressed the button. The gun jerked in my hand, a smear of blue-white light blurred my view of him—

He died. And his death was my own, in agony that exploded like a star and vaporized my soul inside shattering bonds of light. . . .

And it was quiet. Like the place had been full of— noise, something; but now everything was quiet. Everything. All I could hear was the air scraping down my ragged throat into my lungs, my heart still beating. Jule stumbled up from her seat and stared at me for a minute, holding her head, with tears running down her face. I couldn't tell what she was thinking, but then she went to Siebeling. As she knelt down beside him, I knew suddenly that it had been a three-way joining, not two-way. That it was Siebeling who'd known the answer to Rubiy, and made me use it. . . . Siebeling was still alive. I watched her lift his head; she said, "Thank you, thank you, thank you. . . ." But I didn't know who she was thanking. Siebeling's eyes were shut; he didn't move.

I looked down at Rubiy, his body lying ruined on the floor instead of their bodies, instead of my own. The nothingness where his mind had been made me gag. I dropped his gun and wiped my hand hard on my pants. And I wondered what was the matter with

me, I'd seen plenty of death, I'd seen it happen before.
But never because of me, I'd never brought . . . *death*.
There was too much death behind my eyes. . . .

I looked back at Jule and Siebeling, blinking hard,
fastening my jacket because I felt so cold, as if the
death had gotten into my bones. My mouth tasted like
death; death stank in the air around me. Because I was
Hydran, body and soul, and to kill was the unforgivable
wrong; but I was human, body and soul, and I'd wanted
to kill. . . . I pulled my hands in against my chest,
against death that stood with me, death that filled the
halls like a static cloud, death that was a wound inside.
I felt my mind trying to get away, with nowhere to
turn but in on itself. Panic rose up in me, knowing
what it would mean. "Jule—!" The whisper echoed.

I saw her glance up at me. I reached for the gentle
thought of her—(Help me!) But I couldn't find her.
The words fell away into the nothing hole I'd made
of Rubiy with my mind and a gun: all I could see, all
I could feel, all I could remember . . . a wound bleeding hate and terror, a wound that would never heal.

There was no aura shining around her head or Siebeling's anymore. There was no trace of them in my
mind. And I knew my thoughts wouldn't cross the
endless silence to find them, ever again. I'd never know
what I could have done with my Gift. Because I'd
killed myself when I killed Rubiy . . . I'd felt both of
us die together. My psi was in ashes, it was gone, and
everything it had given me was gone with it, forever.
I'd never be a telepath again, I'd never be Hydran,
everything was gone. I'd killed and I'd survived it, and
that was my punishment: to come full circle, to be a

walking dead man, blind and alone and going nowhere. . . . Only this time it would be worse. This time I'd know what I was missing.

I stood shivering beside Rubiy's corpse, with my hands pressed against my chest, and started to cry.

Jule teleported to the mines to bring back help. Somewhere in the silent hours while she was gone, Siebeling called my name. I went to him, sat beside him listening to the words that slipped out of his mouth like the hot tears sliding down my face: asking me to forgive him, but I didn't know why; telling me that he'd make it up to me, that he'd make me whole again. But the hole was in my mind and words didn't mean anything anymore. And after a while the words stopped and the tears stopped; I sat with his head on my knees and death watching over us with empty ice-green eyes.

Jule came for us, finally, her eyes swollen and tired, a cold wind behind her like a slap in the face. I watched her kneel down beside me while the doctor looked at Siebeling; but she only saw Siebeling. There were others standing behind her; I didn't look at them. There was talk, and maybe they were telling me to get up; I didn't listen. I just sat staring, until somebody shoved me with a foot and I fell against her. She caught hold of me, startled. Her face looked confused, she was frowning, "Cat . . . where are you? Cat? Oh, God. . . ." They tried to pull me away but she said, "Leave him alone!"

The hands let go of me, except hers. The guard said, "Bunch of freaks, they're all crazy." She didn't look up, holding onto me, "Cat, oh Cat, what's wrong—?"

I pulled at my jacket. "I can't feel you, Jule. I can't feel you, it's gone." My eyes were like sand; I thought there weren't any tears left, but they ran stinging down my face again. There wasn't enough room in the galaxy to hold all the pain inside me. "I'm all alone." I started to hiccup. Somebody laughed.

But Jule wiped my face with her sleeve and held me close. "I know, I know. . . ." Her voice shook. She took my hand, then; I got up and followed her outside.

I sat beside her in the snowtrack, with my head on her shoulder and my hands bound together. She murmured, "It's going to be all right," over and over, but I couldn't feel her at all.

". . . This is insane. You can't still want him. . . ."

I remember the mines, sitting quietly in a strange/familiar room while Jule stood over me, protecting me, as she argued with someone: ". . . . of the taMings who ship your ore. My credit is *very* good. . . ." But the words didn't mean anything anymore; I couldn't feel them. No one hurt me, they just came and stared. They weren't real anymore either, so it didn't matter that a couple of them looked familiar. After a while I noticed that my hands were free. Then there was a flash at my wrist and something fell off, a red band; but my wrist still wore red. Somebody wrapped it in white. And all the while I was getting farther and farther away. . . .

I pulled at her jacket. "I can't feel you, Jule. I can't feel you, it's gone." My eyes were like sand, I thought there weren't any tears left, but they ran stinging down my face again. There wasn't enough room in the pain to hold all the pain inside me. "I'm all alone." I started to hiccup. Somebody laughed ...

Rit? Jule wiped my face with her sleeve and held me close. "I know, I know ..." Her voice shook. She took my hand, then I got up and followed her outside. I sat beside her in the snowtrack, with my head on her shoulder and my hands bound together. She murmured, "It's going to be all right," over and over, but I couldn't feel her at all.

"This is insane. You can't still want him."

I remember the time, sitting quietly in a strange/familiar room, while Jule stood over me, protecting me; she argued with someone. "... of the taxman, who shut your eye. My death is not good ...." But the words didn't mean anything anymore. I couldn't feel them. No one took the that just came and shook them. There weren't any more either, so it didn't matter ... they, a couple of them looked familiar. After a while I noticed that my hands were numb. Then there was a tingle at my wrist, and something felt off, a red band ... but my wrist still work out. Somebody wrapped it in white. And all the while I was getting number and further away.

PART III

CROSSROADS

22

I was human; so I survived. I'd even come home to
Ardattee: the crossroads of the Federation. Gray sky
and flowing towers and silvered glass—every day I sat
in the dome lounge at the Sakaffe Institute, staring out
over the city, and by now they knew enough not to
bother me. The techs had put me back together, with
Siebeling making sure they did it right this time. They'd
used everything they had to bury the guilt and stop
the pain, to mend my torn mind. They filled the nothingness piece by piece; they were tough and patient and
they wouldn't leave me alone.

Because Siebeling had forced me to kill Rubiy, he
didn't have any choice. But he'd known what it would
do to me, better than anyone, and I guess he wanted
to make it up to me now. So the wound healed, but
it left scars that no one could help. Scars that sealed
me off from the past, cauterized nerve endings that
turned everything that had happened to me into something happening to someone else. All the memories, all
the feelings, all the gifts of a psion, that had been
mine once, were behind a glass wall now—where I
could see them but I couldn't touch them.

The techs had told me there was no reason I couldn't
be a telepath again; but they were wrong. I couldn't

project anymore; I'd lost all my sense of direction, I couldn't find anybody else's mind. I didn't even know where to start. And if someone tried to break through to me, my mind would shut them out, I couldn't stop it. Even Jule. Every time we were together, she tried to reach me, but all I could see was her smile that stopped at the skin. And when I believed finally that it wasn't ever going to change, I got up and left the room; I wouldn't see her again, or Siebeling either. Because it wasn't enough, after what we'd had before, and knowing that I could never have it again was more than I could stand.

She and Siebeling had gotten married as soon as he was out of the hospital. I remember how strange it had made me feel, surprised, when she told me. Not because they were actually married, but because I finally realized that I wouldn't be with them anymore. I wondered what I'd expected: the job was done, and they were married. That wasn't any surprise. But it mattered, more than I wanted to admit; and hurt more than I ever let her know. Because I'd loved her more than a little for a long time now. But I'd had time to realize she didn't love me the way she loved Siebeling . . . and sitting alone for hours watching the sky, I finally realized that maybe it wasn't the same way, how I loved her, either. They'd have a lifetime together, in happiness; time to make up for all that had happened to them before. . . . And if they were married, the last thing they needed was me around reading their minds.

But I couldn't read their minds, after all. I had to keep poking myself just to remember someone was in the room. And no tech was ever going to fix that, no matter how long I stayed at the Institute. I had a clean record with the Corpses and a data bracelet to hide the scar on my wrist, and nothing else, and I guessed that now maybe it was time to go home.

I turned back to the window, leaning across the sleek, leathery coolness of the seat. I could see the towers pushing up pale and gleaming through the shadowmist of winter snow, like a picture out of a fairy tale. I remembered the endless fields of silver and the crystal forests of Cinder.

But suddenly I was remembering a part of the city you couldn't see from here. Where there'd never been a crystal tree, or even a blanket of fresh white snow— where winter was icicle-hung sewer pipes and dirty slush in Godshouse Circle, frostbite and pneumonia. . . . Where the icy wind sucked in from the sea cut through your worn-out clothes like a knife, and nobody would let you sleep where it was warm. Where dreams rotted and the darkness ate its way into your soul like worms. . . . Oldcity. Home sweet home. *Dream of a life, dream of a time.* . . . My mother's voice still sang about broken dreams, somewhere in my mind behind a wall of glass. . . . If she was really even my mother. I'd never know for sure, now. I looked down at my twisted thief's hand; it made a fist. *God, you freak.* . . . *Now you've really got nothing. Not even the gutter.* My mouth started to tremble. I dropped in a piece of sour candy and cracked it with my teeth. I hadn't touched a camph since I'd come back from Cinder; every time I saw one I thought of Dere. Poor Dere . . . lucky Dere, honored in death like he'd never have been alive. All his troubles were over now. I rubbed my eyes.

Someone had come into the room, I felt—I *heard* it; and I looked up. Jule and Siebeling were standing there, each with an arm around the other. Siebeling's other arm was still bandaged. "Hello, Cat."

I grinned without thinking, but then I pulled my mouth down again. "What are you doing here?"

Siebeling said, "It's no better, then?"

"No. I told you; it's not going to get better." I looked away, out the window again. "So what else is new?"

They stood there, invisible, for a while, before Jule asked, "Did you get your commendation from Corporate Security?"

"You mean this?" I reached into a pocket and pulled out the message 'cast, all in a wad. I'd been too embarrassed to ask anyone to read it to me; and then I'd forgotten about it. I smoothed it on my knees, and found my name printed at the top. "Is that what it is?"

Siebeling actually laughed. "And that's all the attention it probably deserves."

I smiled. "I didn't want to get a swelled head. What's it about, anyway?" And I knew how glad I was to see them; the tension eased inside me.

"We were the heroes of the moment, all over the galaxy—for about that long. At least we forced them to admit psions had done something to save the Federation, as well as something to try to destroy it. . . ." They sat down and told me more than I really wanted to know about what had happened because of us. ". . . So Galiess and the other psions will be in prison somewhere for a long time for what they tried to do, if they aren't executed for it."

I wondered how much harder their punishment would be just because they were psions. "What about the ones who put 'em up to it? There were combines backing Rubiy. . . ."

"And whichever ones they were, their identities died with him. Not even Galiess knew who his contacts really were." Siebeling leaned back against the window. "The FTA has its suspicions, but they have no proof. Even they don't have the power to act unless they can prove something without question."

"There was no proof?" I looked at Jule, remembering what we'd both heard Rubiy say about her family and Centauri Transport.

"No." She shook her head, answering the question I didn't ask. "Some things are more important—some ties never come unbound, you never get free of them, no matter how much you think you want to. And maybe that's only right."

"I guess maybe it is." I thought about Dere again. "But you saved their ass in a big way. Did it . . . did it make any difference?"

"Just a little." She smiled, just a little. "They didn't ask me home to take my place on the board. But they offered me a substantial settlement for staying away, to go with what the FTA owes us. That means more than they know. . . ."

"They bought you off," I said.

She nodded, and she didn't say anything more.

I leaned back in the seat. "So that's it. That's the end of it, huh?" The Federation kept going, because

of us. And the telhassium supply on Cinder was safe
because of us. The bondies were still dying there because of us, the Hydrans were being "investigated"
because of us . . . and Dere Cortelyou was dead. I
stared at the half-hidden scar on my wrist, and felt
the new-made barriers in my mind come down to cover
the old pain. *Me, a big hero. . . .* I wadded up the
commendation and threw it on the floor; and I said
something I shouldn't have, too softly for anybody to
hear.

But Jule said, "Don't you think that what we did did
any good?"

I tried to think about it. "I don't know. If it meant
the ones who run this screwed-up universe got some of
their own from me, then maybe. . . . But we didn't
change *any*thing; that's for damn sure."

"Maybe we changed something." Siebeling touched
Jule gently, and smiled. "And Cat—the Federation
keeps going, because of us. That means that at least
there's something that tries to restrict the whims of a
Rubiy. This galaxy would be worse than it is—damn
it, there'd be no end to the misery and pain—if there
wasn't something."

I glanced up at him, angry. But his voice was bitter,
and I realized what it meant for him to be saying
that, after what the Federation had done to his family.

"By the way"—he looked past me out the window—
"Corporate Security is looking for replacements for
Cortelyou. They're offering us an opportunity to do
more work for them."

"I ain't Dere." I shut my eyes for a minute, trying
to see Dere's face. "Are you—?"

"No." He looked back at me. "Then I take it making the galaxy safe for hypocrisy doesn't really appeal to you . . . either."

"No. What are you gonna do, then? Go back to the Colonies?"

Jule shook her head. "We've been making plans for staying here in Quarro. . . ." With the money they were getting from her family and the FTA, they were going to work with psions. Not just the ones who could pay, like Siebeling had done before, but the freaks who really needed help, the ones in Oldcity whose lives were being ruined by what they were. And there were a lot of them; it was hard to be human and a psion.

I thought about Siebeling's son, wondering whether he thought . . . But then I knew they felt that even if they never found his son, they'd find something that was worthwhile. I smiled.

"That's why we're here, Cat. We thought maybe you'd want to work with us." More than just professional interest showed on his face; but I couldn't read the feeling.

"Work with you . . . ?" I stopped, feeling the smile go flat. "Just what you need, a basket case. Try and tell me from the patients."

He said, "There's nothing wrong with your psi ability; except that now you control it too well. You aren't ready to use it again. And I can't change that for you this time; because it's not my right. You need to be in control, only you can decide what you need the most now. But I think you will be a telepath again, when you're ready—when you've had the time that you need to heal."

I shook my head. "I'm glad I've lost it, I don't care why. I hope it never comes back! It's too *hard*. . . ." To think I'd found everything, because of what I'd become . . . and because of what I'd become, to lose it all. The pain started and choked off again inside me. I couldn't even feel anymore . . . because I'd already died. "I wouldn't be any good for what you want."

"I think you'd probably be very good. More than anyone, you'll never forget how hard it is—or how much it can mean—to be a psion. Even if you never use your talent again, there'd always be a place for you."

I stared at the floor, eating a piece of sour candy.

After a minute I heard them get up, and Siebeling said, "It's up to you, Cat. Whatever you decide to do, from now on; it's finally up to you." He smiled.

Jule caught his eyes; he nodded and moved away, leaving us alone together.

"Cat." She touched my face; I saw her ring flash in the light. "I know . . ." Her hand dropped away. "But you didn't lose everything. The things that drew us all together are still stronger than the things that separate us now. They can't be changed, not for the three of us. You'll always know where to find us. It doesn't matter why you come—but come and see us, please. Don't forget us. . . ." She turned away as if it hurt.

Siebeling came back again, and put his arm around her. He reached into his coat pocket and brought something out. He held out his hand, offering it to me on his open palm. It was the Hydran crystal ball I'd stolen from him once, somewhere in my former life.

I took it from his hand, my own hand slow and uncertain. It was warm, like a living thing, like it always was.

There was a nightflower plant blooming inside it—
midnight petals streaked with silver like the light of the
stars.

"A promise," he said.

I cupped the ball in my hands, looking up at him.
For a minute I couldn't even speak. Finally I got one
word out: "Thanks. Thanks."

He nodded. I watched them start away together. As
they reached the lift, Jule stopped and looked back
at me, and I heard something in her voice that I
couldn't feel in her mind: "We never get everything
we want, Cat . . . but sometimes we get what we need."
The lift chimed, its doors opened and closed, and they
were gone.

They were gone, and it was a while before I really
understood: that they were gone forever, this time.
That what I did with my life really was up to me now.
I was free, I was rich, I was . . . nobody again; like
always, like I'd been at the start. And once I would
have gone out to the Colonies, if I was rich; but my
back was scarred, and I remembered too many lies.
And once I would have searched for my mother's
people, if I was rich; but my mind was scarred, and I
couldn't face them—because I'd killed, because I wasn't
Hydran enough. And once I would just have done
dreamtime for a month. . . .

The past was dead. The past was in a museum. And
the price for bringing it back was too high . . . I
couldn't pay that price again, I didn't have the strength.
But I didn't have the strength to forget. What was the
use of a future, if I couldn't stop wanting the past?

I looked down again at the Hydran ball in my hands,

alive with captive light, potential energy, pr.
And suddenly I remembered that final frozen mc   .c
in the mines back on Cinder, when the Hydrans left
their farewell in my mind. They'd shown me the future—their future, my own future, splitting apart from
that moment on: theirs blazing up in a moment of
triumph, then fading to black; the fragile threads of
possibility fraying, breaking, disappearing one by one.

And mine—blackness and ashes; but not an end,
only a new beginning. The threads of my life tangled
and frayed, but didn't break. Weaving the pattern
of the future they multiplied and grew until the choices
I had were like the stars in the sky. And as grief started
in me for the Hydran's loss, their hope for my new
beginning had filled me. . . .

I tightened my hands over the crystal ball again. The
nightflower would bloom in there forever, if I let it;
but more strange and beautiful things than I could
imagine would always be waiting for me to set them
free. I closed my eyes, trying to focus, trying to call
them out—

When I opened my eyes again, the nightflower was
still there. Nothing had changed. Jule had said it: to be
alive was to be disappointed. You tried and failed and
kept on trying, never knowing whether you'd ever get
what you wanted. *But sometimes we get what we need*.
Now I had everything I needed to start over again, with
even odds this time. Only a fool would throw all that
away. This was the place where the past and the future
came together: I held them both here in my hands.

Nothing's changed—yet. But it will. I got a few lives
I ain't even tried yet.